MY
HUSBAND'S
LIES

MY HUSBAND'S LIES

MARYANN WEBB

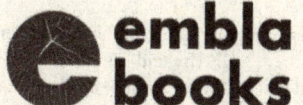

embla books

First published in the UK in 2025 by

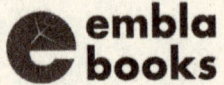
embla books

An imprint of Bonnier Books UK
5th Floor, HYLO, 105 Bunhill Row,
London, EC1Y 8LZ

A CIP catalogue record for this book is available from the British Library.

ISBN: 9781471419614

Also available as an ebook and an audiobook

1

Typeset by IDSUK (Data Connection) Ltd
Printed and bound in Great Britain by Clays Ltd, Elcograf S.p.A.

MIX
Paper | Supporting
responsible forestry
FSC® C018072

The authorised representative in the EEA is Bonnier Books
UK (Ireland) Limited.
Registered office address: Floor 3, Block 3, Miesian Plaza,
Dublin 2, D02 Y754, Ireland
compliance@bonnierbooks.ie
www.bonnierbooks.co.uk

To Les, who always listened to my earliest stories.

Epigraph:

Uxoricide – The killing of a wife or girlfriend

Prologue

She crosses the road without a care in the world. So confident the life she knows will be hers to enjoy forever. Untouchable. She grips her purse strap—not to deter a would-be thief, but as another tool. She hikes it higher on her shoulder as she passes through the crossing before the traffic moves again, her elbow out as a defense mechanism for anyone who might trample her, even though she's the kind of woman that people make room for.

You might say she's entitled, though it's carefully masked as confidence. She's a nurse, so she seems caring, hiding who she really is. Her black boots pound the walkway like a pestle, grinding the concrete as she heads east.

I've been watching her for three weeks now. She hasn't noticed, perpetually focused on herself, lost in her thoughts.

Not for the first time, I struggle to understand what he loves about her. I suppose it could be the obvious things. Anyone can see she's beautiful, but so are a million other women in New York City. She's caring, but everyone cares about something. What makes her so special?

Her gray knit dress moves with her as she walks, accentuating the way her slim waist curves into round hips. He wasn't supposed to fall for her, but I think he has. She was supposed to be temporary, a fleeting chapter in his life, but she has become a permanent fixture.

I watch her as she lines up at a street vendor and orders a pretzel, refusing the change offered by the mustached man who delivers the freshly baked knot with a smile that reaches his eyes. She doesn't appreciate the life she has been given. She spends *his* money as if it's hers to waste, buying new things for their home. Treating herself to expensive clothing.

The vendor waves a hand in her direction and thanks her with a wink. She takes her time gathering her things, but he waits patiently, as if he has forgotten the line of customers. Her smile suggests she notices him checking her out, and that she likes it.

This is not how things were supposed to go. People who do bad things shouldn't get away with it. There are meant to be repercussions. I'm not superstitious enough to expect justice, but she did what she did and now there should be consequences. Order maintained. Rules followed. But it seems like the opposite happens to her. She is rewarded for the awful things she's done.

I can't let that happen. I need to put a stop to it, remind her that beneath that expensive skin cream she likes to apply is the same blood as the rest of us.

She will walk down the alleyway and exit out the other side, close to the Starbucks on the corner, like she always does. It's a shortcut she takes home from work sometimes, unburdened by the fear someone might slip behind her and take her by the throat, demanding her money, stifling her screams until they die on her lips.

I follow her down the lane, trailing like I have many nights before, far enough away that she won't notice. Seeing her like this helps me figure out what I should say to her, if I should say anything at all. But most of all, it feels good knowing what I might do when it's time.

I slip a hand into my pocket and feel the smooth metal, imagining what it would be like to sink it into her side. I would leave her there for everyone to see who she really is instead of the perfect avatar of a loving wife she's created. She's hiding her true self now, but all she needs is a nudge for her real nature to surface. He won't love her once he sees that.

I curl my fingers around the knife and increase my pace to catch up. She's fast, but I'm taller, lengthening my strides so I don't lose her. She's a few feet ahead, hair bouncing around her shoulders, the clang of her boots drowning out my footsteps.

The smell of unemptied trash in the alleyway fills my nostrils, growing more pungent, but I press on. Tonight may be the night I end her life, like she ended mine.

I'm close now. Much closer and I risk being noticed. I promised myself that if that happens, my choice will be made, and I will kill her. The decision weighs on me as heavily as her conscience should weigh on her, yet she walks as if she's unburdened by what she has done, my ruin nothing more than a footnote in her life.

With a flick of my wrist, I pull my jacket hood over my head. It does nothing to drown out the sound of cars one street over, but it shields me from passing eyes.

I think of things I may have overlooked. Like testing the knife is sharp enough to cut through her skin, burying itself to the hilt. I've never done this before, and I don't have a plan B if things don't go smoothly. If I mess this up, I might not get another chance.

I don't see the obstruction before I reach it, so there's no time to sidestep it as I plow straight into a dented trash can lid. It rings out in the night, a discordant cymbal announcing my presence.

She turns, and despite the shadows, I'm sure she's seen me.

I run back the way I came, pocketing the knife to pump my arms harder.

She calls after me, her words muffled by a bite of pretzel. It sounds something like, "Are you all right?"

It's only when I round the corner that I slow down and pull off the hood, trying to steady my ragged breathing. Maybe she thought she saw a startled animal, something she'll easily forget.

I doubt it.

I can only pray she didn't recognize me, that she doesn't tell *him* what she saw.

Chapter 1

There was no fanfare when my husband, Ethan, announced he was going away on another business trip. It wouldn't be for long, he promised. A week at most.

I've noticed evenings out being replaced by weekends away for work. Going to dinner and holding hands through Central Park—a cliché that I didn't mind being a part of once I finally understood why it existed—is little more than a memory. He promised we would have a date night when he got back before he packed his things to take on the trip.

How did we become strangers sharing an apartment instead of the couple who used to be so in love that we eloped for our wedding and went on an extended honeymoon?

My friends hadn't been able to make the ceremony. The travel cost alone was extravagant. I asked only my closest friends, because it seemed insensitive to ask work friends when most of them lived in small apartments and scrimped and saved for everything they had.

Even my best friend, Cassandra, couldn't make it at such short notice. I tried not to take it personally, but even now I wonder whether it was because she didn't like Ethan.

Honestly, I was relieved not to have to plan a wedding on top of crazy shift hours as a nurse. I thought it would end up being just Ethan and me there. I was more than a little surprised when Ethan's best friend from college, Jason, and his then girlfriend—whose name I no longer remember—attended, happy for the excuse to go on vacation.

I loved my job, but I thought I was ready to take a break from other people's problems and focus on my new husband for a while. After our wedding, it seemed we might not get another chance between work, friends, and possibly starting a family, which we had already talked about.

I didn't expect that three short years later I would wonder where he really was when he said he was away for work. Yet here I am. I know Ethan is lying to me. I have known for a few weeks now, but with no proof, it's still just a feeling deep in my gut that churns in the background—there, but in that intangible way that isn't fixable.

There's no way to prove he's lying, and I know there's no way he would admit to seeing another woman. I'm not even sure he's still seeing her. Perhaps it was a moment of weakness and nothing more.

That's the problem with feelings. They can't tell you why they exist. Sometimes they seem inexplicable, but it doesn't stop the whisper in your ear or the prickle at the back of your neck telling you that something is wrong.

Another feeling hits without warning. Trepidation? What if it isn't over, and this is just the beginning?

My phone beeps. It's Cassandra, asking me to come out for Thursday night drinks. Usually it's Cassandra, Isla, Zoe, and me. I haven't been for months—ever since Ethan and I got serious about trying for a baby. I don't want to explain myself when they realize I'm not drinking, but Cassandra still sends the invitation every Thursday, pleading with me to come.

Cassandra's message arrives, like always, four days into Ethan's latest business trip, and I realize that despite what Ethan and I decided about not drinking, I don't want to stay here. I will just be wondering what he's doing and who he's with, hating myself for it. I never saw myself becoming one of those jealous wives who obsess over what her husband gets up to when she's not there, but that's exactly what I'll be doing if I stay home.

I'm still considering going when Cassandra messages again.

Aria, you're going! I have big news! xx

Sure. I'll be there.

Chapter 2

The bar is vibrant and full of energy when I walk in. Cassandra is already there and Zoe and Isla enter soon after.

"There she is," says Isla, pulling me into a hug. She leans in, her tone intimate. "I've been trying to call you, but it's like you disappeared." She frowns, suddenly serious. "We need to talk, but not now. I want to know why Cassandra dragged us here. Later?"

"Sure," I agree, not sure what I'm agreeing to. I notice Zoe watching us. She shoots Isla a look, like a warning, but Isla ignores it and the moment passes.

It's Thursday. Not quite the end of the week, but close enough to wind down and relax. Some will be nursing hangovers at work on Friday but aren't as likely as the Friday crowd to end up in emergency, getting their stomachs pumped to relieve them of whatever substance they ingested that night. None of the hospital staff like the Friday night shift.

I notice a woman a few tables over, my eyes drawn to her. She holds a glass, elbow resting against the table. Ethan might be sleeping with this woman. Or maybe I'm paranoid and we just caught each other's eye.

She's the most beautiful woman in the room, her smile unburdened and genuine. Ethan's usual type. Long, dark, highlighted locks frame her face. The edges of her curtain bangs catch on her long lashes when she looks up. There's something alluring about the way they settle when she blinks. Her simple black dress highlights her sensuality, the fabric clinging to the curve of her hips.

Perched on the bar stool, she looks like a goddess, set apart from the rest of the crowd. She's older than most of the women here—I can tell by how self-assured she is and the lack of showy, strappy clothes. Early thirties, maybe? Just a few years older than me.

She rearranges the little umbrella in her drink, oblivious to the attention she's drawing from the men in the room. She doesn't acknowledge them, even when they try to get her attention.

Maybe Ethan met her at a bar just like this while he was out entertaining clients around New York, making sure they didn't miss the best dive bars or restaurants that were so new they were open by invitation only while the chef tested variations on what would become the menu for New York's elite.

I try not to stare, but she notices me watching, her swimming-pool-blue gaze meeting mine. Instead of looking away when our eyes meet, she smiles warmly, holding up her glass as if wishing me a good night. Her stare makes me uneasy, as if I'm exactly what she was looking for tonight, making me think we might know each other.

I can't have seen her before. She has the kind of face you don't forget, but she seems to know me.

Is she the person who has been following me? At first I thought I was being paranoid, but I've heard footsteps behind me on the way home from work, heard someone lingering outside my apartment, which I was too afraid to check, imagining their ear pressed against the door, listening to the sounds inside.

Maybe I really am paranoid, the growing sense of dread that I'm replaceable getting the better of me. If Ethan chose her, maybe I could understand why.

She turns away and says something to her friend, making me wonder if I imagined her gaze fixed on me tonight.

I take a slow breath, centering my thoughts, trying not to wonder if this is the retribution I've been waiting for—this woman, swooping in to upend my marriage. When will I stop obsessing, stop waiting for the punishment I think I deserve? Not only do I imagine my husband seeing someone else, she's nothing short of perfect.

I look at the jagged scar snaking its way up my arm. It looks like something got under my skin, leaving a trail of destruction in its wake. I used to hate how damaged the scar made me feel. Now, it doesn't seem like enough to make up for what happened.

The woman's lips move, but she's too far away to be heard. Her friend laughs again. She isn't Ethan's fling, or she would be with him now. She's just a stranger on a fun night out with her friends. They are carefree, unattached. There are no rings on their fingers, except the ones they bought for themselves. They're here for fun. None of them cares what anyone else thinks of them.

They laugh loudly, talk, and are open to wherever the night takes them in a way I haven't been since *that* night. I haven't told Ethan, which I felt guilty about until I realized he was keeping secrets of his own.

It happened before I knew Ethan, whereas his secrets feel like they're about us, and the ways we aren't working.

Chapter 3

Later in the evening, I catch the brunette watching me again, and I wonder if I might've known her a long time ago, before she looked like *that*. Maybe she's trying to figure out where she knows me from too. Is she a former patient? People don't look like themselves when they arrive at the emergency department in need of medical assistance. Bloated. Swollen. Broken.

It's possible, but I'm sure I would remember her even then. Her intense blue eyes give her an ethereal glow. If I wasn't afraid of dredging up the past and things I'd rather forget, I'd march right over and ask.

She raises her eyebrow, asking a question. I turn away, wondering how long I'll need to stare at the glossy floor before she looks away. I try to stay interested in the spot I've fixed my eyes on, wondering if that's dirt or an unfortunate texture, but I can't help thinking about her, about why she seems so interested in me. Would Ethan hire someone to follow me while he's away?

Maybe she's supposed to find out whether I'm drinking cocktails, to help him figure out why we haven't been able to have a baby. He seems to think there's something stopping us from falling pregnant. It would explain why this elegant-looking woman is at a bar, but surely spies don't take their friends along to stakeouts, and suddenly I'm sure she's just a woman, and I'm the paranoid wife I didn't want to be.

If it wasn't so stupid, I'd laugh. My husband wouldn't spy on me. He trusts me. Besides, if he wanted someone to follow me, a beautiful woman in a black dress would draw too much attention.

My gaze is pulled back to the table as Cassandra returns with our drinks, setting a whole bottle of champagne down with a thud. "We're going to finish this," she says with a grin. We don't usually drink enough to get tipsy, but most of us don't have shifts tomorrow, and Ethan isn't back from Los Angeles until late Friday evening.

I can't face sitting around waiting for him to get back, trying to figure out whether he's with her.

A pang of jealousy at this nameless, faceless woman who may or may not exist creeps through me. Ethan and I used to travel together. It was a shared love of ours, and the reason we got married somewhere new and exciting, placing some names in a hat and pulling one out to decide where to go.

I try to stop myself from going down that path. I shouldn't be sad or jealous—I should be furious. I should be demanding answers, telling myself he doesn't deserve my tears, but all I feel is an overwhelming sadness threatening to engulf me.

When Zoe and Isla see the bottle of champagne, they make their way back from the dance floor, unsteady on their feet from the blue heaven cocktails they've been drinking all night.

I force a smile as Cassandra pours four glasses of pink, bubbly liquid, accepting one distractedly, looking for the woman in the black dress. She has left her table, disappearing into the crowd. It's not that late, but maybe she went home for the night.

What kind of place would she call home? Maybe she shares an apartment with a friend. Or perhaps she lives alone with a pet. I can see her going home to a dog that wags its tail to greet her.

"So, what are we celebrating?" asks Zoe, her voice somehow carrying despite the din of the bar. She leans on the little bar table we're gathered around and takes a glass, handing one to Isla, who is distracted by something just beyond the dance floor.

"Aria, are you there?" asks Zoe in a singsong tone, waving a hand to get my attention, champagne sloshing inside her glass.

"Sorry, I guess I zoned out," I say, feeling selfish. I snap myself back to reality, focusing on the cold glass in my hand to keep myself present. It's a trick I learned to address the intrusive thoughts I had after the *incident*.

"Well, don't. Because I have some great news, and you're gonna want to hear it!" Cassandra squeals. She looks at Isla's glass, which is already a third empty, and her smile fades. "Save some for the toast," she says, her eye roll giving away the joke as she pours more into Isla's glass.

"Here, you can have mine," I say, starting to hand the glass to Isla.

"Are you still on that health kick?"

I nod. It's not a complete lie. I haven't told my friends we're trying for a baby, that I'm cutting out things that could make it harder to fall pregnant. Isla is reaching for my glass, but Cassandra stops her and says, "Tonight you're not. I need you to celebrate properly."

I can't refuse without making a scene, and I'm not sure I want to tell them we've been trying to conceive when it feels like it might never happen.

Lifting our glasses in anticipation, we all wait as Cassandra clears her throat, making a show of announcing her news. I can't imagine what she's about to say, and my first thought is that she's going on an overseas adventure, or maybe she's eloping with some guy she just met, and is planning on living in Spain for a year, doing nothing except eating food and making love.

She speaks loudly to drown out the music, which thumps with a club rhythm. "Well, you all know I've had my eye on that promotion . . ." She stops, waiting for us to acknowledge that she has indeed been working hard to get promoted. We all nod, and Isla rolls her eyes dramatically. "This is about work?" she asks, clearly disappointed.

"And," continues Cassandra, not allowing Isla to steal her momentum, "it looks like I finally got it! They're moving me up to Assistant Nurse Manager of the ER."

I know what this means to Cassandra. I've known her longer than I've known Isla and Zoe—since we were just a couple of student nurses figuring out how to hold a stethoscope properly while taking a blood pressure reading. She works harder than anyone I know. She has a way with patients that makes them feel special, and uses humor to keep the nurses on track during long, grueling shifts.

When we were still learning, I wish someone had warned me that no matter how much training you did, nothing could prepare you for that first life-or-death situation when a patient is struggling to breathe and you have to act fast while waiting for the doctor to arrive. I wish I knew that sometimes the doctor is busy with another emergency and all you can do is try to keep the patient alive until they get there.

I raise my glass and call a toast to my best friend. Isla and Zoe raise their glasses, echoing my sentiments that Cassandra will be great in her new role.

"Does this mean you'll be our new boss?" asks Zoe, laughing. "Like Murphy?"

Cassandra almost chokes on her champagne, swallowing the fizzy liquid quickly. "God no! I will never be like Murphy!"

Murphy has been in the job too long. She never takes vacations and never smiles. She also wears her socks unevenly and we joke that she doesn't know what a smile is because she mustn't have any mirrors in her house to see her own expression.

Zoe has a point. She might not be Murphy, but Cassandra's new role will take her one step away from being one of the girls.

Chapter 4

When Isla and Zoe finish their drinks, they make an unsteady return to the dance floor.

Cassandra looks at me with her big brown eyes, and I know my best friend is sizing me up. "Okay, honey. What's up with you?"

I've always admired her directness, the way she gets to the point but makes you feel like she's doing it for your own good. I wish she hadn't noticed anything was wrong. I don't want to spoil her celebration.

"It's nothing," I lie, knowing before I get the words out that she isn't buying it.

She folds her arms across her chest and sighs. "Let's try again. I love you. You know I do, but you've been so distant. Is it work, or something closer to home?"

Since we work together, she knows things are good there. That means she's asking what's going on at home.

She doesn't say it, but I can feel the real question. *What's up with you and Ethan?*

"I'm fine," I say, hoping she'll let it slide.

"Okay. I'm gonna tell you how it looks from where I'm standing, and I'm gonna try my best to be gentle," she says.

Here we go. My stomach somersaults. I sip my pink champagne, taking in too much, so the bubbles fizz in the back of my throat, almost choking me.

Cassandra unfolds her arms and takes hold of my hand. "It's been a while since you came out for drinks with us. And I mean a *long* time. You've avoided my messages for a solid month, but I'm still your best friend, and . . ." Cassandra pauses. This must be the bit she's trying to deliver "gently."

I'm not sure I want to hear the rest. I haven't been the best friend I could be. I've canceled lunch dates and after-work drinks to avoid Cassandra seeing through my fake smiles and wandering mind, but she's noticed anyway.

"I thought you were avoiding me. I don't know what's going on," she continues, "but you're not going to talk because in the time I've known you, you've never talked about it when you've been hurting. You've never been able to let yourself just feel it and admit when things aren't perfect. You get all hermit-like and bottle it until it explodes, except it never explodes. It just stays bottled up while you keep on struggling."

I'm about to protest, but her knowing gaze stops me in my tracks.

"What has he done? I'll kick his ass if you want me to," she jokes, and I can't help but laugh because she's the kind of friend who would make good on her promise.

"He didn't *do* anything. I'm just being silly. Ethan's always working. It feels like he's away more than he's at home."

Cassandra considers my words, her face obscured by strobe light flashes as they dance around the room, giving me glimpses of her changing expression. "He's always worked a lot," she says. "I can keep you company while Ethan's gone. Willow can make one of those amazing dinners you've told me about."

I smile weakly. I hate that Ethan feels the need to hire someone to cook and clean up after us. I've offered to do it myself, but Willow has worked for Ethan since before we met and it's something he insists on, claiming that he wouldn't want to leave her out of a job. The truth is, I miss cooking. I like throwing ingredients together and making something, or having an excuse to order takeout if I feel like it. When Ethan's away, I insist on making my own dinner, usually something simple like warm grilled chicken salad, which used to be one of my favorites. I assure Cassandra that's why I haven't invited her over. I'm hardly a chef and I doubt my cooking could compare to the culinary dishes Willow prepares.

My purse buzzes and I reach in, retrieving my phone. It's as if Ethan knows we're talking about him. I hold up the screen to show Cassandra. "Ethan just texted."

I read the message quickly. It's short and has the feel of being rushed so that whatever business he's attending to isn't interrupted. There are multiple typos, and a few words out of place, unlike his usual carefully edited messages.

"You look like I just told you to drink your own pee, so I'm guessing it's not good news."

I shrug. "He was just letting me know he needs to stay a couple more days. They didn't close the deal yet, but it looks like they're not done trying."

"He's just *letting* you know? No phone call saying, 'Hey baby, I'm sorry, but it looks like I have to stay'?"

"It's fine. If he needs to stay, he needs to stay."

She doesn't come out and say it, but I can see by the twist of her lips that she doesn't believe I'm as OK as I'm trying to sound. Ethan's trips are getting longer, and I feel his absences more acutely. I've convinced myself he's not where he says he is.

This must be how a reasonable, trusting person becomes neurotic and paranoid.

It's never just one thing. It begins with an instinct. Something you can't quite name, but has the ability to jolt your stomach into a rubbery mess, spurred by tiny changes you haven't recognized yet that agitate your subconscious like something just outside your peripheral vision.

And then it happens. He says something out of character. It could be as simple as saying he loves you. Except it's too much, or not as much as usual. But when he does, you notice the spark is gone from his eyes. He's relaying a line he's said a hundred times, but this time, you can see he's going through the motions, that he doesn't *mean* it.

That's when I noticed something was different. When Ethan left for LA, he went through all the usual rituals. Getting his travel bag ready, packing an extra set of earbuds in case he needed them. Zipping everything inside, only to unzip to make sure he had fresh socks.

As he left, he kissed me like he usually does, held me as if he didn't want to let go, but it was when he told me he loved me, his eyes already on the door, like he was already gone, that I heard it. There was a finality in his voice. He was going away to reconsider our marriage.

Chapter 5

I know the company Ethan works for goes through busy periods, and they compensate him well for his time. However, it feels hypocritical to extend his trip when he hated the long hours I used to work.

When we first started trying for a baby, he asked me to reduce my number of shifts. Ethan hated the evening shifts that ended late at night, when I would come home and shower in a hurry before falling into an exhausted heap. He wanted us to make the most of our time together while it was still just the two of us. We woke up late on Sunday mornings, hazy from late nights out.

I think he worried a baby would change things.

His argument made sense, and I agreed, giddy at the thought of becoming a mother. I couldn't wait to tell Cassandra that Ethan and I planned on becoming parents, and that she would make the perfect godmother. She had worked in maternity for a year after we finished our training. She knew things that could help us conceive a healthy baby, but Ethan thought it would be better to keep it to ourselves until it happened. He thought it would avoid added pressure if we didn't fall pregnant right away, but I couldn't help wondering why he wanted to keep it a secret when I was bursting to say something.

I told Cassandra everything. Almost. We used each other as sounding boards when we had problems, bouncing options around until we found a solution. Out of respect for Ethan, I didn't tell her we were trying.

It turns out Ethan was right. Getting pregnant didn't happen like I expected, and the longer we tried, the more grateful I was that I didn't have anyone to update on the lack of news.

Ethan thought it was the stress of dealing with life and death in the emergency room. He didn't understand that being a nurse gave me a sense of purpose. I enjoyed helping people. I didn't say that to Ethan because he was right. My job was stressful sometimes.

I took his advice and reduced my shifts to work on staying physically, mentally, and emotionally healthy.

It's only now I realize giving up my shifts was my misguided way of feeling like I was taking action, ignoring my fear that something was wrong with my body.

Months later, the single blue line on the pregnancy test still taunted me, making me worry we would never be parents. How could I explain to Ethan that it may never happen for us, that my body couldn't seem to do what others found effortless, when I knew it would devastate him?

Maybe he's had the same fears. Has he been distancing himself while he figures out how to bring it up? Maybe he's looking for the right way to say it. Ethan has never been great at discussing feelings, which I assume got worse when his parents died. I still don't know how he managed it, but he graduated from Columbia Business School and has a successful career. I admire his grit and determination, the sacrifices he must've made to get where he is.

Family is important to Ethan. He wants a family of his own. He doesn't talk about them much, but I know he misses his parents, who I never got the chance to know. By the time Ethan and I met, they were already gone, victims of a tragic road accident.

Maybe Ethan was right, and there was more we could try to become parents. So, I cut back on the double shifts. There was always a new patient, a new problem that needed attention. I would pick it up again after. I started doing more yoga, planning healthier meals. I gave up takeout altogether and peed on a stick each month, hoping it would tell me I was about to begin my journey into motherhood. Each time I looked at the single line on the pregnancy test, hoping that a second identical line would appear. I started imagining a faint line just starting to show. I told myself I might be pregnant, but it was just too early for the hCG levels to flood my system.

I showed every negative test to Ethan, who seemed more disappointed with each one. I reminded myself that he wanted this too, that his disappointment hid the same fear that plagued me at night. Anger was an easier emotion to deal with than the hopelessness of waiting.

His workload increased around the time I started giving up on our dream of becoming parents. Clearly unsure of how to comfort me, he listened as I cried about still not being pregnant. He reminded me this affected him too, but it felt like he blamed me. He asked if I was taking multivitamins every day and said I shouldn't be stressed because I had cut back on work.

He questioned how serious I was, despite the extra vitamins I was taking and my grueling exercise schedule.

Now, as my thirtieth birthday approaches, I'm wondering if it's all been for nothing, and I just waited too long and missed my opportunity.

I used to scoff at thirty being too old. There are tons of women having kids well into their thirties—some even in their forties. When I was ready to become a mother, I thought it would just happen.

Eventually, I turned to the facts, searching for fertility statistics by age. What I found shocked me. Even in your early twenties, there's only a 25–30% chance of falling pregnant in any month. By age thirty, that drops to 20% and goes down rapidly from there. That meant that with everything going smoothly, it could still take five months, and it had already been longer than that.

Since Ethan's been gone, I've researched fertility clinics. I know we can afford it, but convincing him to talk to a stranger, let alone go through invasive tests, is another thing.

My phone beeps with another message. It's from Ethan. I read it right away, hoping it will fill the distance. He used to send gushy texts saying he couldn't wait to come home, but this is nothing like that. It's a reminder not to drink if I'm out with Cassandra.

I gaze at the drink in my hand, feeling as if someone caught me doing something I shouldn't be doing. A drink or two wouldn't hurt. It's not like I'm pregnant, and the alcohol will be out of my system by the time he gets back.

"What's wrong?" asks Cassandra.

I'm angry at Ethan, and sick of having no one to talk to about it. Cassandra is my best friend. Why shouldn't I talk to her?

"You're not allowed to drink now?"

She's waiting.

Once I open up, it's like I can't stop talking.

Chapter 6

I start with me and Ethan deciding we want a baby. She listens attentively, but when I explain how long we've been trying, how I'm letting it consume me, her expression changes.

"And you didn't tell me?" she asks, trying to sound annoyed. Behind the fire, I hear the hurt. I've known Cassandra longer than my husband, and I didn't tell her about one of the most important undertakings of my life. "Is that why you've been avoiding me?"

Her words sting. I haven't intentionally avoided her, but the sadness I've felt has been eating away at me, and I didn't know how to be around her bubbly personality without being a downer. "I wanted to tell you. Ethan thought we should keep it to ourselves, just in case. And he was right. I'm still not pregnant."

She makes a face, one that I've seen her make when a celebrity does something stupid but predictable and makes headlines for it. "Since when does Ethan decide what you're allowed to tell me and when you should say it?"

I know there's more on her mind, but she's holding back. When I don't answer, she moves to my side of the table, placing a hand on my arm. "Honey, you shouldn't have to go through this alone."

I'm about to protest that Ethan is going through it too and it's every bit as difficult for him, but the past months have made me wonder if that's true.

I feel a flood of tears well up. It feels good to talk to someone who's on my side, but I refuse to ruin Cassandra's celebration by fixating on it.

"Getting pregnant can take a while. Even when you're fit and healthy and doing everything right. It's not an exact science." I smile at her tone. She sounds just like Professor Delaney from our college days. Professor Delaney had a unique lilt to her voice. Sometimes her lectures felt like a junior high class, but she meant well and we still managed to pass, despite worrying all semester that we were failing because we never got our assignments handed back on time to review them before the test that usually came after.

Cassandra's trying to cheer me up and I love her for it, but somehow it makes me feel worse. What if my body isn't working and I can't have children?

"You're right, but I'm scared it won't happen."

I've always wondered if Cassandra dislikes Ethan, but I've never had the guts to ask, so I'm surprised when she says, "Don't give up. I know this is important to you, but you have options. A friend of mine is a fertility specialist here in New York. It can take ages to get an appointment with her, but she's great. She is expensive, but I can ask her to squeeze you in?"

"Really?" The squeak in my voice betrays my excitement and I almost reach over and squish her in a hug.

I should talk to Ethan before agreeing to see a fertility specialist, but I'm worried we might miss our opportunity, and who knows how long we will be on a waitlist?

I can talk to him about it when he gets back. If we can't have a baby naturally maybe a specialist can tell us what happens next.

"Really," Cassandra confirms, a smile playing on her lips.

Images of Ethan holding a tiny bundle wrapped up with a little beanie atop its head almost overwhelms me. My body aches to hold that little bundle between us and I use that feeling, willing my body to make it happen. I almost convince myself that this will solve all our problems.

"You're the best." I don't need to feign excitement—if there's anything I can do to become a mother, I'll do it. I think of the tests they can run to check my egg count and how healthy my uterus is. There are tests Ethan can do too, but doubt lingers in my mind like an unwanted guest, because there's a chance Ethan won't agree to it.

I mentioned seeing a fertility specialist a few months ago, but he dismissed it, confident that if we waited, things would happen on their own. Perhaps he's changed his mind since then?

Maybe he was avoiding it. He had mentioned the cost, which seemed strange because we could afford it. I didn't push, but I got the feeling he was hiding the real reason he didn't want to see a specialist.

Cassandra's smooth alto tones interrupt my thoughts. "Aria, are you all right?"

I assure her I'm fine. She smiles but doesn't look convinced. "I'm glad you told me, even if you waited a millennium. Is there anything else you want to talk about?"

I smile back at her. She's giving me an opportunity to talk without being pushy. Cassandra has always been able to read me. Usually I'd tell her if I thought my husband was having an affair, but I don't want her second-guessing her offer to set up a fertility appointment. I can't risk her changing her mind.

Besides, what if Ethan isn't having an affair, and my imagination is just running wild because I'm stressed out? It could cause a bigger problem than necessary if I say something now. I decide to keep it to myself, ignoring the flash of red-hot guilt when Cassandra gives me a warm look.

"It's good talking to the *real* Aria again. I was worried you disappeared on me." She laughs, trying to lighten the mood. Humor has always been her go-to tension breaker. "I read a NASA article that made me think of you. It said aliens could be real, and I thought, yeah, I can believe that. Maybe they've taken over Aria's brain."

I laugh at her joke to cover my true feelings, pushing the guilt down as far as it will go. It feels like the half-truths I'm telling are nothing more than thinly disguised lies. I can't think of a comeback quick enough because she's right. She isn't getting the real Aria, not even by half thanks to Ethan and the person following me.

I can't tell her because I'd have to admit that I think the person my husband is seeing might be keeping tabs on me and risk sounding paranoid.

Cassandra beats me to a comeback with another quip. "It may be selfish, but I'm kinda relieved you weren't avoiding me."

"Never." That's not quite true either. I've missed Cassandra's humor, her bright energy that never seems to dwindle. I don't know where she gets it from, but she's generous with her time and gives it freely to others. It makes it impossible not to love her. It's why she's a great nurse.

I don't tell her I would believe her alien theory, given my husband's recent behavior.

She turns to the dance floor and my eyes follow. I see Zoe dancing right away, somewhere close to the middle of the room, her hips moving to the music. I search either side of her, looking for Isla. First my eyes roam toward the exit, then to the front of the stage where a fresh-faced DJ is mixing music like he's been doing it for a lot longer than his smooth, baby-faced features would suggest.

I look back at Zoe. A man in a tight T-shirt joins her on the dance floor. The sequins of her glittery dress snake around her waist like scales, reflecting off his arm. I look away as they dance closer, embarrassed to have stumbled across an intimate moment between them.

"Well, there's Zoe." Cassandra stares openly at our friend, trying to catch her eye. "Who's that guy? He doesn't look like her usual type. Too pale."

It's impossible not to smile at that when I look at her own smooth dark skin. Everyone must look pale to Cassandra, but she's right.

"Yeah, but where's Isla?" I scan the dance floor but don't see her.

"Probably fixing her face in the restroom. That girl wears more makeup than I knew could fit on one face," she says affectionately.

It's an ongoing joke in our group. Isla is always in full makeup, including lash extensions, hair, and salon nails. We rib her about how she finds the time to work to pay for it. It takes hours to get ready, but between hanging with us and making time for her latest boyfriend, she manages just fine.

I sneak a glance at the brunette's table. Her friends buzz back and forth, congregating at the table to sip cocktails before disappearing like bees. Now that I'm paying attention, they have the distinct uniformity of a bachelorette party, but I can't see a bride-to-be donning a gaudy veil or sash.

The brunette is still gone. A woman with rich red hair and a round, doll-like face has taken her seat, waving her arms to the music and singing along. Tomorrow, she will most likely forget about her drunken freedom.

Cassandra and I talk with an ease that was missing when we arrived, clearing the air between us, clearing layers of dust that have settled over our friendship. I reluctantly agree to another bottle of champagne when Cassandra promises it will lure Isla back to our table.

An uneasiness washes over me when the champagne arrives and there's still no sign of Isla. I announce I'm going to check the bathroom and slip off my bar stool with my purse, so Cassandra has one less thing to babysit. I make my way to the back of the venue, but when I get to the bathroom, the line is as long as ever, with at least six women waiting before me. The line spills outside and into the corridor.

Maybe the line was this long when Isla got here. That would explain her absence. I stop, hoping to catch Isla on her way out, but the line isn't moving.

I cut in front, ignoring the grumbles from behind, and try the handle. The door doesn't give, and a few moments later, a bartender steps out of the restroom, worry lines creasing her face.

"Sorry, but we're going to have to close these up," she says, ushering the line backward, her blonde ponytail flicking back and forth.

The woman at the front of the line makes an exaggerated, incredulous expression. "What are we supposed to do? I'm about to pee my pants."

"Uh, just use the men's bathroom," says the blonde distractedly, ignoring the woman, who protests sarcastically that she hasn't mastered how to use a urinal yet.

"Why can't we just use this one?" the woman asks indignantly, so busy complaining that she doesn't notice two women trying to brush past her to get to the front of the new line. I look at their makeup-enhanced faces, but neither one of them is Isla. Maybe she's still finishing up inside?

"We need to close up for cleaning," says the blonde woman, but I crane my neck to get a peek inside before she closes the door behind her. I can see an arm, as if the person it's attached to fell asleep there for the night. The longer I look, the more apparent it becomes that whoever it belongs to is completely still, more like an object than a living thing.

Perhaps whoever's in there drank too much and passed out on the floor. I hope that's all that has happened.

"Well, can't I just be quick? I don't care if it's messy." The woman at the front shifts uncomfortably as the rest of the line dissipates, probably because she's causing a scene. Ironically, she doesn't seem to realize she'll be at the end of the new queue.

The woman ushering everyone from the bathroom has her back to the door, guarding whatever's inside. A nervous feeling begins low in my stomach. She's clearly waiting for someone to arrive, but I approach her anyway. Her name tag says her name is Billie. "I'm sorry to bother you, but I think my friend's still inside."

Billie's eyes flash at me, as if she's not sure whether to respond. "I'm sorry, but that's everyone out for now."

"Would you mind having a quick look? Two people came out, but there are five stalls," I press. I've been here before, waited outside this exact bathroom, and I know they're usually full.

Billie averts her eyes, looking over my shoulder as if the person she's waiting for has arrived.

I turn, expecting someone laden with cleaning products to appear, ready to clean up whatever drunken mess the passed-out girl in the bathroom has made.

Instead, a man in a black T-shirt and jeans who looks as frazzled as Billie arrives. A somber look passes between them, and I can see it's more than just an unpleasant mess that has them acting so subdued.

When he notices me, he looks me over, trying to figure out if I'm meant to still be here. I save him the trouble and ask if he's seen Isla, giving a vague description of the red dress she was wearing tonight.

He apologizes, unable to help, and turns to Billie. "In there?" he whispers, choosing his words carefully. Whatever's in there, they don't want to make a scene about it.

Billie nods, knuckles on her hips, as if steadying herself before moving aside to let him through.

He reaches into his pocket and takes out his own set of keys, sifting through for the right one. I'm guessing from the way Billie interacts with him, staying out of his way, answering his questions, that he must be her boss.

He hesitates before he goes in, clearly uncomfortable about entering the ladies' room. He disappears inside. The door thuds behind him.

"Are you sure you didn't see her inside?" I press, anxiety seeping into my tone. "She has long hair with highlights kind of like mine."

"Sorry," Billie says, her tone the right mix of sympathy and distance. She's probably had plenty of practice dealing with drunk, disgruntled customers. She apologizes so well I can't tell what she's apologizing for.

My stomach is roiling now, preparing me for what comes next. What if she's sorry for what's on the other side of the door, not for leaving my questions unanswered? My phone beeps and I check it, hoping it's Cassandra sending a photo she just took of Isla drinking at our table.

Did you find her??

My hope fades. It can't be Isla in there, can it? Did she pass out? If she did, why isn't someone calling an ambulance or something? It's possible that situations like this are common at bars, and they handle them quietly. They could be splashing water onto her face and coaxing her off the floor right now.

Still, my nerves bite at me. Something about this doesn't feel right. I'm about to find out what when the man in the black T-shirt leaves the bathroom looking rattled. "Jesus," he says, locking the door behind him. I don't have to ask to know he won't forget what he saw in there.

His breathing is shallow and fast, the composure he had when he entered almost shot. He doesn't meet our eyes when he says, "Call the police."

Chapter 7

Those three words set off alarm bells in my head, prompting me to call Isla. The thought of her leaving with a random guy who might be a weird sex freak isn't as scary as the idea of her going into the restroom tonight.

I hear a ringtone coming from the bathroom. What are the chances that someone's still inside? That their phone rang at the same time I called Isla? It rings three times before I hear her voice, bright and friendly. I almost start speaking before I realize it's just her voicemail.

My heartbeat echoes in my throat as I leave a quick message, telling her to call me back.

I glance at the locked door, recalling Billie's reaction as she emerged and swiftly locked it. I remember the expression on her boss's face, confirming what I already knew.

There's a body in there. The hand I saw wasn't moving because the person inside was already dead. I only saw the curve of an arm, not enough to say whether it could be Isla.

Billie and her boss have vanished to call the police and handle the necessary arrangements. I'm still standing there, afraid to move. I should search the bar, in case Isla's somewhere I haven't looked yet, but I'm rooted to the spot, wondering if Isla's behind that door.

I expect the music to stop, for someone to send everyone home, but the steady rhythm of drums continues. In the dampened light, it feels as if I'm in a creepy fun house, ready for the monster to jump out of the shadows and scare me.

I step back into the darkness, away from the disco lights that sweep the dance floor like a searchlight. No monster is as scary as not knowing where Isla has gone. I go back and try the door handle to the bathroom again, just in case the manager forgot to lock it properly in his shock, but the handle sticks.

A sense of foreboding grips me as I hold my breath and sidle up against the door. I press my ear against it to listen as I raise my phone to my other ear and hit redial. A bright ringtone chirps from the other side. My knees weaken and I lean against the solid frame for support as my call goes to Isla's voicemail.

"Isla?" I call against the door, my voice a weak thread.

I wait for her response, hope leaching from my voice each time I call her name.

A sound behind startles me, and I jump back from the door to find Cassandra. "What's going on? I waited for you. I had to give up our table. Did you find Isla?"

Zoe appears behind Cassandra. "There you are. I was talking to you back at the table before I realized you left, and I was actually talking to complete strangers," she says playfully. Her tone turns serious. "I couldn't find Isla anywhere, but I didn't see her leave with anyone. She's not answering her phone either. I'm worried."

If they were playing a prank on me, Isla would walk in now and say, "Gotcha, bitches." But there's an eerie absence where Isla would usually be, and Zoe's tone suggests if this is a prank, she's as much in the dark as I am.

"Was she in the bathroom?" asks Cassandra, already trying the door handle. She uses more force, cursing when it refuses to turn in her hand. She knocks on the door in frustration.

I try to tell them what happened when I dialed Isla's phone, but Cassandra already has her phone to her ear. As the music dips, a ringtone echoes from inside the bathroom, stark in the sudden silence. Cassandra's head jerks toward the sound.

"That's Isla's ringtone," says Zoe as two men in dark chinos and shirts try to move past us, accompanied by the manager who went in earlier.

"Excuse me, but we're going to have to ask you to leave this area," says one of the men in an authoritative tone. I know immediately that he's a cop, and that there's definitely a body in the bathroom.

"I think our friend is in there. We called and her phone rang from inside," I say, pointing, desperate to find out if Isla's in there. Until I know for sure, I'm willing to let myself hope she dropped her phone in there without noticing. It's a long shot, but the alternative is unfathomable.

"It couldn't hurt to have someone identify the body." The man I'm talking to introduces himself as Detective Kinsley Scott. He has a handsome face with soft lines that make him seem approachable for a cop. I absently give him my name.

All I can focus on is his confirmation of a body inside. Even if it's not Isla, someone's life has ended here tonight. What if, while we were sipping champagne, someone committed a murder just a few feet away from where we were sitting?

"What do you think happened?" I calm myself with a deep breath. Being a nurse, I know that if someone ODs and dies, the police are usually called. Maybe they were partying too hard with a bad batch of party drugs, and the police were looking for the dealer?

An EMT waits patiently as the door is unlocked before disappearing inside.

The detective holds up a finger as if asking me to wait a minute. I stand there awkwardly, aware of the small crowd gathering to see what the fuss is about. A uniformed officer moves them back with an authoritative tone.

The detective emerges moments later and shows me a close-up of a woman's face.

The angle he chose makes the picture look like an arty amateur selfie. The damage to her face is almost hidden, but a sliver of blood edges into the shot. Though it just happened, it's clear that the girl in the photo is dead. Her eyes will never open again, resting heavily like windows that have fused together from being shut for too long. Her face is relieved of expression, the stillness of death taking the sharpened angles of her cheeks and slackening her jaw. I can tell she hasn't been dead for long.

Cassandra and Zoe look at the image over the detective's shoulder. He retracts it a little, as if he doesn't want too many people to see her yet. Maybe he thinks we're involved and doesn't want to compromise the investigation. Or he just wants a chance to tell her family first.

Waves of nausea ebb deep in my stomach, growing into a cascade before I can stop them. They spill over in a rush and I turn and duck my head into a pot plant, releasing the contents of my stomach.

The detective looks at me with an expression somewhere between sympathy and repulsion, waiting until I've composed myself before speaking again.

"Is she your friend?" he asks, but the question is clearly a formality because Zoe is swaying, unsteady on her feet, and not just from the alcohol. She emits a deep cry of grief before being led away by one of the EMTs. I hadn't noticed them come in, but suddenly there are people everywhere. I watch as two of them disappear into the cordoned-off bathroom while another stands to the side, redirecting people to use alternative restrooms instead.

A look passes between me and Cassandra, each waiting for the other to confirm it, just in case we've got it wrong.

"It's her," I say. "It's Isla."

Chapter 8

The police have more questions. They want to know how long we were at the bar, whether Isla talked to anyone outside of our group, if she took any drugs that we knew of, and a slew of other questions I can't remember.

By the time I arrive home, it's almost two in the morning. I can't sleep, so I let myself cry. Ugly, racking sobs that feel like I might stop breathing.

Eventually there are no tears left, and I'm numb, thinking how I'll never see Isla again. Never hear her share gossip she learned while getting her nails done or give us a rundown on the best thing about her latest boyfriend. It's always something unexpected. Things I wouldn't think to notice, but Isla always found something beautiful in everyone. She told us the last boyfriend she dated had fingertips that made her skin tingle when he ran them down her thigh, prompting Cassandra to ask if he used hand cream with menthol while the rest of us laughed.

Usually, Isla would bring her new fling along to drinks, where we would get to know them a bit. We all knew it was her way of seeing what we thought of them when we went out for coffee and tore them apart later in the week, but we never got to meet Tingling Hands, as Cassandra dubbed him, before Isla moved on.

Isla's love life became a real-life version of *The Bachelorette*, with her as the star and the rest of us acting as armchair psychologists, analyzing her compatibility with prospective partners and predicting how long it would last.

We hadn't come across anyone who seemed likely to hold Isla's attention long enough to make it past six months. Now, the realization that no one would sets off a fresh wave of tears.

I roll over in my empty bed, wishing Ethan was here to tell me everything will be okay, even if it isn't true. I could ask him to come home, but it's still early morning in LA and I don't want to disturb him.

Eventually, I decide this is different. He won't mind being woken up when he hears what has happened. These aren't exactly normal circumstances. I quickly type out a message, hesitating when I try to mention Isla.

I need you here . . . can you please come home?

I can't bring myself to say one of my best friends just died, that what I saw when I looked at that picture will never be gone from my mind. I'm used to death, but seeing Isla feels different from the strangers in the ER who I know might not make it. They're already sick or injured when they come in, and when they die it's sad, and I feel a pang for what's lost—but knowing Isla's mannerisms and the way her lips curled at the edges when she smiled, to see that taken from her, not in a hospital but in a bathroom stall at a bar, feels wrong.

Ethan doesn't answer my text, and eventually I call. He doesn't sleep well when he's not at home in his own bed, so I don't want to wake him, but I need to hear his voice.

The phone rings four times before he answers. His tone is formal. It sounds like the voice he uses when he's with a client. "Ethan Dolan speaking."

I check the time, raising my eyebrows when I see it's almost nine in the morning. I have been lying here thinking about Isla for hours. Did I fall asleep without realizing it?

He waits for me to say something. "Ethan?" I say, trying to sound calm.

"Hi." He maintains the formal tone. I get the feeling I've caught him at a bad time.

"Should I call back later?"

"No, that's okay." His voice grows distant—he must have covered the receiver. I probably caught him during an early morning meeting with a client. He introduced them years ago as a way to fit more into his day. "Excuse me for a moment. I need to take this," he says.

He's quiet for a few moments while he finds somewhere to talk. "What's wrong?" he asks, his voice softening. "Is everything okay?"

"Yeah. Um . . ." I stall while I figure out how to tell him that Isla is dead and that it looks like someone murdered her. I want to say that until I find out why someone killed my friend, who worked at an advertising agency and still visited her grandma at least once a week to make sure she was eating well, I won't be able to sleep. We might never have answers.

"Actually, things aren't okay at all." I pause, steadying my voice.

"What happened, sweetheart?" He sounds worried now, but the words don't want to come out, no matter how I try to phrase them.

I fight the sinking feeling that threatens to consume me. "I went out for drinks with the girls, and . . ."

He sighs, like I've just confirmed something he already suspected. "You were *drinking*?" The way he asks makes it sound like he's already pinpointed drinking as the reason something bad happened. Maybe he thinks I've done something drunk and stupid, but I force myself to continue and ignore his judgmental tone.

"I only had one glass," I say, rushing to tell him why I'm calling before he has to get back to his meeting. "It's Isla . . ." I swallow back a heaviness in my throat. "She left to go to the bathroom, and someone killed her."

"In the bathroom?" he asks, as if that's the strange part of the story, even though I just told him my friend was murdered. He clears his throat, processing what I've just said. "Aria, I'm so sorry. I wish I could be there."

I tell him how I waited while the police went in, how awful it was to wait for confirmation it was her, knowing but not really knowing until the police showed me her picture.

"I don't want to be alone. Can you come home?"

I thought my husband, who used to be so attentive and concerned about my feelings, would hear how upset I was at losing one of my best friends. I figured he would tell me he was already packing, that he was just as upset as I was, and that he would be home soon.

Instead, a silence stretches over the line, so absolute that I can almost hear him thinking it through. I can tell what he's about to say before he says it.

"Honey, I'm so sorry, but I just can't right now. My boss is expecting me to close this deal."

What about what your wife is expecting? The words flare on my tongue, almost spilling over, but I'm too worn down to fight. "Okay," I say weakly, hit by a sudden numbness. If it were him, he would expect me to be there. He would take my absence as an indication of how little I loved him.

I guess the rules are different for each of us, and I end the call feeling more alone than ever. I lie there in the silence afterward, trying to get comfortable.

I see Isla as she was last night, promising she was going to give the dance floor a run for its money. Giving Zoe a hard time when she complained she was wearing four-inch heels and recovering from a double shift on a busy night, plying her with alcohol to numb her aching feet until Zoe caved and agreed to dance with her, making it less obvious while they were together that Isla was there to pick up, even if she was.

I laugh into the darkness at the memory, a sad, stark sound with no one else to hear it.

An intrusive thought strikes, demanding to be heard. What kind of business deal is so important that it trumps being there for your wife when she's just lost her friend?

I try to look at things from his perspective. In a week or two, Isla will still be gone and Ethan can comfort me then, but the business prospects might move on. I never ask him to skip work commitments, not even when I had a panic attack about my body housing a baby. And thank goodness for that. I'm not sure I would've wanted to know that when I needed him, he wouldn't have been there.

I spend the entire morning irritated by my own thoughts and angry with Ethan. I pick up my phone to distract myself, trying not to remember that Isla is gone.

An emoji-laden name catches my eye that I don't recall seeing before. Wedged between a stack of emojis is *Cassandra*, and I realize she must've done it herself while my phone was on the table and I wasn't looking. It's something we used to do all the time, though usually we would change each other's ringtones to something cheesy or embarrassing, a race to the bottom of all-time bad songs to show whoever happened to be there when your phone started ringing that you had awful taste in music.

I call, ready to question her choice in emojis, which feature a lot of eggplants. She answers on the first ring, as if she's been awaiting my call. She was probably just scrolling her phone, trying to distract herself too, but I'm glad to hear her voice.

"Hey. It's me," I say. "I'm guessing you can't focus on anything either?"

"You too, huh?" she asks. "I've been thinking about it all day."

"I mean, I'm calling you," I answer automatically, trying to keep my tone light but failing.

"There's a reason it's called a rhetorical question," she fires back.

"Sorry. I didn't really sleep last night," I say. I couldn't sleep after my talk with Ethan either, and I'm feeling it. "I can't stop thinking about the way Isla looked in that photo."

"Me either," she says. "I was thinking about the blood on the back of her head. Where did it come from? Did someone hit her with something?"

"I know," I agree. "I noticed it too. It wasn't much, but just enough to see. I wondered if there was more. Maybe the detective edited it out before showing it to us."

"Damn. I didn't even think of that. It's scary if someone did that to her."

"Do you think she fell and hit her head? Or did someone kill her?"

"I mean, she was drunk, so she could have fallen." Cassandra's tone tells me she doesn't believe that. "But I've seen her drunker."

She's right. Isla held her alcohol well. "I feel it too," I say. "Something happened to her. She didn't just fall. But why Isla? If someone had a reason to kill her, then no one's safe."

"I know," Cassandra says in a low tone. "The girl was like a big puppy dog."

I smile. It's a great way to describe her. Boundless energy. Friendly. Trusting to a fault. There can't have been many people who would want her dead, but why would someone murder a random girl in a bathroom when they might get caught? It seems too risky.

"Wasn't she wearing a necklace?" I say. "She was fidgeting with it, pulling the charm around the chain."

"Yeah, I think so. Why?"

"I didn't notice it in the picture," I say.

"Maybe an ex killed her? Did any of her boyfriends buy her that jewelry? Maybe he wasn't ready for her five-second 'thanks and goodbye' breakup speech. He might've been angry she was dumping him," says Cassandra without missing a beat, as eager as I am to find out why Isla met such an undignified death in a bathroom stall.

She makes a good point. Isla doesn't have the best track record for sensitive breakups. When Cassandra brought it up to her once, Isla said that she didn't like the part where it ended, that she would want it to be quick and clean if she were the one being dumped, but she hadn't been on the receiving end often enough to understand how hurtful it was.

The line goes quiet until Cassandra changes the subject, saying she thought lounging around the house at this time of the day was an urban legend her twenty-year-old self knew might exist but hadn't experienced.

We stay on the line for the next twenty minutes, our conversation drawn out and sleepy, neither of us wanting to plunge back into the reality that just hours ago, we hadn't noticed our friend being murdered a few feet away.

Our call comes to a natural end and my mind slides back to Isla and how the killer must have stopped her from screaming. Why didn't we hear her cry for help? Maybe they struck her, knocking her unconscious before she saw them coming.

Maybe she did scream, but the music was too loud to hear it.

Or she didn't scream because she knew her killer. She would've thought they were approaching her to say hello, maybe coming in for a hug. A sudden act of violence from someone she knew wouldn't give her time to scream.

I can't think of anyone who would want to harm her.

A man entering the women's bathroom would attract attention. Was Isla's killer a woman who wouldn't be noticed, or had Isla gone in there with someone?

Hookups happened all the time. Most people pretended not to notice a couple sneaking into the bathroom together.

Zoe was dancing with someone that night. They were so close they looked amorphous, but Isla had seemed happy dancing alone, and I hadn't seen her talk to anyone for longer than a minute or two.

A knock at the door interrupts my thoughts.

My heart stalls in my throat, and I try to remember to breathe. What if it's the person who followed me last week?

Their presence had creeped me out then, but it feels even more menacing now.

Chapter 9

I stare at the door handle but don't answer it. I consider calling out, just a simple hello to see who answers, but if I do that, they will know I'm home.

What if it's the killer?

I shake the thought away. A more likely possibility is that it's Ethan coming home because he realized I was serious when I asked him to, waiting with a bunch of flowers, ready to apologize for being such an ass.

Except that doesn't make sense, because Ethan has a key. He wouldn't need to knock. Instinctively, I know it isn't my husband. I approach the door carefully, as if I can figure out who's there, but my door doesn't have a peephole. If I want to know who knocked, I have to open the door, but it's late enough that I don't want to be stuck making small talk with the neighbors.

A voice rings out, startling me and making me wish I'd armed myself with a hairbrush or a nightlamp—anything—before moving from the safety of my bedroom.

I know that voice.

I slide the lock and pull open the door. "Cassandra! You scared the shit out of me."

"Well, if I told you I was coming over, you would've made up some crap about why I shouldn't, when neither of us wants to be alone right now."

She looks at me pointedly until I look away. She's right. On both counts.

I think of Zoe at home, probably obsessing over what happened to Isla. I hope someone is there to keep her company and make her warm tea. It might be good to talk to someone who didn't see Isla's lifeless face.

I think about calling her myself and decide against it for now. She might need more time to process what happened.

Cassandra studies my face. "You look like you've seen a ghost," she says, realizing too late what she's said. "Shit. Sorry. I didn't think."

A wan smile crosses my face. "Isla would've laughed at that if one of us had died. Even if we were murdered," I muse, and Cassandra agrees. Isla used humor when things got uncomfortable.

I pull two mugs from the cupboard without asking Cassandra if she would like coffee before brewing a pot. It's getting late in the afternoon, but I need a little pick-me-up and I can see Cassandra does too.

Moments later, we sit side by side on the sofa with steaming coffee mugs. "There's a reason I'm so jumpy. I didn't say anything because I thought I was being paranoid, but now I'm not so sure."

"Okay," says Cassandra slowly, and I know my tone is scaring her.

"Last week, I caught the subway home from work, and I thought someone was following me. They ran off when I called out. I don't think they wanted me to know who they were."

"Did you see them?"

I shake my head, thinking of the woman with dark hair and blue eyes, wondering where she disappeared to. Maybe it was gaze perception and I noticed her watching me. Perhaps someone sent her there to monitor me, but why would anyone want to spy on me?

"But what if they were at the bar? Maybe they thought I was going to the bathroom when it was really Isla. Maybe it got her killed."

"You think someone was deciding whether to kill you?" Cassandra sounds alarmed. She watches me over the top of her mug.

I wasn't sure until I heard her say it out loud, but that's exactly what I think. Ethan has been acting strange, and my imagination is running wild after Isla's death, but my gut is still telling me something's wrong, that whoever my husband is seeing wants me out of the picture.

If Ethan's fling believes I'm the reason they can't be together, maybe she thinks eliminating me will mean she can have Ethan all to herself. What if she's just waiting for the right moment to kill me?

"Tell me why someone would want you dead." She sounds skeptical. "Have you done something I don't know about?" she jokes.

I can't remember if I mentioned Ethan's possible affair in my drunken state last night, but I'm hesitant to talk about it now.

Cassandra's fertility specialist may be my only chance to have a baby of my own. I want that referral so badly that I consider making something up, but I can't pretend Isla isn't dead, and if she's dead because of me, I owe it to her to be truthful.

"I'm not involved in anything," I say. "But I think Ethan might be." I stop talking. It's out there now. No more pretending to myself that I don't think it. The fact that I've been hiding my suspicions makes this feel like a confession.

Cassandra wouldn't hide something like that. She wouldn't ignore it either. She would take the bull by the horns and make it sit. But I'm not Cassandra, and I'd probably just aggravate the bull and end up with a nasty scar to show for it.

"What did he do?" She says it like she's been expecting Ethan to mess up but hasn't been able to say it.

"It's not criminal activity," I say, attempting to downplay it. I hold my mug between my hands, one hand gripping the handle, thankful for the warmth and a barrier between Cassandra and me. I hide behind my shame as if Ethan's actions are my fault.

I inhale, letting it out in a rush. "Ethan might be having an affair. I don't know if it's still happening."

Cassandra's eyes widen. She looks genuinely surprised by this. "Are you serious? How did you find out?" Her voice goes up an octave as she questions me. Her posture hardens against the soft fabric of the sofa, and she sits forward, the caffeine taking effect and perking her up. But something about her reaction is too dramatic, the shock too theatrical. Did she already know about his affair, or did she suspect it would happen eventually?

"I don't know for sure. It's just a feeling I get. I thought it might all blow over. We've been going through a rough patch. I would've told you last night, but when you said you knew a fertility specialist—"

"You didn't want me to change my mind about introducing you," she finishes. "Honey, I won't change my mind about that. If you want to talk to someone about fertility, whether it's something you do with Ethan, or without him," she adds, "that's your decision. You know, I'd recommend you go anyway to see what your options are. You don't need a husband to have a baby anymore. If Ethan's not the right guy, that's not your problem."

Relief rushes through me. Why was I ever worried Cassandra might judge me? Now I remember why I used to tell her everything. Even after months of barely speaking, it's as if nothing has changed between us. She's still my best friend. She's still got my back, even if I haven't had hers.

"But I have to ask. What has Ethan cheating got to do with Isla?" Sudden recognition dawns on her face as she tries to piece it all together. "Oh, my God! You don't think that Isla and Ethan were . . .?"

She doesn't finish her sentence, and for that I'm grateful. Ethan with a random person is bad, but Ethan and Isla—two people I loved and trusted—is too much.

"No," I say, "I don't think it was Isla, but she's about the same height and weight as me. If the killer is Ethan's fling, maybe she's angry that it didn't work out and followed Isla into the bathroom, thinking it was me. It was dark enough in the bar to confuse us. Maybe she was going to confront me."

Cassandra looks skeptical—she doesn't believe that's what happened. She's trying to figure out if I'm telling her the truth or feeding her part of the story like I did earlier. "You think they found out about you and snapped? No guy is worth jail time. And if they wanted to kill you, wouldn't they make sure they got the right person?"

"I don't know if it's really about me or something else," I say carefully. "But I think it's suspicious that in the same week I noticed someone following me, Isla ends up murdered."

"I know how to find out if he's seeing someone," she hints, as if she's about to suggest something illegal.

"How?" I ask, curious, even if I don't intend to do it. If I could find out what Ethan is up to, would I want to know?

"He's not home, but maybe he left something in the house? We just need to find it."

What does she think he's hiding?

I've lived with Ethan long enough to know he isn't sloppy. If he wants to hide something, he'll make sure there's no trail. Even if he forgot something, he has Willow cleaning up after him. She's never liked me much. Her loyalty has always been to my husband. I doubt she'd think twice about keeping his secrets.

I tell Cassandra as much, but she stands and places her mug on the cedarwood coffee table. When she gestures for me to stand too, I know that if there's evidence that Ethan's seeing someone, she will find it.

Cassandra's great at piecing things together, figuring out how to get the best results and predicting the truth behind people's stories when they come into the ER.

I've watched her uncover the exact drug a kid ingested when the police did a raid on their home and their mother had to make a quick decision about where to hide it. The bag popped, and the kid was lucky to survive thanks to Cassandra's quick thinking and ability to stay calm.

Then there was the guy who brought his girlfriend in because they thought she might be in labor. Cassandra thought he was nervously sweating until she realized there was more going on. No one had noticed the badly infected gunshot wound he was hiding under his hoodie until then, but Cassandra noticed he looked more uncomfortable than his very pregnant girlfriend, trying to sit without putting pressure on his abdomen.

Cassandra documented the contractions, but they were sporadic. It was a false alarm. She convinced the guy that fatherhood was worth more than hiding his infected wound, regardless of how it happened, and dying before he could meet his newborn baby. When she finally convinced him to let her take a look, she discovered a necrotizing soft tissue infection. He'd been shot in an altercation with a rival gang and hadn't wanted to get his friends in trouble, so he had tried treating the wound himself and hidden it from his girlfriend.

That's how I know that if Ethan's hiding something, Cassandra will find it.

Cassandra dives into analytical mode, while I pretend this isn't just a distraction from Isla's death.

"If you're somehow right about being the target, it's only a matter of time before this woman realizes she killed the wrong person. I'm not sitting around waiting for her to come back and kill another one of my friends. We're going to figure out who this bitch is and shut her down," says Cassandra, her eyes ablaze with determination. She has the same look in the ER when everything's burning but no one can extinguish it.

Cassandra searches the apartment, examining each room. She won't find anything. Our home looks unlived in. Since Ethan's been so busy with work trips or in the office, I've barely left my room, except to cook dinner and use the bathroom. I've spent the majority of my time obsessing over what's going on, waiting for an epiphany so I can stop feeling so ridiculous.

"Your place looks like a display home," she marvels. "Not even a coaster out of place."

I'm not sure what Cassandra was expecting to find—Ethan's hardly stupid enough to leave a pair of his mistress's panties out on display. I imagine him trying to explain if he had, insisting I must've bought them and forgotten. Or worse—saying he bought them and was going to give them to me as a present. I feel annoyed at Ethan for the imaginary conversation he's not even here to have.

"Willow's a perfectionist. I don't think she even buys commercial cleaning products. She makes her own. She says they get to the layer under the grit."

I follow Cassandra from the living room to the kitchen, still going on about cleaning. She stops. Thinking.

"Have you checked his pockets?" she asks.

"No," I laugh. "No one keeps evidence of their affair in their pocket. People keep things they're trying to hide in their phones, and Ethan takes his with him wherever he goes."

She raises her eyebrows, and I almost expect her to ask if I want to make a bet. We used to bet on silly things all the time—like who would laugh first at a joke, with the loser shouting the winner or who would get the most demanding patient of the night a coffee—but this isn't a joke. This could change my marriage forever, my whole life even, and I'm glad she doesn't want to bet on it, because that would mean she knows she'll find something. "I've found crazy things in people's pockets at work. People store things in pockets and forget about them. Out of sight, out of mind."

What does she think we'll find?

Chapter 10

Cassandra wouldn't be telling me we should snoop through Ethan's stuff if she didn't think there was a reason to, and for one paranoid minute I wonder if she knows something that has always made it difficult for her to warm up to him.

Is my husband the person Cassandra thinks he is?

"What are we looking for?" I ask.

Cassandra marches through my bedroom, the thick covers still pulled back on the bed and crumpled from my futile tossing and turning. The amber lamp on my nightstand is on, lighting a path to the closet.

We stop and Cassandra almost opens the shutters, then flicks the light switch instead. "Better to keep those down. If someone sees us, they might tell Ethan."

I blink against the sudden brightness as Cassandra inspects the closet Ethan and I share like a shopper browsing the racks at Bloomingdale's, looking for the perfect buy.

For the first time, I notice how Ethan's endless suits, ties, and shirts for every occasion drown out the few clothes in the closet that belong to me.

She inspects Ethan's row of business suits, each one still wrapped in plastic film from the dry cleaner's.

"I don't like to speculate. We could be looking for anything from a note to a key to her house. Is anything different from usual?"

I take a moment to look around. Everything is tidy, shoes lined up in shoe boxes, hangers all facing the same way, holding variations of the same suit repackaged over and over in different shades. It looks the way it always has, a work closet for a person who likes nice things but doesn't want to spend too much time getting ready for work. A few shirts hang on the other side of the closet, all white with a few exceptions for special events, like the party hosted by a client of Ethan's a year ago. He hadn't been sure what to wear and decided that smart casual—which to Ethan meant losing the suit jacket and wearing a blue shirt instead of a white one—was the right way to go. I only remember it because we don't usually go to those events. Ethan prefers to go alone, claiming they would bore me.

It annoys me he never bothers asking.

I scan the clothes again in case I've missed something. Everything is aligned. Among Ethan's clothes, there isn't a single pattern or variation. "No, I don't think so," I say.

"Wrong," says Cassandra, as if she's a game show host and I've just missed the million-dollar question.

My eyes brush over the clothes again, looking underneath for something that might've fallen to the floor below, but there's nothing that stands out.

Cassandra dives deep into the closet, making a beeline for something. She goes straight for a suit that hangs in line with the others, tucked between two laundry bags. A creased black sleeve pokes out, waving a casual hello. If it had been covered in the same plastic as the rest of the suits, Cassandra wouldn't have thought anything of it as it blended in with the rest of Ethan's standard work lineup. Something to wear on a Wednesday.

"He left for this latest trip without much notice. An opportunity came up, and he ran out of time to get this one to the cleaner's," I muse.

It was also too important to leave, even when I needed him home, I think, but I'm not ready to talk about the way he brushed me off.

"Can you smell that?" Cassandra asks, her nose crinkling as she inhales, leading her to the lapel of the unbagged suit like a puppy sniffing out a treat. She pushes the hangers on either side so that the suit stands alone.

"Smell what?" I ask, to make sure she's talking about the floral perfume I think I can smell and not something else.

Her nose is almost against the lapel when she stops sniffing, taking in one last breath before turning to me, the conclusion all over her face. "It's perfume."

Willow usually drops Ethan's clothes off at the dry cleaner's and picks them up, placing them back in his closet before he's even noticed they're gone, so seeing a suit that clearly doesn't belong is strange. If Cassandra's right, if there's still the scent of perfume on the jacket, the suit's not only missing a plastic covering, but it hasn't been to the cleaner's.

I push into the closet, moving a set of hangers aside so I can squish in beside Cassandra. She steps back, giving me room to investigate. I don't need to get too close before the clear scent of women's perfume fills my senses in a heady rush.

"Is it yours?" she asks, but she knows I wear Eternity for Women, has even borrowed some when we've gone out after getting ready at my place, and this is not the smell of Eternity for Women.

"Maybe he was going to buy something for you and tried out some scents at the store?" she says. I can tell by her expression she hopes I won't believe something that lame, but a part of me wants to believe there's a reasonable explanation.

"I don't think so. He knows how picky I am. There's no way he'd try to guess what I like without taking me along." I sniff again, my nose close to his suit. Now that I'm focused on it, I can smell the slight scent of Ethan's cologne mingled with the perfume, and the faint, salty smell of sweat. The jacket wasn't washed before he slipped it back in the closet—he must've thrown it back in while he was getting ready for his trip. He must've forgotten to tell Willow it was there.

"I've smelled this perfume somewhere before." I try to remember where, but it's just a faint recollection. There must be thousands of people who use that same scent. I would have smelled it a dozen times in the ER.

"Listen, smelling like perfume doesn't mean he's seeing someone. Maybe he wanted to feel pretty," says Cassandra with a mischievous smile, fluttering her eyelashes.

In my tired state, I laugh at her joke, even though inside I'm doing everything but laughing.

Cassandra moves the fabric and digs her hand into the left pocket. "Let's see what you've got for us," she says to the suit. She upends the pocket, finding nothing—not even lint scraps—and repeats the same on the other side.

As she retracts her hand, I notice something clenched in it. "If this is a candy bar wrapper, I'm putting it right back in there," she promises, but it's not what she's holding that concerns me.

The gray jacket lining has what looks like a small, almost round stain. I don't mention it to Cassandra, not wanting to draw attention to it, but from where I'm standing, I imagine it could be one of two things. A red ink stain from a misplaced pen, or a smear of blood.

Why would Ethan have blood on his clothes? Maybe he got a paper cut and wiped at it to soothe the sting that followed? Or perhaps he cut himself shaving and a drop of blood escaped unnoticed. Except Ethan always shaves and brushes his teeth before he dresses to avoid spilling toothpaste or shaving cream on a thousand-dollar suit.

I curse his absence. If he were here, it would be easy enough to find out if he had any nicks and cuts and figure out if it was his blood or someone else's. I consider calling him and asking outright, but after our last conversation, I doubt he'll receive another call well, and I'm not sure he'll tell me the truth over the phone, especially if he's with a client.

Cassandra holds out her hand, ready for me to take whatever she's found. She's giving me the opportunity to see it first, to decide if I want to share it with her.

I shake my head and she knows I'm asking her to do it—I don't trust myself to interpret our findings correctly. I'm already feeling sensitive about the whole thing. Whatever she finds in

Ethan's pocket is less personal to her, so she may know what it means better than I will.

"You sure?" she asks.

I want to say no, but it doesn't matter how sure I am. If I want to stop myself from obsessing over it, this is something I need to know. "Very." I nod as she unfurls her fingers, revealing a folded-up piece of paper. She opens each fold, careful not to rip the thin paper. It looks like a receipt, with black ink letters on the inside.

I watch Cassandra's face change from curiosity to a perplexed frown, unraveling Ethan's secret one crease at a time.

"What is it?" I ask, before she can decide to tear it up and swallow whatever she's found, like people do in movies to hide something. I can already tell that whatever it is, it's not good news.

"How long has Ethan been gone on his business trip?" she asks.

"Since Sunday. Why?"

"This is a receipt," she says. "For Matrix." She clears her throat before continuing. Everyone knows Matrix. It's an upmarket sex store. "The date stamp says he bought it on Saturday." She looks at me with sad eyes.

"Saturday? Like, last weekend?" I ask, already knowing the answer. I need to hear it out loud before I can believe that my husband made the purchase the day before his business trip.

We spent Saturday morning together. He couldn't have done it then. He must've stepped out when I took a nap later that afternoon because I had a throbbing headache and felt worn out.

Cassandra nods, looking to me for my best guess as to why my husband's suit smells like perfume with a receipt for a sex store in his pocket.

I'm as stumped as she is. It makes no sense. "Maybe you read the store name wrong," I say, a tiny sliver of hope creeping in. If Cassandra misread the store name on the receipt, it could explain everything.

Cassandra looks again and shakes her head. "Sorry, honey."

I try a different tack. "Maybe he ordered it online and printed the receipt for taxes. It could be a gift box for someone at work. Maybe everyone in the office pitched in."

But there's an obvious flaw in my logic, as Cassandra reminds me, holding the thin, curling slip of paper up for me to see. "This came out of a cash register. The fucker went in and bought it."

I check the receipt to confirm the date stamp. It says Saturday, just like Cassandra said. Maybe he returned the jacket while I was out for drinks, and that's how he knew where I was?

Matrix is known for their popular range of adult toys and lingerie, but Ethan would never buy a colleague something like that, even as a joke. I'm glad Cassandra doesn't mention the perfume on his jacket is fresh, belonging to someone who got up close enough to leave their scent all over him.

Cassandra holds out a hand for me to grab. The room is suddenly cold, and I want to go back to the warmth of the sofa and forget about the receipt and the smidge of blood, which most likely means nothing more than Ethan cut himself on his razor while shaving.

And yet he said he couldn't come home when I needed him. The thought is unstoppable, making me feel annoyed at Ethan all over again.

What was more important than Isla dying for him to reschedule his meeting?

I force my brain into solution mode, refusing to feel sorry for myself. "What did he buy?" I ask.

Cassandra's frown deepens. "It doesn't say. It's just a list with a bunch of prices and a total."

Matrix isn't just an adult store. It's *the* adult store, known for customizable designer gift boxes to suit all kinds of occasions. They're especially popular with a rich clientele and cater to bachelorettes and women looking to spice up their sex lives. I would guess that there are plenty of men who shop there when they want to say sorry—adding an arrangement of flowers, chocolates, and candles to add a little sugar to the spice.

An affair seems more likely by the second. If he had purchased a gift for me, wouldn't he give it to me before leaving?

Unless he was saving it for when he gets back?

"Well, how much did he spend?" I ask, already guessing he might spend a hundred dollars.

Cassandra gives me a four-figure amount, and my jaw drops. He either wants to make a good impression on this woman, or he's done something that will require a lot of forgiveness.

What have you done, Ethan?

We throw around theories, each one more outlandish than the last, talking until Cassandra starts long-blinking, looking as if she might fall asleep right there. It's too late for Cassandra to go home, especially if the person who has been following me is still out there. If I'm wrong, and it's not the woman I think Ethan might be seeing, what's to stop them from following Cassandra too?

I set her up in the guest room and try to get some rest, haunted by my waking nightmare, but glad to have some company.

Chapter 11

Ethan calls Saturday morning while I'm in the kitchen and asks how I'm doing.

I'm surprised to hear from him. I listen for background noise, trying to figure out where he is and if anyone is with him, but I can't tell. "I'm sorry I can't be there. It's crazy busy right now. I'll make it up to you when I get home."

Does his promise involve thousands of dollars spent on candles, roses, and bath salts? Or does he want his apology to be more memorable than that?

It doesn't matter if he "makes it up" to me. He wasn't there when Isla was murdered. That's when I needed him. I thought Ethan would understand. He lost his parents, although it's not the same thing. His parents weren't murdered.

I know it's crazy. I don't have any proof, but I still can't let it go. I feel it in my gut. There's someone else. Does she want to be with him badly enough to remove me from the picture? Does he care enough to lie for her, to cover up a murder? I can't ask him because he will just lie to protect himself.

I need to find out who that gift was for, and how he got blood on his suit jacket.

Cassandra is still sleeping, and I don't want to pick an argument while Cassandra is here. I need to see his face when I ask if he thinks his lover would try to kill me, and what reason they might have to kill Isla.

I want to see for myself how my husband looks when he's lying.

But here I am, surprised by his call, spaced out from lack of sleep. My eyes are open, but my brain is still sleeping.

When I don't speak, he asks if I'm still there. I would almost believe he's concerned about how I'm handling Isla's death. "Do the police know who killed her?"

Is he asking, or is he looking for information?

I focus on his voice, trying to figure it out. He sounds worried. Maybe he's afraid of what I know.

Ethan is so familiar, almost an extension of myself, but for the first time in our marriage, it feels like I'm talking to a stranger.

"I haven't spoken to the police since it happened." I stop abruptly, the words catching in my throat.

"Maybe you should call and ask if there's any news? If you think it might help you," he adds.

Does he want me to fish for information? I get the feeling he's worried how close the police are to finding Isla's killer. If the police discovered Ethan's girlfriend killed Isla, his lies would unravel too, ruining his reputation and destroying our marriage. If I'm right about this, Ethan's whole life could end up in shreds.

I take a long breath and exhale. I still don't have the evidence I need, but I know Ethan's reaction could give me some answers. Maybe I should give him the benefit of the doubt, but the uneasy feeling in my stomach won't budge until I know for sure.

I make a noncommittal sound to Ethan's request as Cassandra appears in the doorway, tying her hair in a messy bun. She's wearing the clothes I lent her the night before. She slows when she sees the phone in my hand and mouths Ethan's name.

I nod slightly and she rolls her eyes and I try not to laugh, only half listening to Ethan's rundown of a situation with a client the day before. His acting unnerves me, the lies smooth and rehearsed. He sounds as if he's on a regular business trip, but I'm not sure anything about this situation is regular.

Have there been other trips like this—Ethan pretending with me oblivious to what he's really doing?

I don't tell him Cassandra stayed over, or that we found a receipt for the exorbitant amount of money he spent. I don't ask what he bought and what he plans on doing with it.

Cassandra holds up a gift tag attached to thin silver thread with Matrix's logo on one side. On the other side of the tag is a handwritten note in Ethan's lopsided script. A name?

I tune out, vaguely aware he's still talking. Once he finishes, he excuses himself, saying a client is taking him on a tour in an hour, but he needs to get ready because his hotel is further away from the city center than he thought. "Which is ironic, because it's called the Central Palais Hotel, but it's not central to anything." He stops himself, as if realizing he's said too much.

I'm surprised he needs to travel an hour. Usually he stays somewhere closer in case there are any last-minute changes to his plans. Come to think of it, this is the first time he's even mentioned where he's staying. Is he lying?

"I can tell you about it later," he mumbles.

Cassandra is dancing from foot to foot like she needs to use the bathroom, waiting for the call to end so we can discuss what she found.

"I miss you," he says, and it sounds so genuine that I almost believe him. "I can't wait to see you."

There's a silence. He's waiting for me to reciprocate, but all I can manage is a half-hearted, "Yeah, you too."

The call ends, and Cassandra exhales as if she's been holding her breath. "Thank god. I thought you'd never finish up."

"Where did you find that?" I ask, pointing to the tag. "Was it attached to a gift box?" I expected that if there was something to find, he would have taken it with him.

Cassandra shakes her head no.

"What does the note say?" I ask.

"I don't know. I wasn't just gonna read it without you. It seemed too personal." Her mouth twitches, the rest of the reason spilling not long after. "And Ethan writes like a girl. I couldn't read a damned word of it with all the twirls and swirls." She makes an exaggerated gesture like she's writing in the air, giving a huge flourish at the end, the silver threads on the tag swinging back and forth.

She offers me the tag. I take it from her hand as if it might strike at me. The tag is large enough to write a message on the back, the kind of message you might get your secretary to write, but Ethan's handwriting is scrawled in black ink, each loop feeding into the next, making the gift seem personal. I've had practice reading his writing, and it doesn't take me long to decipher the message.

Babe, I'm so sorry.
Let me make it up to you.
Love, Ethan
xxx

I read it out loud to Cassandra, sighing with disappointment. There is no name. Nothing to suggest who it's meant for.

"Babe? That could be you, right?" says Cassandra enthusiastically, as if we can still come up with a reasonable explanation.

"Well, the only thing this shows is he's groveling to someone about something he thinks he shouldn't have done," I say dispassionately. "And he spent a lot of money on it."

"Well, who knows? Maybe he realized all those years of leaving the toilet seat up and you almost falling in when you got up to pee in the middle of the night is as annoying as you say it is," she jokes.

I smile weakly. Ethan hasn't called me "babe" even once in the time I've known him. Whoever he's apologizing to, I doubt it's me.

I almost tell Cassandra, until I notice something strange on the corner of the tag, just at the bottom. A red stain, like the one I saw on the inside of Ethan's jacket. Had the tag fallen out of his pocket when he dropped off the suit? And where was the expensive gift?

Perhaps whoever he gave it to didn't accept his apology.

71

Chapter 12

Cassandra watches me pace for a full minute, tapping the gift tag against my hand while I think. Perhaps the note was for me, the "babe" meant ironically. I've never liked the term, so if he's apologizing for something serious, there are a hundred better names to call me.

He wouldn't use the word *babe* in an apology. Ethan knows how to build trust. He grovels for a living, and I've seen him in action. He's good.

The note isn't for me. If I knew what he spent all that money on, it might make things clearer. "Let's go to Matrix's site and match up these prices with some of their products."

"Smart," says Cassandra. "While you do that, I'll keep searching to see what else I can find around the house."

"Thanks," I say. "I know this isn't how you want to spend your day. Especially after . . ." I stop before saying Isla's name. There's no point distracting ourselves if I'm going to bring up the thing we're trying to forget. "Don't you have a shift today?"

Now it's Cassandra's turn to sigh, and the sound is deep and deflated. "I did, but given what happened to Isla, they canceled, told me to take a couple of days to get my head around it."

I know Cassandra, and she's not a sit-around-and-process-what-happened kind of person. She'd prefer to do something.

"It's not even that my shifts were canceled. It's that they didn't bother asking. They just decided. I bet they wouldn't do that if I were a man. Or white."

She looks at me apologetically and I wave a hand; she has nothing to apologize for. She's right.

I don't have any shifts until Monday, but I still check my phone. There are no messages from the hospital.

"Well, thank you for being here and helping me figure this out," I say.

"No problem. I hope this other woman, if we find her, had nothing to do with Isla's murder, or I might have to kill her myself," jokes Cassandra, but something suggests she isn't really joking.

It's unsettling, given that Isla's death and Ethan's fling seemed to coincide.

I have questions I want answered, but not with words. There are things I will be able to tell about my husband by looking at her, but first I need to find her.

While Cassandra rummages around in the next room, I stare at the empty computer screen, wondering if it's worth a shot asking Ethan outright, even if he lies. It feels like we're almost beyond the point of being able to sort things out between us but I'm not sure I can give up on him completely yet. Not until I know for sure he's cheating.

Maybe I can figure it out for myself.

I go to Matrix's site and filter a price range for the most expensive items listed on the receipt. Jewelry is at the high end of the list, studded with crystals and diamonds. By page two, the prices drop a little and are mostly lingerie. A pretty lace corset exactly matches the amount on the receipt, but so does an elaborate vase with flowers and an aromatherapy set. The pessimist in me knows which one he bought, but the optimist tries to temper it, reminding me I know nothing for sure yet.

For the last three years, I thought I had the kind of marriage where if something like this happened, Ethan and I would resolve whatever misunderstanding led us here and move on.

Now, I'm wondering what else he's been hiding from me.

Have I happily buried my head in the sand, ignoring the coming storm until it rushed in and swept me away? Was it my ignorance that got Isla killed?

When Cassandra walks back in, it looks like she's seen a ghost.

Chapter 13

She pulls up a chair beside me at the kitchen table. "You said you thought someone was following you?"

"Yeah."

"How long ago did you notice?"

I think back, trying to remember the first time I felt the creepy sensation of someone behind me, far enough away that I questioned it, but close enough to know they were a threat.

I remember sensing something outside the apartment, and the time I called out to someone in the alleyway before they ran off. Until then, I might've thought I was imagining someone on their way home walking a little too close, mimicking my movements. I had stopped to get a pretzel, waiting a good five minutes in line, giving them plenty of time to pass, but they began following me again when I walked on.

There haven't been many opportunities to follow me lately. Besides working a few shifts, and buying a few groceries, I've been home, trying not to obsess over ovulation or which fertility vitamins I should be taking.

Until Thursday night drinks.

"I guess the alleyway was the first time, but they took off," I tell her. What if they're still watching me at home? The thought sends a shiver down my spine, and I make a mental note to check the doors are locked and the shutters are closed so no one can see inside. "And the time it felt like someone was lingering outside the apartment. Why?"

"I noticed something . . ."

Her expression is the same as when we realized Isla had been gone for too long, that she wasn't out on the dance floor having a good time like we thought she was. That same look of horror I had when I realized Zoe was busy dancing with some guy instead of our friend.

"What?" I ask, but she doesn't reply straight away. "Cassandra, you're scaring me," I say. Cassandra isn't lost for words very often.

"It's probably nothing. There was a car outside. I noticed them when I went into your room to recheck the closet. They can see inside your room from the street, but when I approached the window, they drove off."

"Maybe they were just visiting someone in the building, or maybe it was another resident."

Cassandra clears her throat, uncomfortable but firm. "They had binoculars or some crap. They were looking right in, like they were scoping the place."

Isla's death obviously has both of us rattled, but Cassandra sounds certain that someone was looking inside my apartment. What did they want?

I move the mouse around, bringing the computer screen to life. I show Cassandra the screen, littered with tabs of potential purchases from Matrix, but she's still obsessing about the person she saw outside.

"Do you think it's the woman Ethan hooked up with?" asks Cassandra, keeping her voice low as if they can hear us.

An email pings on my computer, and I glance at it. I don't recognize the address. It's from a random email account, but the headline catches my eye.

I can't tell if it's a question, a warning, or a threat.

How well do you know your husband?

If Isla hadn't died and Ethan wasn't having an affair, I might've marked the email as spam without reading it, assuming it was a virus or someone trying to extort money in some new online scam.

Instead, I open it up. The body of the email is empty.

A key turns in the locked door, taking my attention from the strange email. Cassandra seems as startled as I am. "She wouldn't have a key to your house, would she?" she whispers in a frantic tone.

"I hope not," I whisper back just as frantically. "I thought you said she drove off?"

"Maybe she came back."

The thought of someone in my house when I'm not there makes me feel claustrophobic, like I'm trapped in a fun house, waiting for the next thing to jump out and scare me.

"Maybe Ethan came home after all. You asked him to." Cassandra sounds hopeful, but I know Ethan's footsteps, the sound of his briefcase dropping to the floor as he sifts through his keys. Whoever's at the door, it isn't Ethan.

I stay silent, afraid of what they'll do if I startle them, moving quietly behind the kitchen bench, where I have access to a weapon if I need it. I'm not sure how I plan to use it from here, but the door is already opening, and it's too late to come up with a better idea, so I stand there and watch a woman step through the entrance as if she's done it a hundred times and has every right to be here.

Cassandra is sitting as straight as a board where I left her, her hands clasped in resting fists. When she sees who walked in, she gently closes the laptop, hiding our activity.

"Oh, I'm sorry. It's Saturday. I thought you might be out," says Willow, startled to see Cassandra and me at home.

Willow is wearing a pair of jeans and a knit sweater. It's strange seeing her in regular clothes instead of her cleaning uniform of slacks and a shirt with her hair pulled back from her face.

This Willow looks younger and more vibrant, unburdened by other people's mess. Her hair billows around her face, untamed.

"Cassandra and I were just hanging out since we don't have to work today," I say, wondering why I'm explaining myself for being home. I don't mention Isla's death.

"Mr Dolan asked me to come by."

Her language when referring to Ethan is formal, although I know she calls him Ethan when they're talking.

She smiles, her lips thinning as she steps around me.

Sometimes I feel like a stranger in my own home, like I have less right to be here than the people Ethan lets pass through. It has always felt like Ethan's. He was the one who wanted this place. He bought it without really asking what I thought.

I don't make way for her, standing my ground, not satisfied with her explanation for being here. Why did Ethan send her? "I've got things under control," I say. "Why don't you tell me what needs to be done and I'll make sure it's taken care of."

"I'm not here to clean," she says indignantly. "Mr Dolan asked me to pick up a few things. I'll just grab them and be on my way."

If she's just picking something up, it can't be too big a job, but I'm curious why Ethan would ask Willow to come by on her day off. What is she supposed to pick up that I couldn't take care of?

"Cassandra and I are busy working on a project," I say, a subtle hint for her to leave, but she doesn't seem to realize. She continues around me in a large arc, as if she can avoid me, moving across the kitchen. Her ballet flats are silent against the porcelain tiles. If Cassandra hadn't been here, if I had still been asleep in bed, I mightn't have heard her at all.

If Willow can walk in unnoticed, perhaps anyone could.

"What did he want you to pick up?" I ask, trying to sound conversational. It's a lot to make a one-hour trip each way to "pick up a few things" when I'm already here.

My words stop Willow in her tracks, and I can tell she's deciding how to respond. She's never blatantly rude. Her disregard is usually more insidious. A disdainful expression when I do or say something she doesn't agree with, a curt nod when Ethan disagrees with me, or avoiding me altogether, speaking only to Ethan.

Her expression tells me what she wants to say, even if she doesn't say it. *That's between me and Ethan. It's none of your business.*

"Nothing much. Just some dry cleaning."

Cassandra shoots me a look. She still has the receipt in her pocket. What if that's Willow's real reason for being here—to remove the receipt before I find it? Or maybe she's just following orders, and I've become too suspicious.

Either way, I need to stop her because Ethan will know it's missing if he's looking for it. "That's okay," I say, the words tumbling out in a hurry. "I'll do it. I don't have much on today, and Cassandra and I are looking for a reason to get out of the house. Aren't we?"

Cassandra nods enthusiastically. "Absolutely. Go. Enjoy your day off!"

Despite our best efforts, Willow brushes off our offer and makes her way to my bedroom. Something about the way she disregards my request irks me.

Willow and Ethan have known each other for so long that their relationship is sometimes a little too comfortable. Willow lost her mother, and since Ethan lost both of his parents, he felt she understood what he was going through. They are close in age, and Willow is one of the few people Ethan listens to.

She's one of the few people I've seen Ethan be himself around, flaws and all, but I guess you can't hide those things from someone who's seen you grow up. Willow's mom used to be the Dolans' housekeeper, so they've known each other for a long time.

If anyone knows who Ethan is seeing, it's Willow. If she's here to retrieve the receipt, maybe she knows.

When Willow disappears into the bedroom, Cassandra strides toward me and whispers, "How are we going to stop her?"

"We're not," I say, catching myself before I chew the edge of my thumbnail, a habit I developed as a teen when I felt vulnerable or unsure of myself. I sometimes revert to the gangly girl who never knew how to hold herself or what to say when someone spoke to her.

Cassandra's voice drops further, and she says, "What if Ethan finds out we've been snooping?" The implication hangs like an uncoiled snake, still capable of inflicting a nasty bite if you're not careful.

"Even if I told her to leave, I don't think she would," I hiss back. "She's always been Ethan's employee. She's never cared about what I have to say, so she's not going to start now."

"Do you think she knows about Ethan?" asks Cassandra, craning her neck toward the rustling hangers, trying to see what Willow's up to even though it's impossible from here.

"Maybe," I say absently, expecting Willow to come out of the bedroom at any moment. "Let's wait and see what she brings out of there. She's obviously looking for something because Ethan leaves his dry cleaning in the laundry room."

"Well, she is *not* in the laundry room," says Cassandra.

Willow comes out of the bedroom a few moments later with the unwrapped suit on a hanger. My eyes fall to the lining, but the jacket is wrapped around the hanger, fastened with a fixed button, hiding the stain on the inside. I no longer question whether it was blood I saw as Willow walks quickly to the front door, throwing an uncomfortable goodbye over her shoulder.

Cassandra raises her eyebrows so they sit high on her forehead. "She knows."

I think Cassandra is right. Willow was too eager to leave once she found the suit. What does she know, and what is Ethan hiding?

Chapter 14

I wait on the sofa as Cassandra makes coffee. I love her for trying to cheer me up with a stimulant. She plucks two mugs from the cupboard, the ceramic clinking as she sets them on the bench, moving with efficiency.

I think about what we've uncovered so far. Ethan bought a gift for someone, but it wasn't for me. It was something you'd only give to someone you were intimate with or risk coming across as a creep. He must have given her the gift, since I couldn't find it anywhere.

I feel certain she was following me, but I don't know why. Maybe she was figuring out how to remove her competition. There's a chance she wants to harm me, and she may have killed Isla, who is like me in height, build, and hair color. What if she followed the wrong person into the bathroom in the dark bar? By the time she realized it wasn't me, it might've been too late to abandon her plan.

I scroll the internet on my phone while Cassandra finishes making coffee. I can't focus on anything other than Isla's ashen skin and lifeless corpse. Was it supposed to be me lying there? It wouldn't be the first time I had escaped death.

The media outlets have already caught on, and because Isla died in such a public place, they're running stories about the nightclub murder, already speculating about the killer's motive. I read a few, wondering what kind of person takes a life.

Maybe the killer is curled up in a ball at home, only just coming to the realization they actually killed someone. Maybe they're sorry, agonizing over whether to confess their crime. If only they would. Do killers think about things like easing the grief felt by their victim's family by letting them know why they did it? Are they unaffected by the lives they impact?

Would the killer ever confess to what they'd done, or would they keep the darkest parts of themselves a secret, so they were free to act on the urge to kill again? Had they started something they just couldn't stop? Just one more. Maybe another after that.

Even if they wanted to confess, I know how difficult it can be to disclose a secret, especially when you're ashamed of what you've done. I know what it's like to keep it in until it rots you from the inside, even when no one suspects you could do something like that. You can spend your life quietly trying to make up for what you did, choosing a career to help others, atoning for the suffering you caused.

Or maybe they don't care. They might've read the articles online about Isla and realized they killed the wrong person. They might kill again, this time getting it right.

They could be coming for me. When the media attention from Isla's death dies down and the police stop searching. Once everyone has forgotten what happened to her. Or will they do it now, before the police figure out who they are?

I look out the window, trying to sense if they're still out there, but the only movement is from the street noise, the muted sound of neighbors and their weekend routines.

I fight the urge to draw the shutters closed, eventually giving in to the fear and yanking them down by the cord.

Cassandra smiles weakly. "I opened them to let in some light."

I flick the light switch. "What if the killer is out there, watching us?"

Cassandra shudders at the thought, and I can tell she doesn't need any more convincing. I search for new articles about Isla's death, looking for information regarding any possible leads.

"I'm making a sandwich. Do you want one?" asks Cassandra.

"Sure. Thanks."

I scroll past an image of Isla, her youthful innocence jumping from the picture, her parents standing beside her after high school graduation. It looks like she's beaming because she just graduated, but I know she's smiling because graduation was the first time her parents let her go to a salon to get highlights in her hair. It's not that she didn't care, but by the time she graduated, she knew what she wanted to be and had already applied to NYU.

The article mentions her parents, who cried about their "vibrant daughter's murder". There's a quote from her sister describing Isla as a "true and loyal friend to those closest to her". It's the kind of thing you only say once someone is dead.

I have almost reached the end of the article, hoping they saved the details about suspects and leads they're following up on, keeping people reading to the end. By the time I reach the final period, I've given up on the police having a suspect.

Does that mean they don't know who killed her? Or are they keeping any information they have to themselves?

I can hear Cassandra rummaging around in the kitchen.

I copy the link to the article and send it to Ethan, showing him that things are as bad as I said, because he seems to be under-reacting to Isla's murder.

I expect a reply, something to acknowledge he's seen the article, but I'm partway through a second article and I still haven't received a text from him.

One line in the article mentions a potential suspect. I forget about Ethan, giving the article my full attention. A man Isla was seen talking to is listed as a person of interest.

Just days before the incident, a neighbor says she saw a man she describes as at least six feet tall with wavy brown hair and a scar on his jawline leaving Ms Diaz's apartment. According to the neighbor, while they usually stay out of their neighbors' business, it caught her attention because she heard a heated argument and had been contemplating knocking on Ms Diaz's door to make sure she was safe. It's uncertain whether the police are questioning this man, or whether he's a current suspect in the murder investigation.

It doesn't sound like anyone I saw Zoe or Isla talking to on the dance floor. It also doesn't sound like any of Isla's ex-boyfriends, but the detail about the scar on the jawline catches my attention immediately and I think about the scar in the hollow of Ethan's right cheek, a scar that would be easy to mistake as snaking deeper to cross his jawline, but only if you were close enough to see it.

My stomach lurches, sending me racing to the bathroom, where I throw up in the toilet. With my stomach emptied, I sit on the bathroom floor, exhaustion catching up with me.

My life has unraveled in a few short days, and I'm not sure how to put it back together.

"Aria?" I can tell by the sound of her tromping around the apartment that Cassandra is looking for me. She stops at the bathroom door. "Are you OK in there, honey?" Her tone is sympathetic, telling me I've been here for a while. She probably thinks I'm crying about Ethan, and I let her. "I just checked the balcony. It doesn't look like they're still there," she says.

"That's good," I say and promise to be out in a minute. I sit until the nausea fades and go back to checking my cell for a response from Ethan. He knew Isla, and while he wasn't close with her like I was, he must be upset by the news that she's dead. It's not every day someone you know has their life stolen from them, but he seems unperturbed, to the point of avoiding talking about it.

I should stop feeling sorry for myself. It must be harder for Zoe, losing her roommate. I make a promise to myself to call later and see how she's feeling, but right now, I'm struck by how closely the description in the article matches Ethan.

Why would Ethan visit Isla's apartment? They hardly knew each other, never discussing more than the weather at parties. I doubt they would be visiting each other alone.

I close my eyes, thinking back to the times I'd seen them together. I never thought to question their interactions, blindly trusting them. The most I've seen them talking together was a few weeks ago when Ethan asked Isla for makeup advice, saying he was thinking about buying me something nice.

Maybe he was really asking so he could buy her something from Matrix. I didn't go through everything, but I'm sure Matrix sells makeup. It's exactly what she would want.

Why would Ethan be buying Isla presents?

I have never worn much makeup because it feels greasy on my skin after a ten-hour shift at the hospital. I prefer a good skin tint with sunscreen and a swipe of mascara and lip gloss. Why would Ethan buy me something I wouldn't use?

I stand slowly, another wave of nausea assailing me, reminding me I've barely eaten since last night. The thought of food makes my stomach roil, but I need to eat. I go to the kitchen, throwing open the pantry to grab a few crackers to tide me over. I crunch into one, savoring the flavor, which seems both saltier and sweeter after hours of not eating.

Stress rarely has such a physical effect on me, but my stomach clenches, readying itself to bring up the crackers. I tell myself it's because I'm not usually faced with so many awful things in such a short space of time. I wipe my hands on my jeans and head back to the bathroom.

I rummage around in the back of the cabinet until I find an open box containing an unused test. It's a one-in-a-million chance, but it can't hurt to be sure. I stopped testing to see if I was pregnant months ago, because Ethan was barely interested in sex, but I never threw out the last test, finding comfort in knowing it was there, even if the other tests had taunted me with a single line month after month. I tap a finger against the packaging, convincing myself it might not be so crazy.

My hands shake and I need to concentrate so the pee hits the stick.

I hate that I'm torturing myself again. It always ends the same, but this time feels different. My emotions don't have the trepidation of months-ago Aria, who thought she wanted a baby at any cost, who couldn't bear the sadness each failed test caused her.

The sadness is replaced with horror at Ethan's affair. Ethan, who might have known Isla better than he pretended to. Who might have secretly visited her and never mentioned it.

Maybe we were never meant to be parents, I think, as I wait for the test to process.

The wait is long as I ponder what Isla and Ethan might've talked about if they met up and why they never told me.

Isla was always a bit wild, but I never believed she would betray her friends. So what were they hiding?

I try to stop the intrusive thoughts, telling myself I control them, that I don't have to believe everything I *think*, just like my therapist taught me to do all those years ago, when everything

I believed about myself was laced with self-loathing and self-depreciation. Dr. Jain had tried to help me understand that I didn't deserve the punishment I was inflicting upon myself, but if she had known where it came from, why I was so critical of myself, it would have changed her opinion of me.

My phone beeps and I place the pregnancy test on the basin with the test window facing down, hoping Ethan has finally responded, but it's not a message from Ethan. It's a new email with the same headline as before. But this time it's not just a heading. There's a message in the body.

You are living a lie. Ask Ethan . . . I have the proof if you want it.

Seeing Ethan's name is a surprise. It's not in the greeting, like an automated message might be. This isn't just spam. Whoever sent it might really know my husband.

Chapter 15

There's a knock at the bathroom door. "Are you good?" calls Cassandra.

"Yeah. I'll be out in a minute," I say, rattled. The emailer is inside my head. It feels as if they're inside my personal space and I remind myself it could still be a sophisticated spam message. They will probably offer to send proof if I pay for it. If it's a scam, their timing is impeccable. I might even consider paying just to see what they have.

Nausea hits me, strong enough to disrupt my thoughts. I'm aware of a dull ache in my boobs.

It couldn't be, could it?

For the first time in a year, the thought of a negative test doesn't seem so bad. But as Cassandra said, people can raise children on their own. I would have to rearrange a few things, but I think I could do it.

Ten minutes pass, and I know I need to read the result if the test is going to be accurate, but I avoid it a moment longer, wondering which would be worse—finding out I'm pregnant under the current circumstances, or finding out I'm not and might never be.

As the test window comes into full view, I look for remnants of the winky face taunting me. I must be imagining it. The face is always there. Sometimes I imagine it's *his* face, telling me he'll be back to make up for what happened, even if that's impossible.

I look closer to make sure I'm reading it right. Two pink lines stain the nitrocellulose paper.

It isn't the first time I've imagined a phantom line on the test. Usually it's barely a shadow, practically there, but not really. Almost a baby. Days after a test, I wondered whether the second line was even there and not just my imagination willing it into existence. A whisper to let me know I would have been a mother, but that something hadn't quite worked out.

Maybe this is my punishment. It's crueler than I could have imagined, but perhaps it's the karma I deserve.

Had I waited too long before checking the result? This could just be a false reading, perhaps the cruelest punishment of all.

I close my eyes for a moment, trying to get a sense of my body and what's inside. Trying to feel if anything's different. I think maybe I can feel it. Something intangible, a slight shifting of energy, but eventually decide I can't be sure either way.

You shouldn't be a mother. People who do what you did aren't fit to take care of children.

There it is again, the voice inside my head, making me feel as if everything that's happened since that night is irrelevant.

I believe I deserve to be punished. Even the aspects of my life that seem good at first end up twisted.

Maybe not being able to have a baby is a hidden kindness, sparing any children from ever finding out who their mother really is.

But the face on the pregnancy test isn't winking this time.

It's smiling knowingly.

Chapter 16

I'm not sure whether to believe the test, but if I'm pregnant, that's even more reason to figure out who killed Isla and how Ethan's involved, because it's not only me who's affected now. If Ethan's fling wants to lash out at me because he's married, I can only imagine how she will react to us having a baby.

I won't be able to hide the pregnancy for more than a few weeks. People will notice my belly growing bigger and rounder, my clothes fitting more snugly, new curves forming with each passing week.

I have no choice—I need to ask Ethan who he's seeing, and it probably has to be an in-person conversation if I want the truth.

I'm not sure I can wait until he comes home. He's probably with her right now, so the risk of her contacting me is low. It could be a while if he extends his trip further, giving her more time to decide how she's going to remove me from Ethan's life for good.

What are they like together? Are they all sparks flying and passionate kisses, interested in each other's bodies more than they're interested in an engaging conversation? Or is it something more? Do they have an easy familiarity that comes with knowing someone well? Do they hold hands, fingertips buzzing with electricity as they lace them together?

A sudden resolve rushes over me, and before I can stop myself, I've booked a last-minute red-eye flight to LA with my credit card, not even looking at the price. If Ethan can't come home, I'll go to him. If we're having a baby together, I owe it to them to find out who their father really is.

I think about keeping the test to show Ethan, but it has pee on it, so I reluctantly place it in the bin. I can always do another later.

Cassandra is waiting when I emerge from the bathroom, and I tell her I'm going to talk to Ethan. She's supportive, and keeps me company while I pack what I need, tossing everything into a backpack and zipping it up. I don't mention the description of the man seen with Isla before she died, or the positive pregnancy test. I need to talk to Ethan first.

There's a couple of hours before I need to be at the airport. I tell Cassandra she can stay as long as she wants, but she says she wants to go into the hospital despite her couple of days off and that she needs to go home and get changed. She always turns to work for comfort.

I grab my keys and walk her out, locking the door firmly behind me. I promised myself I would check in on Zoe, and there's just enough time to stop by her apartment before my flight. I hope she doesn't mind me showing up this late in the evening.

I take a cab to Zoe's place. The driver agrees to wait while I speak with her, but I take my backpack with me, just in case he gets a better fare. Hauling it over my shoulder, I climb the stairs to the third floor and knock on her door.

I look out the window and see the cab waiting for me, the bearded driver obscured by his beret, head bent, lost in his phone. In my rush, I forgot to call ahead to tell Zoe I was stopping by. She might be out. I send her a quick message to let her know I'm standing at her door.

I'm about to leave when a bleary-eyed Zoe opens the door. She leans against the frame, trying to smile for my benefit but failing. Smudged makeup around her eyes gives the impression that she hasn't slept and hasn't bothered to wash her face since Isla's murder. I hug her and ask how she's doing. When she moves back to let me inside, I can see she's been crying. Purple splotches across her cheeks blend with her tears to make a watercolor.

"I can't stop thinking about her," she says, and I can tell by the way she says "her," choking it out, that she can't say her name yet. "I can't believe she's gone," she says, and I know what she means. It seems impossible for someone so vibrant, so alive, to stop existing so suddenly.

She moves out of the doorway and I follow her inside.

"Do you want something to drink? I think I have soda?" she says, leading me through the tiny kitchen and opening the fridge. The counter doubles as a table and I stand on the opposite side, not wanting to crowd the cooking space. I've eaten here enough to know food is rarely served in the kitchen. Zoe and Isla prefer to snuggle on the sofa with a steaming bowl of whatever meal they've thrown together and an old sitcom.

I hoist my backpack higher on my shoulder, my thumb jutting from the strap. "I can't stay," I say. "I'm surprising Ethan. I wanted to see you before I left."

Zoe gestures at the backpack. "I wasn't going to ask," she says in a tone that makes it clear she wanted to. "I thought you might be here to crash for a bit, while Ethan's away. Which would've been fine, by the way." She smiles, and it reaches her eyes.

Throwing my bag down, I lean on the counter and watch as she removes two cans of diet cola and places them on the counter slightly too hard. She seems jittery, like she already finished a can or two before I arrived.

She drums her fingernails on the counter before spinning around. "It doesn't feel real," she says. "I keep waiting for her to walk in and say Thursday night was a write-off, that she came home. Alone." She pours soda into pretty, double-walled glasses and hands one to me. I take a sip, thanking her.

I look around the little apartment they shared, not sure how they lived in this tiny space together without getting fed up with each other. Isla used to joke that she couldn't find the right guy because she already had the perfect woman.

I take another sip, wondering if her comment was more than an off-handed joke.

"Why would someone want to kill her? How could they do that?" asks Zoe, her voice cracking.

I shake my head, feeling guilty for not telling her what I know. But I still don't know for sure that the mystery woman Ethan's seeing could have done this, and it's a big accusation to make. "Was she acting the same as usual?" I ask instead. Maybe once I have more information, I can talk it out without sounding crazy.

"She seemed to be," says Zoe, her eyes falling to her glass. The lilt in her voice tells me she isn't being completely honest. I wait as she takes a slow sip. She looks up to see why I've gone quiet.

If I wait long enough, she'll probably tell me what's on her mind.

"Have the police talked to you and Ethan about what happened?" she asks.

The mention of Ethan throws me, triggering a nervous response. Ethan wasn't in town when Isla was murdered. "Why would they talk to him?"

"They wouldn't. I mean, they might, if they were looking for you, and he answered the door. I didn't mean anything by it," she says. "It's just, they came by my place last night. They asked a bunch of questions and went through Isla's things like they were looking for something," she says in that hopeful tone that suggests talking might uncover some answers.

"What did they ask?"

"They wanted to know if she was seeing anyone. If she had any enemies, anyone who might hurt her. I don't know, it made me think they're looking into an ex-boyfriend or something, but then they started asking whether she was secretly seeing someone."

"Was she?" I ask, thinking of the article I read about the man who was seen leaving her apartment. There was still a chance it wasn't Ethan but one of thousands of guys in New York who matched his description.

"I don't think so. She would've told us if there was someone— she usually tells us the minute she's even thinking about dating someone. I doubt she could keep a secret like that for long."

"Unless it was someone she didn't want us to know she was seeing," I say, leaning on my elbows, coffee in hand.

Zoe studies me. "Do you know something?" she asks, and I sense she's about to come clean with whatever she's hiding.

"Not as much as I'd like. Did the police find something to suggest she was seeing someone?"

"They wouldn't tell me anything," says Zoe, rubbing her hands together with nervous energy. "But there's something you should know."

She sets her coffee down, frowning as if she's about to deliver bad news. "I don't know for sure what it means. It could be nothing, which is why I didn't mention it." She's preparing me for the worst, trying to soften the impact with pretty words that tell me she doesn't need to know for sure—*she already suspects whatever it is to be true.*

I check the time on the microwave clock. I need to leave for the airport soon if I'm going to make my flight. The cab downstairs is probably costing me a small fortune.

"What is it?" I ask, trying to sound like I'm not afraid to hear it.

"I don't know if I should tell you just before your flight. I know you hate flying."

I could turn and walk away, but I know the flight will be worse if I leave here wondering what Zoe knows, obsessing over the possibilities. "I can handle it," I say, hoping I sound believable.

"Before Isla died, she wanted to talk to you about something. I told her she should wait until after Cassandra's big news, because it was Cassandra's night. I don't think she wanted to wait. She thought it was too important. I think she'd been holding on to it for a while, but she was afraid of hurting you."

I set my mug down, preventing it from slipping through my fingers, just in case. Does she know about Ethan's affair? How could she know about it when I live with Ethan and I've just figured it out?

Suddenly, Isla and Ethan being together doesn't seem like such a long shot. It would explain why she was afraid of hurting me, why she hadn't told me right away. They weren't around each other much, but perhaps it was enough to ignite a spark. Enough to wonder what it would be like in the dark, just the two of them with the lights low, keeping warm in each other's arms.

"She was worried you wouldn't believe her. She wouldn't tell me what it was because she wanted you to know first. I'm sorry," says Zoe.

"What do you think it was about?" I ask, hoping she has a theory.

"It could be anything. All I know is she was worried about how it would affect you. I think she was scared of what it would mean for your friendship."

Zoe's mug is almost empty, and I'm not sure if it's the caffeine making her seem jittery, or what she's trying to tell me. If Isla was scared, maybe Zoe's afraid to mention it too.

"What makes you think she was scared?" I ask. Did Ethan tell her not to mention his visit, or was it more than that? Was she afraid of losing our friendship once I found out her secret? I wish she was here so I could ask. I reprimand myself for thinking like that—it wasn't as if she had chosen to die.

"Even before she started keeping secrets, she had changed. On the surface, she was still loud and bubbly, but she started doing things she hadn't done before. She was easily scared; she would hesitate before answering the door when someone knocked. I think she was in danger and didn't know how to get herself out of it."

When I was followed, it was scary not knowing what they would do next, or what they wanted. Had Isla felt that same fear? Did she know someone was going to hurt her?

"I had to tell the police," says Zoe, as if I might hate her for it. "I told them she was keeping a secret, and that it involved you."

"I would do the same," I say. There was no reason not to tell them. I hadn't done anything wrong. It wasn't like Zoe was implicating me by telling the police that Isla had a secret.

I look at the time. It's later than expected. If I'm going to make my flight, I need to leave now. I want to stay and talk some more, to figure out what Isla was hiding, but it's too late to cancel my flight, and I have just as many questions I need to ask Ethan.

"Sorry to leave like this," I say, squeezing her hand. "Can we talk when I get back?"

"Of course." Zoe gets up to see me out, holding the door open while I wrestle with my backpack. I hug her goodbye. "Stay safe," she calls as I'm leaving, her voice catching. I nod. After what happened to Isla, we will all be more cautious.

"You too," I say, looking back and giving a wave.

Zoe waves back, her hand barely moving with the gesture. I notice something I didn't pick up on before. Zoe's expression is sad and pitying, as if she feels sorry for me. I realize that despite her claim, Zoe knows more than she's letting on. Suddenly, I feel certain she knows what Isla was going to tell me before she died.

So why is she keeping it a secret?

Chapter 17

I make it to the airport and my flight is delayed by hours, so I try to get some sleep despite the uncomfortable chair until it's time to board. I rub the sleep from my eyes and file onto the plane to take my aisle seat next to a guy who immediately starts talking. His nervous rambling tells me he doesn't enjoy flying. I would almost feel bad for him if he didn't keep looking at my chest. I give noncommittal answers to his barrage of questions as the crew gets ready for takeoff.

It's like Zoe said. I hate flying at the best of times. The motion of the plane turns my stomach into a turbulent ball, and the delay and the lack of sleep have enhanced my fear. As the plane speeds up and I feel the wheels leave the tarmac, I place a hand against my stomach protectively, as if I can stop the little life growing inside of me from the nauseating g-force. The nausea hits me in waves like it usually does, but it's made worse by the fact I was already feeling sick. I had convinced myself it was just stress, but now I'm wondering if it was morning sickness. I take a ginger candy from my pocket—I always carry them when I travel—and pop it in my mouth, hoping it soothes my stomach.

Once we are cruising at altitude, and the chatter from the man in the seat next to mine has died down, the nausea settles and I can focus again, but once I start, I can't stop thinking about what Zoe said. And what she hadn't. Why was Zoe hiding Isla's secret? It must be bad, because she had lied about it. Was she afraid that telling me could get her killed? Or was it something she didn't think I would want to know?

Hours later, the sun has risen and I lean forward and look past the man sitting beside me, making sure I don't make eye contact, trying to see out the window for a glimpse of the Hollywood sign, which I think I can see in the distance.

My thoughts creep back to Isla as I settle back into my seat. I'm hurt that she felt she couldn't tell me what was going on, and even more hurt that Zoe won't tell me now.

My stomach lurches as we fly through some turbulence, butterflies circling. I'm not sure the Ethan I'm coming to see is the same person I promised to spend my life with.

After my conversation with Zoe, I now believe that Isla knew something about Ethan. Isla isn't the type of person who holds back, so if she couldn't say it, then it's probably not good. Except I'm confident Isla would tell me if she knew Ethan was seeing someone behind my back.

I'm about to turn thirty. What if Ethan was planning a surprise and Isla was helping? No, it didn't add up. Zoe said Isla had feared something, though a party is something she would have offered to help with. Isla had organized Cassandra's thirtieth birthday party but hadn't been able to keep it a surprise (although Cassandra graciously acted surprised). Isla was not a secret keeper. She was more of an information sharer, sometimes an over-sharer.

My nerves kick up a notch as the plane hits another patch of turbulence. I remind myself there's still a chance that Isla's secret has nothing to do with Ethan, that I misinterpreted the description of the man Isla talked to because I know Ethan, so it's easy to imagine him fitting it.

Still, Ethan has changed. I had heard him on multiple nights tiptoe into the kitchen to whisper into his phone when he thought I was sleeping. He was clearly trying to hide that he was talking to someone, and while I couldn't hear his words without getting closer, his tone was smooth and almost flirty, immediately making me suspicious. They weren't emergency work calls, which he kept friendly but brisk while he sorted out whatever problem had arisen. It was a tone you reserved for someone you cared deeply about and were happy to hear from. I hadn't heard him speak like that to anyone from work, but I knew the tone well because he used to use it when he called to see how my shift was going or if I wanted him to pick up something for dinner. It was the tone he used to wake me in the morning on the weekend as he kissed a trail up my neck. He had done exactly that last Saturday, and we had ended up naked, warm breath against each other's skin, cocooned in a tangle of sheets.

Maybe it's me who's changed and not Ethan. Isla's death is making me paranoid, less trustful of even the people closest to me. Except I can't blame Isla's death because I know that a part of me has always been like that. I've seen what can happen when reasonable people are forced to make unreasonable choices.

There has always been a little voice in the back of my head telling me this life won't last, that eventually it will disappear, leaving me with the fallout from what I did all those years ago, because if Ethan knew, he wouldn't have married me. Even with cold iced tea in my hand, my feet dipped in the cool water of a swimming pool, I've always been aware that just underneath the calm is the frantic beat of my heart, reminding me to keep an eye out for the warning signs that my past has caught up to me.

I had grown complacent and began sleeping for more than three hours at a time. I stopped replaying what had happened in my mind over and over.

After Ethan and I were married, I forgot that old version of myself, the girl who couldn't face who she really was, who couldn't bear to think about what she had done. It was a nice reprieve, but I knew it couldn't last, and slowly the thoughts crept back in, accompanied by the searing guilt that tried to warn me I should go to the police and tell them everything.

It was the thought of *him* that stopped me. I didn't want to go back there, reliving each moment as I dissected the details one at a time, every word recorded. Once it was captured, everyone would know what I had done. They would be free to judge me, to punish me as they saw fit, never really understanding why it had to be done.

I had spent a long time running away from that girl, trying to leave her in the past so I could forget she ever existed. When Ethan and I were married, I wanted to change my name, to stop being Aria Miller and become Aria Dolan. Aria Dolan would never do the things Aria Miller did. She was a kind person. A nurse who spent her time helping others. She was a loving wife who saved people's lives. She absolutely did not kill people.

It was Ethan who had encouraged me to keep my name. He said that was the person he fell in love with and didn't want to change a thing about me, so unless I wanted to tell him everything—which I didn't—I decided it would be easier to let it go, to be Aria Miller in name at least.

The plane has the static anticipation of people excited to land. They're twisting in their seats to catch a glimpse of LA from up in the clouds. The man in the seat beside mine is snoring, the sound rattling in his throat.

I realize that visiting Ethan unannounced might not be the great idea I thought it was. What if he thinks I've come all this way to spy on him? What if he doesn't want to see me?

I stop my thoughts from spiraling further and take a couple of breaths. I've come this far. I might as well find out what in my life is real and what isn't. Maybe I'll learn what's so important that my husband needed to stay.

I rummage around for my phone and find a message from Ethan. I read quickly, expecting a response to the article I sent, but there is no mention of it, or Isla's death.

Sorry I haven't called to see how you're doing. Things are hectic here, but I think we're a little closer to sorting it all out. x

Something about his message feels strange and unlike him. Ethan's tone is typically warmer. Despite the kiss at the end, his words feel formal, like something you would send an acquaintance to apologize for missing drinks, not something you'd send your wife.

Looking over his message, I eventually realize what seems off. He said *we're* a little closer to sorting it out, not *I'm* a little closer. Maybe he's referring to himself and a colleague, but I've never known Ethan to share credit. I thought this was a trip he was taking alone, which is why he was so nervous about it. He didn't mention anyone else going, and I doubt the company he works for would send more people than they needed to when things were so busy.

What if he's not here on business at all? What if he was lying about going away for work so he could go on vacation with *her*? It doesn't seem so crazy, given everything that's happened over the past few days. That would make it impossible for his secret fling to be Isla.

I curl my arms under my ribs and try to relax. The flight will be over soon, and hopefully so will the sick feeling in my stomach. Now that I've had time to process our conversation, I want to call Zoe back to ask a few questions.

When the plane lands, I wait to gather my things. Afterwards it's late enough to grab some breakfast, and I stop for a bagel and some juice before heading outside the airport. There's a line of cabs, and people clutching their morning coffee all going in different directions, eager to get to their destinations. I wonder if the airport would have been quieter if my plane hadn't been delayed.

I walk until the throngs of people thin, taking the time to breathe deeply, trying to settle my bagel-filled stomach, but with the looming call to Zoe, and needing to face Ethan, it's no use.

One thing at a time, I tell myself. Might as well get it over with. I call Zoe, who answers partway through the second ring.

"Hey, Zo," I say. "Listen, the plane just landed, and I was thinking . . ." I pause, preparing myself to come out and say it. "Were Ethan and Isla having an affair? Is that what you didn't want to tell me?"

"What?" she asks, sounding flustered. "I don't think so. I mean, I doubt it."

I feel embarrassed for asking, for thinking one of my best friends would mess around with my husband behind my back. I've been watching too many dramas on Netflix.

"Do you think Isla was capable of something like that?" she asks, sounding almost hopeful that I might figure it out for the both of us.

I think about the times we were there for each other when life seemed too hard, and decide that I really don't. Isla valued her friends, and I can't see her wanting to date a guy who didn't care enough about the person he married to consider what an affair might do to them. I tell Zoe as much, and she agrees.

"She really didn't tell me what she wanted to talk to you about. I tried wearing her down," she admits. "At first, I thought maybe she did something stupid with Ethan. She could be impulsive," she says. "I couldn't think of anything else bad enough that she'd keep it from me. My next thought was that he was having an affair, but she would have told me if that's what it was."

She seems to think that Isla's secret was about Ethan too. But why? Would she tell me if I asked, or would she lie to avoid answering? It's hard to tell across the phone line, but I'm pretty sure my friends have been keeping things from me. If Zoe and Isla both knew, does Cassandra know as well?

Cassandra hadn't mentioned Isla's secret when she visited. Perhaps she didn't know how to bring it up, or she didn't want to get involved.

"Why do you think Isla's secret was about Ethan?" I finally ask. *The real reason,* I silently add.

She sighs. "I heard a knock on our door a couple of days before Cassandra told us her news. It was late at night. I don't think Isla knew I was at home because I'd been in my room most of the evening, working through a book I wanted to finish so I could return it to the library. The noise at the door was more like a bang. I didn't want to answer, because whoever was knocking sounded kind of angry. So, I ignored it. Honestly, I assumed it was one of Isla's flings coming back for their T-shirt or something."

Zoe's voice wavers, and I imagine how scared she must've been, hearing someone thumping on the door late at night, worrying they were angry.

"When it didn't stop, I got out of bed to see what was happening. I didn't want to wake the neighbors. Then I heard Isla throw the door open. She didn't invite them in. She sounded pissed that they were there."

I want to ask who was on the other side of the door, but I'm afraid to interrupt her.

"She asked what they wanted, and I heard her say they shouldn't be there. I peeked to see who it was. It sounded like their argument could escalate, but I didn't want to interrupt their privacy. I'm sorry I didn't tell you before, but I think it was Ethan."

"Why was Ethan there?" I ask, the words slipping off my tongue. Ethan had only been to Zoe and Isla's a few times. I'm surprised he remembered their address.

"He tried to push his way inside. He was looking around like he shouldn't be there. Isla blocked him from coming inside and asked what he wanted. I listened from my doorway because I was curious," she says, as if she needed a reason to eavesdrop.

"Did he answer?" I ask, dreading what he said.

"He said she didn't show up at eight like they planned. Apparently he waited for over an hour, and she didn't answer his calls."

My stomach sinks. What Zoe's telling me doesn't sound good, but I can't draw conclusions before I know more.

"She told him she had changed her mind. That she was sick of lying to you," says Zoe, her tone apologetic. My instinct was right—she was lying before and this is her way of coming clean.

I don't judge her even a bit. At that moment, I want to confess too. Tell her I've hidden much worse for a lot longer, but I'm a hypocrite, and as much as I want the truth, I can't give it.

"Did they say anything else?" I ask, switching my backpack to my other shoulder, my steps slowing to a crawl as I pace back and forth.

"They were interrupted by Dane, our neighbor from across the hall. Dane asked if Ethan was giving Isla any trouble. After that, Ethan just kind of left. I think Dane scared him off," says Zoe. "I'm sorry. I don't even know what it means. That's why I didn't mention it before."

Why would Ethan be trying to meet up with Isla? And how had she ended up dead just days after their conversation?

"Did you tell the police about Ethan's visit?"

"I said I heard her talking to someone, that I stayed in my room, and that I didn't know who it was," she says. "I'm not completely sure it was Ethan. It was dark, and I was tired. It could have been someone who looked like him. I was so sure when I first thought I saw him standing there, but by the next morning, I couldn't be certain."

I wonder if she really believes that, or if she's just having a hard time reconciling my husband being on her doorstep in the middle of the night and what followed just a short time later.

Maybe Ethan knows why Isla's dead. Maybe that's why he wasn't surprised when I texted and told him she was murdered. Is that why he didn't respond to my messages when I sent him the article? Maybe he's trying to figure out what to do now that he knows someone saw him visiting Isla.

I run a hand through my hair. Ethan's the mystery guy who someone saw arguing with Isla, and now he's hiding out. Is he afraid the police will arrest him if he comes home?

Could that be how he got the blood on his suit? Is my husband a murderer?

Chapter 18

When I arrive at the hotel with just my backpack, I realize how hollow my plan was. I know which hotel he's staying at, but I don't know which room, and I don't have a key to get inside. All I know is that I have to speak to him.

I think about Ethan's argument with Isla, and the email. *How well do you know your husband?* Is it possible that everything—the LA ticket, my surprise plans—is just a distraction from being alone at home, fixating on Isla's death and Ethan's infidelity? Or is it something else?

Do I really believe Ethan could have something to do with Isla's death? Maybe I'm trying to prove to myself that none of these crazy thoughts are real, that our baby can rely on him, but I can't shake the feeling that buying a ticket across the country to see my husband is the beginning of the end.

Before I can change my mind, I force one foot in front of the other and head inside the hotel lobby. It's large and looming, all black-and-white tiles with gray marble. A beautiful water fountain sits in the middle of the lobby, the soothing sound of flowing water giving the hotel a serene vibe. I've never been to the Central Palais, but I expected it to be more businesslike. This looks like the sort of place you come to for a honeymoon or a vacation.

Ethan's personal assistant, Stella, would have reserved the room for him. She may have figured it would be a difficult deal to seal and wanted to make sure he had the stamina to see it through by booking a spa retreat instead of a stale hotel lined with faded red carpet and lobby armchairs well past their replacement date.

I take my phone from my pocket, ready to call Ethan. I could play this off as a surprise visit, just like the weekends we had when we were first dating. Back then, I wouldn't have thought twice about calling, but that seems like a lifetime ago. Now, I stand with my phone firmly squeezed into the palm of my hand, wondering what Ethan will say. Will he be happy to see me? Or, a part of me asks, will he send me home so he can go about his business, uninterrupted by his annoying, clingy wife?

I gaze at the artwork on the wall, procrastinating to avoid calling. The pieces look like the artist was studying human emotion, trying to capture the feel on canvas. They're supposed to be happy, but there is a Bosch-like quality reminiscent of his dark renaissance depiction of hell, the colors bold and expressive.

A painting of a girl catches my eye. She is laughing. Her eyes crinkle at the edges, as if someone just gave her the best news she ever had, but her hands are anxiously gripping something.

I feel like I should be as happy as the girl looks. I finally have what I wanted, something I would have paid a lot of money for, but it feels like something is about to ruin it. Like the girl about to reveal her hand.

I'm still unsure whether to tell Ethan I'm pregnant. I haven't confirmed it with a doctor, and the test could be a false positive.

I've almost convinced myself that not telling him is the right thing to do, until a blood test confirms it, when I notice the woman sitting at the concierge desk looking right at me.

She turns away when I notice her watching and starts lazily tapping away at a keyboard, as if slowing down the typing process will help pass the time until the end of her shift.

I put my phone away and walk forward, wondering how out of place my travel outfit of faded denim jeans and a pink shirt must look here. I can hear her gel nails clipping against the keys like a slowly trotting horse. I wait until she stops typing before I speak.

I smile, apologetic for interrupting her. "I'm supposed to be meeting my husband, but he has the key so I'm locked out."

"No problem. What name is the booking under?"

I hope the booking was made under his name and not Stella's. I try to remember back to when she booked us a weekend getaway down the coast. I'm sure it was booked under Ethan's name. What if the mystery woman made the reservation? I have no hope of guessing her name. I take a shot, hoping it pays off. "Dolan," I say, trying to sound certain despite the little niggle in the pit of my stomach that tells me I'm going to show myself up as a fraud.

I wait as she types something into the system. Her big blue eyes scan the screen and eventually she looks up and asks innocently, "Did you misplace your key, Mrs Dolan?"

My heart stops. Never have I gone by the name Mrs Dolan. I've always been Aria Miller. Is Ethan playing house with his girlfriend, pretending Isla isn't dead and that he's not about to be a suspect in her murder once the police realize he paid her an angry visit?

Maybe it was an honest mistake from the receptionist.

I smooth the tensed muscles in my face with a smile. I mentioned my husband. It was a reasonable assumption.

She mistakes my hesitation for confusion and continues, "The system says you were each issued one when you signed in."

Her words leave me breathless, like a gut punch. "Yeah. My husband has them. Both of them," I clarify. "I put them in the backpack."

I fight to keep the smile on my face, the effort becoming more difficult as I process the weight of what she said. Ethan is here with someone, playing the happy couple with a matching set of keys.

"No problem," she says. "I can unlock the room for you until you can get your key back?"

My mind races. What if I go up there and she's with him? I don't want to make a scene at the hotel. I could slink out and wait until Ethan comes home to confront him?

He's been lying for so long, so why trust him now? I need to catch him in his lie if I want the truth. I should go up and pretend I'm here to surprise him, see if he continues lying or comes clean.

I want to ask if he had any part in what happened to Isla. A part of me is hoping that somehow I've got it all wrong. That Ethan is still the guy I married. A guy who wouldn't secretly visit my friends in the middle of the night.

My stomach cramps, like it does before my period, but that shouldn't happen when you're pregnant. I place a hand over my abdomen, hoping that all this stress isn't hurting the baby that I'm too afraid to believe is really there.

"Thank you, that would be great," I say, and wait as she calls someone to let me inside Ethan's room.

Chapter 19

"Hey, Lenny. Can you please help Mrs Dolan? She's misplaced her key," she says. I peek at the tag as she hands the key to a bellboy. The top has the number 1026 printed across it. Now I have their room number.

I follow Lenny, who seems nervous. He looks uncomfortable in his uniform, and I assume he hasn't been working here long. He barely seems old enough to have a job at all, and he offers to take my bag as we walk, an offer I thank him for but decline.

"Happens all the time," he says.

"What's that?" I ask, surprised by the sudden conversation. For a second, I think he's realized I'm not the same Mrs. Dolan Ethan arrived with, but Lenny continues to walk down a hall and past generously spaced doors, which suggest large suites. I wait as Lenny stops outside the one marked 1026.

"People forgetting their keys," says Lenny. "Don't worry about it."

"Thanks," I say and wait as he retrieves the key from his pocket. He frowns when he takes it out and turns it over to look at the number. "Did you say Dolan?" he asks.

"Yeah." I hear the question in my voice, inviting him to explain his own. "Is everything all right?"

"I thought Mr Dolan checked out early this morning. I carried his bags to the cab and loaded them up for him while he was on a phone call. His booking was until Tuesday, but he told me he wouldn't be coming back. Maybe he forgot to check out at reception." Lenny shrugs—Mr Dolan's reason for leaving isn't his problem.

I suddenly feel nervous. What if he recognizes I wasn't the woman who was with Ethan when he left, unless he left alone? I desperately want to ask, but I can't ask if I left with him without seeming a little flaky, suspicious even.

"Yeah," I say, playing along as if I already knew Ethan had checked out. "That was the plan, but I think I left something inside. Is it okay if I go in and quickly get it?"

If Lenny suspects something is off, he doesn't show it, and willingly unlocks the door. "Sure. Housekeeping hasn't come by yet, so go right ahead. I'll wait outside to lock up once you're done."

"Thank you," I say with a grateful smile. This is my chance to look around. I wonder how well my husband has cleaned up after himself and what I'll find inside. I hurry past the door, knowing I don't have long. Lenny is waiting outside for me to retrieve my imaginary forgotten thing.

My shoes spring against the luxurious carpet. My gut was right. This isn't a quick business stop hotel. The room is beautiful, decorated with light wood and blue accents, making me want to breathe in the freshness. It looks like a honeymoon suite, with a view of the pool from the window, and a separate, more private space at the back with a bedroom.

I walk inside, bracing myself for what I might find. On first inspection, the room looks tidy but lived in, missing that sparkle that comes from a deep clean. He's even tried to make up the queen-sized bed, the luxurious bedding crumpled on both sides, pillows thrown crookedly over the covers. I usually make the bed at home. Perhaps *she* made up the bed. Thinking about it, Ethan probably wouldn't bother. I look underneath the bedframe, searching for anything they might've forgotten, but there's nothing.

Next, I look inside the ensuite, knowing I'm walking into the aftermath of a life-changing disaster. Dirty towels hang on a rail next to a giant spa bath and two empty champagne glasses.

I hear the door to the suite open, and Lenny's voice calls out uncertainly. "Uh, sorry to hurry you, but I need to close up soon. I have a few things to get to before my shift finishes."

"Be out in a minute," I say, hoping Lenny doesn't feel compelled to come in after me as I try to figure out where to look next. I move to the cupboards, opening each one until I find what I'm looking for.

The trashcan is hidden, and almost full. I bury down my guilt and embarrassment. If I dig through, the last shreds of trust between Ethan and me will be gone. Is this how people turn into stalkers, paranoia slowly setting in until they're sure their marriage is no longer just between the two of them? Until they search for evidence of a third party, snooping like Cassandra and I had, unable to go on wondering what has changed, feeling like the only person who still doesn't know their marriage is a lie.

As I root through the trash, I remind myself why I'm doing it. This isn't just about me anymore. My baby deserves a chance at a stable family. "I'm sorry, Ethan, but I need to know," I say, digging deeper until my hand stops at a hard rectangular box.

I pull it from the garbage, bright pink and ornately detailed, seeming too pretty to throw out. A little logo tells me the box is from Matrix. I remove the squished lid, hoping Lenny's patience holds up for a few more seconds.

The box is empty except for crumpled tissue paper cut in the shape of a heart. Whatever was inside, Ethan's girlfriend must've liked it enough to keep.

I look at the heart-shaped paper, tearing it in two. This wasn't just a fling—nobody spends a small fortune and delivers it with love hearts to someone they don't intend on keeping around.

A fling might get some mid-priced underwear to remove without worrying whether it might get ripped.

I try to remember the last time Ethan surprised me with a lavish gift for no reason, but I have to think back further than I expected. One month. Two. Six. A year. My memory races back to the time we booked a vacation in the Hamptons, nearly two years ago. He'd bought me an ugly bathing suit, expecting me to protest, claiming that my real present was a fully funded shopping spree once we arrived so that I could choose something nicer.

I told him I liked the suit and asked if we could spend the money on a trip to an art gallery or a museum along the coast— my real reason for wanting to go on vacation.

The memory makes me smile sadly. Less than two years ago, I thought my marriage was unbreakable. I couldn't have imagined that two years later I would wonder whether Ethan could be involved in a murder.

I put the trash back quickly and rinse my hands. There's nothing left to do but get out of here and figure out what to do next.

At least the trip wasn't a complete dead end. I know Ethan was here with someone, and that it wasn't for work. Will he head home now that he's finished with his trip, acting as if nothing's changed?

If he left a few hours ago, that means he might be on his way home now. What do I tell him if he gets home before me? I could just confront him, tell him what I know, and hope he comes clean.

I indulge the thought, seeing myself showing him the email she sent, gauging his response. When I told him someone was following me, he shrugged it off as someone probably just heading in the same direction as me. He probably knew it was *her* all along.

The thought makes me mad, but I don't know if I'm ready to be that confrontational, not until I have evidence he can't explain away, and I can see him finding a reasonable explanation for the hotel. Sharing the hotel with someone from work. Ethan swearing that nothing happened between them.

There is one way I could find out more. I find Ethan's PA's number in my phone. She answers in her usual bubbly tone and I apologize for interrupting her weekend.

"Hey, Stella. It's Aria," I say in the happiest voice I can muster.

"Aria! How are you?" asks Stella.

I don't answer immediately, listening to the sound of muted voices in the background, but I can't tell who they belong to. I think I hear a car pass.

When I realize what I'm doing, I clear my throat and remind myself to take a step back, almost getting caught up in the stereotype. There is no way Stella would be the person Ethan is seeing. She's about our age, but she's happily married with a couple of kids, and talking with her for even a few minutes, you get the sense that she's dedicated to her family.

Stella is probably somewhere with them right now, enjoying their time as a family. I listen for their voices, but all I hear is the sound of engines roaring to life as the traffic finally moves on.

"I'm great, thanks. Do you know where Ethan is? I've been trying to call his cell, but it must've gone flat." The lie comes easily, a means to an end.

"Oh," she says awkwardly. "I'm sorry, but Ethan hasn't been in the office all week. Have you tried leaving him a message?"

"That's right. He had that thing in LA," I say, playing along. "Sorry, I've been so busy. I completely forgot."

"LA?" she asks, as if that's news to her. She seems to realize she's let something slip, but it's too late to take it back now that it's out there.

"Some business trip?" I say innocently, a question at the end of my tone suggesting I'm not sure.

"There's nothing scheduled. Would you like me to call Ethan for you?" she asks, sounding concerned. Whatever's going on, Stella's just as in the dark as I am.

"No, that's okay. I think I just got the dates mixed up." I apologize and wish her a great weekend, ending the call with me sounding like a fool. Stella is far too organized to miss a business meeting scheduled out of town.

I've caught Ethan in his lie.

Chapter 20

I manage to secure a flight home after hours on standby, people-watching as they pass through the gates. Boarding. Landing. Families leaving on vacation. Newlyweds honeymooning, their arms snaking around each other like they never want to let go. Suits attend to business, while nervous fliers grip the handles of their travel luggage.

I wonder if they see me, what they think my story is. Am I a woman traveling alone without much luggage? Am I a carefree, spontaneous vacationer, or a lonely traveler, leaving my life back home for something new and exciting?

As the cab approaches my street, I call Ethan, curious whether he has arrived home yet. So much has happened in the time he's been gone that it feels like forever since I've seen him. Perhaps he's wondering where I am—but not enough to call and find out.

He doesn't answer on the first try. A recorded message invites the caller to leave a name and number so he can get back to them.

It's not the voice of a killer but a friendly person who is genuinely apologetic about being unable to answer their phone. I leave a message to let him know I'm worried, reminding him we haven't spoken in two days. I ask if he got my text message—maybe it didn't send properly—reluctantly ending the call with no answers.

Today is the day Ethan was supposed to be home, and I half expect to find the door unlocked, Ethan unpacking his things like usual, even when it was late enough to justify waiting until the following morning.

When I reach our front door, I slide my key into the lock. It's dark inside. I flick on the light, knowing it won't chase away the shadows. I wait for the emptiness to hit me, the realization that I'm completely alone. I look around the apartment for his travel luggage. Everything is just as I left it, but something feels different. The happy home we built feels like the shell of something that's long moved on.

I move through to the kitchen and drop my bag on the floor. After hours of travel, I'm craving a warm shower. I make my way toward the ensuite, taking my phone with me, in case Ethan calls and check the closet as I pass, rifling through to the place where the uncovered suit was hanging. It feels like so long ago since Cassandra and I searched the house, looking for clues about who Ethan was seeing.

The suit jacket is still missing, but the matching pants are folded over their hanger and covered with plastic wrap. Willow must have returned them while I was away. I remember the spattered stain I saw on the inner jacket pocket, red and angry, as if it had arrived violently and unexpectedly. There is no way that stain was coming out, the sepia tones clinging to the fabric. Just like blood.

I can't imagine Ethan's dry cleaner, Anton, returning a stained jacket. He must've kept it and returned the slacks. Anton wasn't an untidy man. He never returned clothing in anything other than perfect condition. Anton would keep the jacket until he made it new again, perhaps sending it to a tailor to have the lining replaced. But that would raise a bunch of new questions about how the bloodstain got there, and I don't imagine Ethan would enjoy that.

Maybe Willow didn't pick up the jacket to deliver to the dry cleaner's after all. Maybe Ethan had asked her to get rid of it, because keeping bloodstained evidence around would land him in trouble.

It would explain Willow's shock at seeing me when she came to collect the suit. She was right. I'm usually out at the time she came by. Had she intentionally chosen a time when she could slide into my home unnoticed and take what she came for without me knowing? I picture her hesitation at the door.

As I step into the shower, I try to forget about Willow, focusing on the warm water against my skin. Once I'm done, I towel off before crawling into bed, too tired to do much else.

Sleep finds me and I don't wake until the sun is almost up on Monday morning. The sudden upheaval of my stomach is like a physical alarm, growing in intensity, warning me I have limited time to make it to the bathroom before it goes off.

I get there just in time to unleash the contents of my stomach into the porcelain toilet bowl. I freshen my mouth when I'm done, still too queasy to think about breakfast. Cassandra has left me a message, saying she booked an appointment for me to see her fertility specialist friend tomorrow. The message arrived a day ago. She probably expected Ethan would be back by now, and I can't tell her I don't need the appointment anymore, not before I've told Ethan that I'm pregnant, so I thank her and say I'll be there. A better idea would have been to tell her I'm sick and that I can't go. Too late now.

I check for a message from Ethan, but there's no text telling me where he is or why he isn't home yet. No missed phone calls. An uneasy sensation falls over me, ominous and oppressive. Another day where he's not home and isn't responding to my messages.

Enough time has passed with no word from Ethan—is it time to report him missing?

I call again. The message I leave this time is more urgent, suggesting that if he doesn't call me back within an hour, I will call the police and tell them I'm worried that something has happened to him. I don't dare let myself question what I believe. My husband has been uncontactable for days, and I'm not as worried as I know I should be because I'm sure he's with *her*, having too much fun to ruin it by calling his wife. Maybe he hasn't told her about me, preferring to pretend I don't exist when they're together.

But what if I'm wrong? I force myself to consider another possibility. An accident perhaps, Ethan lying in a ditch, unable to call for help. It's this image that is the catalyst I need to propel myself into action.

I call the police but hang up before they answer. What if Ethan has gotten himself involved in something that could get him in trouble, something illegal? Selfishly, I don't want him to be carted away before I've asked some questions of my own. I call Ethan again, willing him to answer, promising myself it will be the last time I try.

The phone rings, the feeling of my pulse in my neck rushing in time with the sound like an accented beat. I feel butterflies, like I used to when we were first dating, the anticipation of hearing the lilt in his voice as if he was happy I had called.

I don't leave another message when the ringtone peters out, replaced by the beep of Ethan's voicemail.

I check my email in case his phone died. I scroll back to the day he left, searching for something I might have missed. There's nothing from Ethan, even in my spam folder.

I stop when I come to the unsigned email asking how well I know my husband. A silly thought crosses my mind that maybe it's Ethan playing an elaborate prank on me that will only end once it meets some arbitrary success criteria he has decided upon. I try to think what that would be. Would he want it to go as far as me calling the police? I doubt Ethan would spend days on a prank, especially when the messages I had sent him made it clear I was worried. But someone had taken the time to send it and it was no longer looking like it was spam or a joke.

The annoyance I first felt at reading the email, when I assumed it was about infidelity, is replaced by an unsettling foreboding. Maybe I've messed up and this is about something more sinister.

My need to follow this through and find out where Ethan is eclipses my fear. I hit reply and type a response.

Who is this? How do you know Ethan?

After I hit send, a panic grips me, reminding me I'm not as brave as I'm pretending to be. Not by a long shot.

Anyone could have sent that message, and I've just responded. Who knows what information I've given them through that one simple action?

But this isn't just some scam to clean out my bank account. There's more riding on this than a few dollars and my interrupted savings.

This is my life as I know it, and an uncertain future that will impact my baby.

This might be my only chance of finding Ethan, of knowing whether he's hurt.

If it is a prank, they might let it go now that I've responded. And if it's not, maybe they will ask for money, or whatever it is they want from me, and I'll have something to take to the police. Because I know if I went to them before I responded, they would tell me to ignore it. They would assume it was one of the millions of spam messages sent every day in the hope people like me would answer.

I would expect a threatening message to appear via Snapchat, disappearing soon after I read it, but the sender didn't want their message to disappear, allowing me to read it over again and again. Daring me to respond.

They did not want to disappear, for me to forget their words. *How well do you know your husband?*

It's what happens next that I care about, now that I realize they're not asking a question at all. They're telling me they know something that I don't. Something I should probably know. It's only now that I've responded that I might find out what kind of game we're playing, and if Ethan has gotten himself into the kind of trouble the police will want to know about.

When a response arrives in my inbox moments later, I get the feeling the emailer has been waiting for my reply since they first sent the message. I open the email and read.

They do neither of the things I expected. There is no request for money, and they haven't ignored my question. They have answered it with a vaguely threatening response of their own. Are they expecting me to react to their words, get angry, and start demanding answers? Or is this a long game they're drawing out to torture me?

**I know him better than you think. And I know you.
I'm surprised you didn't learn about me sooner.**

There is no signature, no identifiers, so I have no way of knowing who emailed, but it feels like it was her. *I know him better than you think. I'm surprised you didn't learn about me sooner.* Both are things I would expect someone to say if they found out their boyfriend had a wife.

Especially if they thought their relationship was over and they wanted to make sure his wife knew what he had done.

The response gives me a better idea of the sort of woman I'm dealing with.

I understand. I'm angry too. I might not be ready to wage war, but I did just fly across the country to find out where he was and who he was with.

Everything points to an affair, but I still don't know for sure. Who else could he be spending time with? Whoever it is, he doesn't want me to know about it. He's never been the kind of person to invite a bunch of people around for drinks and dinner, but maybe he found a friend he wasn't ready to share.

The idea sounds stupid even as I think it—going on vacation with a secret friend to California without telling me, *lying* about it, is ridiculous.

My email pings while I'm trying to figure out who else it could have been from. It's another message from the same email address. This time the words spook me, sounding like someone who wants to be a part of Ethan's life more permanently. Someone obsessive enough to do what was necessary to make that happen.

What if she's got Ethan locked up somewhere, and that's why he hasn't come home? What if she's trying to disrupt his life just as he disrupted hers, thinking she can achieve her goal through me?

I force myself to consider the words on the screen.

You have a beautiful home. I left you a present in the top drawer next to your bed.

I consider going and looking at what she's left, scared I will find a bomb or a severed finger. *Ethan's* finger. I could call Cassandra, but I get the feeling that whoever sent the message could be watching me, just like they had weeks ago in the alleyway.

How long had they been following me before that, before I even noticed them? They haven't said what they want yet, but

I know it's coming. If I involve the police, will it put Ethan in danger? I take a moment to compose myself. I need to stay calm and figure out what they want. There might still be a way to deescalate the situation and get Ethan home safe.

That means not calling Cassandra or doing anything that could trigger a reaction.

Should I check my nightstand drawer? Or is she challenging me, waiting to see what I'll do? Does she want to see if I'm brave enough to face what she's left inside the drawer?

Showing weakness now could push her to act.

My hand has crept to my stomach, across my abdomen, as if I can keep my baby safe in there—the baby that I haven't verified is truly there. The gesture is driven by instinct, and I force myself to move my hand away because she could be watching.

I search the apartment, looking for anything that seems out of place. I think some clothes have been moved in my room, but I might've moved them while I was packing for LA.

I look at the drawer in my room, trying to figure out if it's different, but there is no sign someone has tampered with it. The drawer is big enough to house something sinister, but I usually keep a couple of books inside. Nothing has been left outside the drawer, so I assume she placed the books back if she removed them. Whatever's in there—if she put something in there at all—isn't so big that it'll jump out and bite.

I take a shaky breath, silently relieved that I'm not about to find my husband's severed head inside.

I could still call the police. I imagine her watching me dial, asking for a detective to report a potential crime to. Then what? Will she hurt Ethan when she realizes I've involved law enforcement?

Before the fear takes over, I edge the drawer open, paying attention to its weight as the brackets shift, the drawer sliding toward me, stopping before it's fully open. I can see the edge of a book cover, a thriller I was reading and had forgotten about. I wedge the drawer open a little more and take the book out.

Nothing looks disturbed, and I wonder if this is just an elaborate prank to mess with me, to see how easy it is to scare me. I pull two more books from the drawer and place them on the bed haphazardly, eager to get to the bottom, my confidence that there's nothing to find growing as I pull each book from its place. When I reach the last book, I visibly relax. No bombs or severed body parts.

I pull the last book from the drawer, hearing a little *tink*, like the sound of a key dropping in front of an apartment door after a drunken night out.

I pull the drawer wider, then pick up the little piece of metal at the bottom. I've seen it a thousand times, felt the round band grow warm against my hand as Ethan's fingers wrapped around mine.

It's Ethan's wedding ring.

Chapter 21

I turn the wedding band over, looking at it up close. Could she have planted a replica, hoping I'd think it was Ethan's?

There's one way to tell if it's the real deal. Ethan's ring has a scratch on the metal. I hold the ring against the light, studying the smooth surface. It's almost discernible as I run my finger across the edge of the band. It feels like a paper cut, thinly slicing the gold. Planting my husband's ring seems like a lot of trouble to go to without telling me what they want.

I scrutinize Ethan's wedding ring, searching for any signs or evidence of where he was when he removed it. Had she convinced him to take it off? Maybe she didn't have to.

He still hasn't answered my messages. What if Ethan really is being held against his will? I swallow down bile. What if she was angry enough to do something even worse, and she sent me his wedding ring to see what I was willing to do?

The emailer has my attention now. Full and undivided. I open my inbox, ready to confirm that I received Ethan's ring. Ready to ask what she wants.

Now would be the perfect time to call the police. Except I'm afraid to involve them until I know more.

A fresh email sits at the top of my inbox, waiting to be read.

Are you ready to talk to me?

I look at my cell. I do not want to give her my number and with it the freedom to contact me whenever she wants, but I need answers and she may be the only person who can give them.

I'm typing out my number when another email pings, listing a time and a place to meet.

By now, you're wondering who I am. I know you must be wondering where Ethan is. I also know you checked the drawer in your bedroom. If you're curious about how I got Ethan's wedding ring, I will tell you that too. All you need to do is meet me for a drink. Tonight.

How did she know I checked the drawer? Is there a camera hidden inside my bedroom, or was it a lucky guess? I scan the bedroom for surveillance equipment, but there's nothing obvious.

She didn't need to see me open the drawer to know I would. Anyone would do the same to confirm the emailer wasn't lying.

Below the message is the address of a cafe close to our apartment. Ethan and I go there sometimes. I wonder if that's why she's chosen it. I try to remember if anything significant has happened there, but it's always been somewhere to go when you're waiting for a table you've booked elsewhere, or when you're not quite ready to go home later in the night.

She wants to meet in just a few hours.

I consider what might happen if I reject the invitation. She could be setting me up to walk right into her lair.

What if she's not?

She still hasn't warned me not to involve the police, or anyone else, which is more unsettling than if she had been making demands, giving an ultimatum about what will happen to Ethan if I don't comply. At least I would know what to expect. All she's asked for so far is one meeting. In a public place, with people around us. She wants to talk.

I give myself a moment to process what she's asking, weighing up the risks. It mightn't have been such a hard choice a few weeks ago. I would've agreed willingly, but now that I might be pregnant, there's more to consider. What if, despite the public meeting place, she follows me when I leave and hurts the baby?

Now that she wants to meet with me in person, I realize this might not be a disgruntled lover sending angry messages. What if this is the real deal, and someone kidnapped Ethan? Maybe they want to ask for money and will insist on watching me wire it to confirm the transaction.

I have no bargaining power, but they think they have something I want. *Ethan.* They don't know we had problems, that the only thing I want from Ethan is answers.

I almost agree to meet until I think about what happened to Isla. Was she a warning, letting me know what will happen if I don't agree to their request? I bite my lip, teeth sinking deep into the skin while I think.

The sound of my phone splits the silence. I put in my earphones and swipe to answer, Cassandra's voice soothing my nerves. I'm so relieved to hear someone familiar, someone who I can trust, that at first I don't notice the edge to her voice.

"Hey, Aria. I'm guessing you're still arguing with Ethan? How late did he get home?"

"What? No. Why would you think that?" I ask.

"It's the only reason I can think of that would make you miss your fertility appointment today." She sounds worried, and maybe a little irritated that she pulled some strings to get me that appointment, and I hadn't even shown up.

I curse under my breath. "Cassandra, I'm so sorry. Ethan still isn't home. I haven't heard from him yet . . ." I almost tell her more, hoping she has a better theory than kidnappers and angry exes, but I stop myself, aware someone could be watching. Listening.

I scan the room for a hidden camera, desperate to tell her about the strange emails and the vaguely threatening tone of the person sending them. I can't find any equipment, but it doesn't stop the fear that they will hear me and take it out on Ethan.

"What?" says Cassandra incredulously. "Have you called the damned police?"

"It's complicated," I say lamely, realizing it sounds like I'm giving her one of Isla's flippant brush-off lines just after she's dumped someone and they ask questions she doesn't want to answer. But what would I say? That my husband told me he was staying longer for a business trip and then did? I picture them asking me if there's a chance he left for good . . . and I would have to answer honestly.

Yes. Yes, I think he's seeing someone. I know he was staying with her and that he made up some story about a business trip.

They would ask how I know all this, laughing when I confessed I had gone to see him before heading back home to our empty apartment.

"How complicated can it be?" She sighs.

If only she knew.

"Look, honey. Even if he's seeing someone else, there's no way he would keep you in the dark like this by not coming home. If he's trying to hide an affair, doesn't it look suspicious as hell if he stays for a few extra days without at least trying to cover it up? Trust me. He *wants* you to find him."

Her certainty almost convinces me. Unless someone is keeping him away, why would he want to incriminate himself? Maybe he's taking the coward's way out, hoping I'll put it together without him needing to tell me he has left for good. It would explain why he left his bloodstained suit, and why he "accidentally" left the receipt in his pocket and the tag for his girlfriend's present around.

Maybe they're all just subtle ways of telling me he's not coming back.

Would things have turned out differently if I had just asked him what was going on weeks ago, when I first suspected he was having an affair?

If I can't talk to Ethan, maybe I should talk to the emailer. I promise Cassandra I'll consider her advice, already pulling up the email as we say our goodbyes.

See you there.

It's just three words, but it takes a few tries to type them the way I want. I look at the screen, hovering over the send button. I can feel the escalation. There's a shift. Something made them reach out. The first email didn't have the same urgency, but I don't know what changed.

I try to figure out what it could be. I have a shift at work tomorrow, the first since Isla died. Maybe they can't monitor me at work, and they're worried I'll tell someone about the messages they've been sending.

I hit send. Moments later, I hear someone at the door.

Chapter 22

Keys rattle on a chain outside the door. My ears strain, listening for clues about what to expect when the door opens.

When he walks through the door, Ethan looks like a stranger. I look closer, wondering whether the well-put-together person I know is gone forever, leaving this man in his wake, a shadow of the Ethan I used to know. His hair lacks its usual finesse, falling in ratty knots as if he hasn't combed it in days. His clothes look disheveled, his eyes show signs of redness and puffiness, and I'm wondering when he last had some sleep.

He is not the well-rested person I would expect to see after a luxurious vacation. It makes me curious about where he went after leaving the hotel. It looks like he didn't leave because a better option opened up elsewhere. He's thinner, his jaw hardened with stubble, like he's been roughing it.

Ethan would never meet clients looking like this, so I can rule out work altogether. Wherever he was, it doesn't look pleasant, but I'm not about to ask.

He looks at me and that smile that used to make my knees buckle spreads across his face. He's happy to see me. Relieved even. He moves closer, about to envelop me in a hug.

I fold my arms across my chest. I want answers. How will he explain not calling me back, when I was clearly worried?

He gets right to it, and at least I can give him that. "Aria, I'm so sorry I didn't call. My phone was flat, and I lost my charger. I tried to get home as soon as I could. You shouldn't have had to be alone after what happened to Isla."

I sigh. "No, I shouldn't have." It's impossible to gauge his reaction. I try to see if he flinches, but he's busy locking the door behind him, testing it to make sure it's engaged as if something has spooked him. Usually, I have to remind him multiple times to lock the door. I'm not ready for more lies, so I stand back, figuring out what I'm seeing, trying to piece together Ethan's actions until they resemble something that makes sense.

He leaves his luggage on the floor without unpacking. He looks ready to pass out on the sofa and sleep for days, but he's still figuring out what to say, like he knows it better be good for me to even listen.

Now that I know Ethan's safe, the emailer has lost their bargaining power. What can they tell me about my husband that I don't already know? We've shared a home and a bed for three years. He knows the very core of me, despite hiding so much of himself.

I remind myself that there is one thing I haven't told him. Something I've kept hidden because telling him won't change who I am, but it could change his perception of me. If he had known my secret, he might have decided not to marry me, so I never told him. I'd done everything I could to keep him from finding out, including pretending to be someone else when Ellen

Weathers, a girl I used to go to college with, came up to our table to say hello while we were out at dinner one night.

When Ethan had asked about it later, I said I didn't want to get stuck going out for lunch with someone I didn't particularly like, so I lied. He believed me, never knowing how close we came to losing what we had built together.

He reaches out, and for a moment I almost fall into his arms, but then I remember what he's done, and what I've been through these last few days, worrying someone might have kidnapped him or that he was lying dead in a ditch somewhere. As his arms move around me, I don't throw my arms around his neck and tell him I missed him like I usually would. Instead, I tense up and inhale a deep breath, my nose pressed against his chest. I smell the faint scent of coconut body wash wafting from his skin.

"I'm so sorry," he says again, feeling me tense up. "I got held up, and I had no way of calling you. There was a problem with my ticket and I couldn't get home. I was stuck on standby."

He senses my reluctance and pulls back, looking at me. "I tried calling," I say. "And I messaged." I look at him expectantly, giving him the opportunity to explain. "You didn't respond, so I called Stella."

I see something pass across his face when I mention calling Stella. Does he think Stella would lie for him? Is he worried that she told me where he really was?

I wait for his carefully crafted questions to figure out what I know. I'm ready to admit I know there was no work trip, that Stella didn't know where he was, but the way he just looks at me, keeping the truth hidden when he could explain it, stops me. "I know. I thought you might be worried. I got home as fast as I could. I'm sorry."

"Why didn't you call from the airport?" I ask, playing along. "You could've borrowed someone's phone to make a quick call. You could've found a payphone." I can't stop the anger from creeping into my voice. I know he was there with *her*.

Maybe he really was stuck, and he had to wait it out at the airport because they broke up and he had nowhere else to go. Is that what cut their getaway short?

I want to ask, but I won't let myself. I need to know if he will be honest or continue to lie.

I look away, tucking my arms protectively against my chest, shielding myself from whatever he's about to say.

"I need to take a shower," he says. "And then I'll make us something to drink."

It's a peace offering, but it feels like a slap in the face; him saying it's okay to have a drink when he decides it's okay, even though he was upset with me for having drinks with my friends.

I wait until I hear the shower running. The sound of water cascading changes as Ethan steps inside, and I go straight to his bags. The top of his carry-on is closed, locked with the small coded padlock he uses when he travels.

I look inside the front pocket and find exactly what I'm looking for. Ethan doesn't always trust the airport technology to work, so he always prints his itinerary. I work quickly to unfold the sheets of paper, scanning for his flight date and location. The departing flight was from LAX, but he didn't arrive tonight.

His plane arrived in New York a whole day ago.

I take the itinerary and bury it in my pocket. He'll be out of the shower soon. Time is running out. I dig my hand to the bottom of the bag until I feel a chain.

When I retrieve it, I almost gasp. It's a pretty charm necklace with a heart on it. I recognize it immediately as Isla's. She collected charms and often changed which ones she wore on her necklace.

My hand recoils, dropping the jewelry back into the bag. There must be a reason he has it. I can't remember whether Isla had the necklace on or what charms were on it. She changed the charms regularly, usually in some kind of theme, but she wore it so often that I'd stopped noticing.

I think of Ethan's wedding ring, how someone put it in the drawer while I wasn't there. If she put the ring in the drawer, that meant she wasn't with him, but Ethan has been back from LA for days. Did she slip away while he was sleeping, taking his ring with her?

I place my head in my hands and try to clear the fogginess inside my brain. I'm grasping at straws, trying to understand what's happening, but all the surmising in the world won't give me answers.

I look at the door, tempted to slip out before Ethan notices. I zip the bag closed and step away, almost deciding to ask Ethan questions once he's showered, but I can't trust him to be honest when he's gotten so good at lying.

Right now, I trust a random stranger using a fake email on the internet to tell me the truth more than I trust my husband.

I collect my keys, clutching them in my palm as the shower stops. There are a few minutes left before Ethan dries off and heads out. I tiptoe to the front door, barely daring to breathe as I escape the apartment, leaving Ethan inside.

I'm past the lobby and out the front doors, lungs breathing in the fresh air, before I hear him call out to me. He's at the apartment window, a towel wrapped around his waist, tucked in at the hip. "Aria! Where are you going?" he calls, his voice panicked. I can't tell if he's surprised that I'm leaving, or if he's annoyed at the homecoming he has received.

He has a small plastic stick in his hand and I'm immediately annoyed with myself for not hiding it deeper in the trash can. At least I don't need to worry about telling him I'm pregnant. He knows what the two lines mean.

Ethan disappears from the window. I know he will come down to stop me from leaving. I quicken my pace, not ready to talk about the possibility of becoming parents in approximately eight months after what I found in his luggage.

Chapter 23

I lose pace quickly, and slow down to catch my breath. I've read somewhere that can happen when you're pregnant, even this early on. A flutter enters my chest at the possibility. Slowly, I'm starting to trust the test, still too scared to believe it. I walk slower. Pushing it too hard could hurt the life growing inside me. I know Ethan might catch up and try to convince me to come back inside. Usually all it takes is a flash of his dark brown eyes. He has a way of making things seem like they're going to work out, even when it feels impossible. It's one of the reasons I love him, but it won't work this time. I used to feel like we would face the impossible together, but he created these problems alone, without caring what it meant for us.

There is usually a row of cabs waiting just around the block, picking up commuters who are tired and carrying more prettily packed shopping bags than they can handle after a day of shopping in the city. I am ready to disappear into the belly of a generic yellow cab at risk of extinction thanks to rideshares, but I'm thankful I don't have to book one and wait for its arrival before Ethan catches up and asks about what will one day become our baby.

I wonder if he would have had an affair if he knew I was pregnant. I admonish myself for thinking about it. What difference did it make? He crossed a line, giving up something we can never get back.

I hear footsteps pounding against the pavement behind me, and I know it's Ethan. I stop at a cab just as he reaches me. I could ignore him and get in, but he's close enough to stop me, and I resign myself to a conversation I don't want to have.

"Aria," he says, and I turn to look at him, my face expressionless. Up this close, it feels like I should be able to tell—is my husband a cheater? Is he something even worse?

Killing someone I love is the ultimate betrayal. What did Isla do to deserve that?

I notice Ethan is barefoot, his hair still wet and uncombed. He's pulled on some jeans and a T-shirt, which sticks to his skin. "If you could just let me explain." He grips the back of his neck, frustration tensing his muscles. "I know I should've called. I wanted to, but I had things I needed to deal with." He pauses, like he's thinking about telling me more, but apparently decides not to. "I really couldn't call." He holds out his hands, his palms up in surrender, and I see that he's not wearing his wedding band, which I had placed back in the nightstand drawer.

He notices me staring and I figure I should ask. It would be strange not to, now that I've noticed it's missing. "Where's your ring?"

"I . . ." Thoughts tick by behind his eyes, which dart left, right, and back to me. I used to believe that expression meant he was considering something. It used to seem sexy and thoughtful, but now he just looks like a liar deciding which lie I'm more likely to believe. I never noticed before.

I'm about to walk away, leaving him to think up a lie I won't hear, but he's already talking.

"I don't know what happened to it," he says. "I thought it would turn up somewhere, so I didn't tell you." It feels like there's a whisper of truth to what he's saying.

"How could you lose it? You never take it off," I say glibly.

He moves toward me, as if he wants to touch me, and I step back, recoiling.

He stops. The distance between us is intentional and non-negotiable. "I woke up one morning and noticed it wasn't on my finger." His tone suggests he should've known, that he might've been able to find it if he'd realized it was gone. Was he with *her* when he noticed?

I imagine him getting ready to see her. Combing his hair and removing his wedding ring before they met up, removing any reminders of me, so that when he ran his hands across her body, there was nothing between them but skin. Maybe he had set the ring down somewhere and forgotten about it. I imagine her finding it. Scooping it up and pocketing it before he noticed. Had she known then that she was going to use it to confront me?

Maybe he didn't bother to take his ring off while they were together and she slipped it off his finger while he slept beside her, like a character in a dark fairytale, freeing the prince of his shackles.

A dozen questions build on my lips, each one unasked. If Ethan was involved in Isla's murder, if that's what she meant when she asked me how well I know Ethan, I might ruin my chance of finding out the truth if I ask the wrong thing now.

I want to hear *her* side first, before I confront Ethan. I have a better chance of reading him than I do her.

Is she going to tell me about their affair? If she wants to harm me, she wouldn't ask to meet in a public place, where anyone could see us together. If my body turns up somewhere, people would know she was the last person seen with me. She would become a suspect.

I almost ask Ethan what really happened to Isla, but he's pulling something from his back pocket and the questions I have disappear.

He holds the pregnancy test toward me, the window showing a blurry set of lines. You're supposed to read the results within the specified timeframe or they can be inaccurate. I consider telling him the test was negative but was sitting in the trash can for too long.

"Why didn't you tell me?" I can see him fighting to keep his tone undemanding, and I steel myself. I don't owe him an explanation, but I give him one anyway.

"If you had answered your phone, I would have." I don't mention that I might've kept it to myself a while longer, even if he answered. I don't owe a liar the truth.

He puts the test back in his pocket, the end sticking out.

I turn, signaling the end of the conversation.

"Talk to me, Aria. You can't avoid it forever. We're having a baby," he says. It's a statement, not a question. "How far along?"

"A positive test doesn't mean there's a baby, just that there are pregnancy hormones."

He looks confused. "Which means you're pregnant, right?"

I shrug, hoping he doesn't see through my bravado. I know the statistics. Anything can happen this early on. On rare occasions, pregnancy hormones can mean things like cancer, which doesn't seem so unlikely after trying for so long and getting nowhere.

"You should rest," he says. "Why don't you come inside and I'll make us peppermint tea or something? I want to discuss a few things."

I'd be lying if I said I wasn't curious, but I can see Ethan spitting out more lies to win back my trust.

"I have nothing to say," I mutter.

"I want to ask you something, and I need you to be honest with me," he says, and I fight a derisive laugh.

"Because you've been so honest with me," I shoot back.

A couple in their early twenties pass by, arms linked like they can't bear to be separated, heads tilted toward each other as they stroll. It reminds me I'm having a very public argument, probably making a scene. If they notice the tension between Ethan and me, they don't acknowledge it.

"Come inside. I can explain everything," he promises, but it's not enough to convince me. If I don't go now, I may never know what Ethan has done.

"I know it doesn't look good, Aria. But it's not what you think, I swear."

He's leading me toward our building, feet padding against the pavement. He holds his hands out to me. Could it hurt to hear him out? I don't owe him anything, but maybe I owe it to myself, and to our unborn child, to get some closure. I move toward him, drawn in by my desire for this nightmare to just go away.

I stop, reminding myself that Isla's gone and Ethan isn't the man I thought he was.

I cradle my still-flat stomach. When I calculate the first day of my last period, I can't be any more than six or seven weeks along. I thought my period would come late.

Ethan drops his hands when I don't take them. "I wasn't sure before, but I think it's time we were honest with each other, especially if we're about to become parents."

I feel an old anxiety threatening to resurface. *He knows about Matt. Maybe he's been waiting to bring it up.*

Could that be why Ethan started seeing someone else? Did he find out what I had done and regret marrying me?

I take a deep breath. This is just anxiety talking. Ethan can't know. No one knows except me and Matt. No one else was there when it happened. I left before someone discovered him, but he was already dead.

"Please, Aria. Just five minutes," he says, and I cave.

"Fine. Five minutes," I say, knowing I'll regret it.

Chapter 24

I walk back to the apartment with Ethan. I need to find out if he knows what a hypocrite I am, judging him for his mistakes when I have made worse ones of my own. He opens the door and holds it while I step inside.

If the emailer wants to speak with me, they will wait.

Ethan offers me a seat at the dining table, and I take it. He sits right next to me, his proximity too close. This space used to feel like somewhere to talk, to toss around ideas and eat dinner with one leg curled around his under the table.

Now, it feels stale and hollow.

Ethan looks at me with a strange expression while I try to guess what he's going to ask.

He's right. If we're going to become parents, we can't avoid talking about things just because they're complicated. Maybe now that it's happening, he wants everything out in the open.

When we become parents, we will need to work together. No secrets. No lies. No ghosts from the past or secret lovers emerging from the woodwork.

It's time to be honest.

"Where were you when Isla was murdered?" he asks cautiously.

I look at him incredulously. He wasn't contactable when my friend was murdered, and he's going to question me about where *I* was?

He waits, an interrogator hoping to catch me in a lie. Is he really asking if I killed one of my best friends?

"Were you still at the bar?" he continues.

I feel a stab of guilt. His question has hit a nerve. We shouldn't have waited so long to go after her. We should've known that underneath the sound of the thrumming music was Isla calling for help.

"Yes, we were at the bar celebrating Cassandra's promotion. Zoe and Isla were on the dance floor living it up while Cassandra and I sat at a table."

"So she was there with her friends, but it feels like the killer got away with it by hiding in plain sight, slipping into the crowd unnoticed." His arms are resting on the table, his wedding finger bare, the remnants of a faint tan line staining his skin where the gold band once sat.

The thought chills me. Maybe that's exactly why no one had noticed the killer in the crowd, a drink in their hand, celebrating their own private victory. Maybe they blended in too well.

I didn't pay much attention. The only person I remember is the woman at the table who had noticed me too, but that was probably nothing more than two people accidentally locking eyes.

"It could've been any of you," he says, and for one horrifying moment, I think he's saying that any of us could be a killer.

The worst part? He would be right.

I consider telling him everything. No more hiding.

What kind of life are we bringing a child into? I've heard the nature versus nurture debate, whether it's genetics or the environment that determines who you are. After what I'd done, I worried it was genetic, that our child would inherit it, but if both parents are killers, what does that mean for a child?

"You and Isla are about the same height. You wouldn't look so different to someone who didn't know you well. Not in a dark bar. It could've been you they killed." The lump in his throat bobs as he swallows.

I think again that the killer might have messed up, that they were looking for me that night.

Just a week before, someone had followed me. I had recently figured out Ethan was having an affair. Next, Isla's murdered. It seems like too many crazy things for such a short time. It can't be a coincidence. What if the killer messed up their hit? If I listen closely, it almost sounds as if Ethan's confessing what happened.

Ethan sits at the table, resting his hands on the surface, clasping them together.

Did Ethan arrange for someone to attack me so he could sail away into the sunset with his girlfriend? Is that why he didn't answer his phone for days on end? There were no consequences for ignoring me, because he knew that in just a few short days I would be dead . . .

His hair has dried into wavy clumps he will have to rewash. He's staring back at me with eyes I've looked into a thousand times, but the overwhelming rush of love I used to feel, thinking how lucky I was to have found someone so amazing, is gone.

He looks hollowed. Empty. A guy going through the motions. Why did he come back?

Does he want to finish the job before he leaves for good? He could've told me it was over and started afresh with her. Letting me live would've been enough punishment, watching him move on while I was stuck trying to get over my feelings for him. Some men can't leave things unfinished. They like to tie their loose ends.

I've heard of guys like that, but Ethan never seemed like one until now. They need to control things. Control people. Especially wives or girlfriends. They're insensitive to other people's needs because their minds are over-occupied with themselves.

Is Ethan about to snap and kill me?

It's usually after the wife dies that people wonder how no one noticed the threat. It's called uxoricide. People like that get good at faking it, or risk being found out and stopped.

What would Ethan gain by killing me? Our lives would unthread easily, leaving almost no mess. We could sell the apartment. We don't have children, so we wouldn't have needed to stay in each other's lives. The more I consider it, the simpler divorce seems. I hate him for not leaving before things got complicated.

I would've gone quietly, rationalizing to myself all the reasons it wouldn't have worked out.

It's what I tried to do with Matt. Not break up exactly—that would've been too confrontational, too damaging. It would have meant making him angry and facing the backlash, so I had tried to slip away slowly so he wouldn't realize what I was doing.

He figured it out anyway, and it was hell. If Ethan and I were over, I wouldn't force him to stay like Matt had forced me. That wasn't a life.

I think of the years Ethan and I have spent together. I know things about Ethan that he wouldn't want anyone to know.

I wonder if *she* knows, and if she loves him anyway.

Did she fall for the same things as me? Ethan can be charming, and being on the receiving end of it made me feel loved—an emotion I hadn't felt since Matt made me feel unlovable.

I focus on Ethan. Is my marriage salvageable? Are Ethan and I worth fighting for?

"Willow came by," I say lightly, hoping for a reaction.

"Oh, did she?" he asks, picking at something on the table.

"She said you sent her. On her day off."

He pretends to think, his face moving in an exaggerated expression. "Oh, yeah," he says, as if it's suddenly occurred to him. "I needed some dry cleaning done. Willow said she didn't mind taking care of it if she didn't get to it through the week. I guess she didn't get to it." He tries to sound offhanded, but it seems strained. Ethan is a smooth liar, but I can hear that he's rattled.

"She let herself in," I press. "She seemed surprised to see me. When did you give her a key to our home?"

He shifts, his weight making the chair squeak.

"I don't know. She's had it for a while, I guess," he says, but I think Willow has been letting herself in whenever she wants, acting like it's her home. She's always been too eager to please Ethan. Is it because she needs her job, or is it something more?

Could Willow be the woman he's seeing? They were close, but I had never noticed sparks between them.

She had access to the house. While I was gone, she could have slipped Ethan's ring inside the drawer and sent an anonymous email to meet up.

What would she do if I called her bluff and showed up? She couldn't hide her identity without giving up the game, and if she really had dirt on Ethan, there's no way she would tell me about it . . . unless she thought it would make me leave.

Wouldn't she tell me while Ethan was at work? She had plenty of opportunities.

I think harder, coming up with a new theory. Has Willow been rude to me because she was afraid of Ethan? She's known him longer than I have. Long enough to know what he's like—maybe she was hoping I'd leave for my own good?

How well do you know your husband?

I need to meet with her and stop guessing. If she's not the woman Ethan's been seeing, perhaps she knows who is.

Ethan and I gather our thoughts in silence, gearing up for combat, aware of the stakes.

I think of all the times I've been at work or out running errands while Willow has been home with Ethan. I can't imagine what she's heard while I was away.

Chapter 25

Ethan slams his hand down on the table, ripping me from my thoughts. He's leaning forward, almost out of his seat, reaching across the table toward me. The action frightens me, and I'm momentarily transported back to the past, Matt's angry face glaring into mine.

I recoil instinctively, ready to run if Ethan stands up. His fist rises, palm opening. I prepare for the sting of his hand against my cheek, but he reveals a squished spider.

Something about the gesture is disturbing. I watch in horror as he wipes the squished mess on his pants. The spider didn't even see it coming. He looks up and smiles, oblivious to my disgust.

His display makes me realize I still don't trust him with the truth about my past.

I'm not getting the answers he promised either. I was expecting him to confess to an affair, giving me the answers I've been looking for and gaining some trust back. That doesn't seem likely, but there's still somewhere else I might get them.

I tell him I need to go out to the store for ginger tea to help with the nausea. He doesn't know I'm feeling much better today and could do without it.

He offers to come with me.

"You probably need to unpack," I say, hoping he takes the bait.

I can't let Ethan know I'm meeting up with his girlfriend without him trying to stop me, so I meander to the door, acting as if I have all the time in the world. I turn before I leave, asking if he wants anything brought back.

He tries one last time to convince me to stay, offering to go instead of me. Has he realized I'm lying, that ginger tea is just a cover-up?

What if it's all just a setup, and Ethan received an email too, saying he doesn't know his wife as well as he thinks he does?

A nervous flutter fills my stomach. Has Ethan been chasing answers of his own, finding out the (mostly) white lies that wouldn't make a difference if he knew or not? I don't always put out the trash when I say I'm going to, and I spend way more time texting Cassandra than I let on.

Has he discovered the lies that haunt me in my sleep—lies that would rival his own?

Maybe that's why I'm taking his dishonesty so hard—no one calls out a lie better than a liar.

What if it's not Willow and I'm walking into another disaster? I consider not showing up.

I already know the emailer let themselves into my home while I wasn't there. I shudder. The thought of someone in the apartment while I was gone is creepy. What's stopping them from coming in while I'm sleeping, taking a pillow from the bed and pressing it tight against my face?

What did they learn about me, creeping around in the empty apartment?

Do they know about the baby? No one knows I'm pregnant except for Ethan. I feel my abdomen despite knowing that it's too early to be showing. Would knowing we're having a baby stop them from breaking up a family?

There are so many questions. The need to find out what they know about Ethan is overwhelming. I have to know if he's the person I thought I was marrying, for the sake of our baby.

If I'm being completely honest, I'm curious about her too. Who is she? What does she look like? How did she meet Ethan?

The need to know makes my decision for me, and I blow Ethan a kiss and slip outside.

"Are you coming back?" he asks, as if he knows I might not return. He could be right, but not just because I'm mad at him.

I play the pregnancy card, reassuring him I'm feeling off from the hormones circulating through my body. The door closes behind me before he can start a new round of reasons I should stay. I'm running out of time to get to the coffee house before she thinks I've stood her up and leaves.

I take a cab, thinking about what to say when I arrive, vaguely aware of the driver navigating the traffic, tapping along on the steering wheel to a playlist, over-applied cologne staining the air.

I try to prepare myself, knowing that tonight I might find out my husband wants me dead.

Chapter 26

The driver pulls in a few doors down from the coffee shop, and I'm glad for the short walk to center myself. It's not too late to turn back, but I put one foot in front of the other, clutching my purse like my life depends on it.

The glass front of the trendy cafe is spotless, and I can see inside as I approach.

I can't see Willow, but she's probably seated at the back. Unlike many of the tiny cafes around, which barely have room for a few people standing inside at a time, this one encourages customers to sit in with its warm decor and scattered sofas.

The doorbell chirps as I enter, and I loosen my grip on my purse so I don't seem as nervous as I am. I scan the booths, but as I move through the cafe, I wonder if she changed her mind after all. A group of college students are strewn across a sofa. I pass their scattered array of mugs and iced drinks, trying not to bump into them, scanning their faces for Willow.

I'm about to leave when I feel eyes on me, coming from the left side of the room. She's sitting at a small table, studying me. Definitely not Willow.

Her eyes are curious but carefully guarded. With her dark lips, chocolate hair, and runner's body, she is beautiful. She looks like she might be strong enough to murder someone, her ropy muscled arms holding them in her grasp while she squeezes the life out of them. She seems vaguely familiar, but I can't place where I've seen her. Was she the woman I saw at the bar when Isla died, or am I imagining things?

After a moment's hesitation, I walk across the room. There's no going back from here. Once I know who she is and what she has to say, I can't unknow. I reach the table, unsure what to do next.

She acknowledges me with a silent glance and I wonder if I've gotten it wrong. Her eyebrows raise, waiting for me to explain why I've walked up to a complete stranger and stopped. I'm about to apologize, suddenly feeling foolish.

"Aria?"

The sound of my name surprises me, sounding so different on her lips.

It's her.

"Have a seat." She gestures to the other side of the table, clutching a smoothie in a heavily sleeved hand, pink nail polish peeling at her fingertips. She asks if I want to order, but I decline, not wanting to delay finding out how my life's about to change.

It takes everything inside of me to speak. "You know my name. It only seems fair that you tell me yours," I say.

She smiles as if I'm a cute kitten trying to escape from a cardboard box. "Monique," she says, and I can't tell whether it's real or something she's made up.

I try to remember Ethan mentioning a Monique. An ex-girlfriend or a friend from college maybe, but the name isn't familiar. I resist the urge to ask questions, hoping she'll talk first.

"Nice to meet you, Monique," I say automatically. It's obviously not nice to meet her, but I don't want to piss her off.

"You too," she says, her gaze making me uncomfortable, like she's figuring out what kind of person I am, or how big a hole she'll need to dig to dump my body in.

"Do you know why you're here?" she asks, bright blue eyes peering through her bangs like a tiger watching its prey.

I don't want to steer things in the wrong direction, so I shake my head.

I silently will her to tell me, to put me out of my misery, but she doesn't seem to be in a hurry.

"I didn't think you'd come," she says with a hint of respect. "You're brave. A lot of women wouldn't want to know the truth about their husbands because deep down, they already *know*. But you—you obviously aren't so sure, or you wouldn't need me to confirm it."

She observes me with razor-sharp accuracy, digging at my fear that Ethan has gotten himself into something I couldn't have predicted. I wonder if this woman truly knows things about him I've yet to discover.

I think of the blood on his suit. The crumpled receipt in his pocket. Neither of those things seemed very Ethan-like, and maybe she knows why.

"I couldn't say what I really wanted to say. Not in an email," she tells me, sipping her smoothie, lips pouting like a model as she drinks.

If she couldn't say it in an email, why is she happy to say it in a busy cafe, where anyone might overhear our conversation?

Maryann Webb

As if reading my mind, she looks around the room. Everyone is busy socializing in their own circles, oblivious to the multitude of conversations around them. If I tried to record our conversation, the noise in the cafe would distort it. She leans her elbows on the tiny table, and I instinctively lean toward her.

"I know what happened to your friend," she whispers.

162

Chapter 27

The mention of Isla knocks the air from my lungs. I force myself to recover fast. I don't want this woman to see my vulnerability.

This isn't just about Ethan, but she inadvertently tied the two together, which makes me shift nervously in my seat. I try to stay calm, wishing I'd ordered that drink to wash away the dry feeling clogging my throat. An idea comes to me—a way to find out if she's telling the truth.

First, I acknowledge her claim with a bored nod. "Have you spoken to the police?" I ask. If she really knows, wouldn't that be the obvious thing to do?

She shakes her head. "I'm not even sure I heard what I think I heard. It might've been her footsteps, but I don't think so. I thought you might want to know, since it affects you."

I think of Isla dragging Zoe to the dance floor, the two of them giggling.

I have to do this.

"Why do you care? You don't even know me." If she didn't want the police to know, why would she risk me telling them?

"I wasn't planning to say anything. Then I saw how upset you were when you realized your friend was . . ." She clears her throat and starts over. "When your friend died."

"What happened to her? Did you see the killer?" I ask.

She keeps her voice low, leaning forward, sipping her smoothie as if we're two friends engaged in an especially juicy gossip session. "I was in the bathroom when your friend came in."

Her voice is low, meant for just the two of us, but when I look around, no one is listening. They are engrossed in their own conversations.

A part of me waits for her to confess to killing Isla by mistake, thinking she was me. Monique looks at me, her face softening as if she feels bad. I start to believe she's sorry about what happened to Isla.

She inhales, her shoulders lifting, gripping her smoothie with the tips of her fingers so that it looks like the glass might shatter in her hand. I reassess her expression, realizing she's not sympathetic at all. She *is* sorry. Sorry she's about to make things a whole lot worse.

Her words from that very first email come back to haunt me. I suspect they are the reason we're here. *How well do you know your husband?*

I imagine her telling me she saw Ethan enter the bathroom just after Isla. Perhaps Isla and Ethan were continuing the argument they had when Ethan visited her apartment. Maybe she can tell me what they were arguing about.

"What happened to her?" I ask, my voice breaking. It's not fair that Isla's dead when she should be here, planning our next get-together and sharing news about her latest boyfriend. I would happily listen to her complain about toes that are too crooked or laughter that's so loud it sounds fake.

Monique sets her empty glass down, and I promise myself I can handle what I'm about to hear. I owe it to Isla to share her last moments, no matter how difficult it's going to be.

"There was someone in the bathroom with us. I locked myself in and sat on the lid with my legs folded underneath me. They wouldn't have known I was there. There was a loud bang and a grunt. It sounded like someone was moving something, but by the time I unlocked the door, they were gone and your friend was lying there."

"Why didn't you tell the police?" I ask, hoping I sound as if I would understand being too afraid to speak out when I'm really thinking it seems like she's protecting herself.

"What would I tell them? That I might've heard someone in the bathroom when your friend was murdered? They already know someone was there. What if they thought I killed her?"

Did you? The question remains unasked. If she killed Isla, why would she tell me?

Monique flicks her hair from her eyes. I can tell she's used to getting what she wants. Her long legs stretch out beneath her, and her foot grazes mine underneath the table. She smiles as if it's funny, as if we're destined to share secrets. If she was involved in Isla's murder, she will tell me in her own time.

I widen my eyes and lean forward. "You must've been so scared, being stuck in there with a killer. I can't imagine what it was like to hear that," I say, just like I would have if I believed she was telling the truth. I reach out as if I wish she were sitting closer so I could give her hand an encouraging squeeze, hoping she doesn't see what I'm really thinking. How could she witness a murder and stay so quiet that the killer didn't notice her?

She's either even-tempered or a smooth liar.

Monique looks away. "It was awful. I wouldn't wish it upon my worst enemy," she says, her face a mask.

I force a sympathetic smile, wondering if it's possible to see something like that and stay calm. Why hadn't she intervened? I know I couldn't sit there and wait. I'd have to stop the killer . . . and probably get my stupid ass killed while I'm at it.

Monique's face relaxes back into a slight smile—her resting face. I can't tell if it's genuine or practiced, but I can't help thinking of the creepy emails she sent me, how she let herself into my home, returning Ethan's wedding ring. Did she think it was normal to act like that?

In some twisted way, did she think she was doing me a favor?

"Couldn't you try to stop them from hurting Isla?" I ask, brow furrowed like a concerned friend making sure that Monique's not hiding something so awful it stopped her from trying. Was she just protecting herself, or had the killer threatened her?

Monique's hands go limp. "Was that her name? She didn't look like an Isla." She smiles. It's a strange response, but who's to say how you're supposed to react after witnessing a murder?

"I'm not sure I could've done anything. I didn't realize she was dead. There were a few thuds, but it just as easily could've been a quick hookup. That's what I thought it was at first." She fidgets with her glass, shifting it from one place to another, keeping her hands busy.

"There were hushed voices. I felt embarrassed. It felt like I was spying on them or something, even though I wasn't. It got past the point where I could leave without it being weird."

There was more, I'm sure of it. Something had kept her inside the cubicle even before she realized something was wrong

"I heard the door open and close, and I thought they'd left. When I came out, I saw your friend. She was already dead, and I knew someone would find her. I didn't want to get involved."

I believe Monique waited in the bathroom. I'm just not sure I believe Isla was already dead when she came out of the stall. What if Isla saw something that got her killed? If the killer had murdered someone, wouldn't it make sense that they would check for any loose ends?

"Why didn't anyone else say what they'd seen? It's a busy bathroom," I blurt out.

"I heard him lock the door behind him," says Monique. "After he closed up each of the stalls."

There was a gap under each stall. It wasn't an easy fit, but someone could slide under if they weren't afraid of getting a little dirty. "He? So it was a man?"

She shrugs. "I guess. I mean, I didn't see, but their shoes went by and it looked like they were wearing black kicks."

I look away. It sounds like Monique saw more than she was first willing to admit. What else is she hiding?

"I should've gone to the police. I think I convinced myself that they would figure it out. For a while I told myself that maybe she overdosed, that the bang I heard was your friend—Isla—stumbling around, trying to find her way to the door before she . . ."

167

I'm grateful when she doesn't finish her sentence. Each time I hear Isla referred to in the past tense, or as being gone, it's jarring.

My dry throat sticks as I try to swallow.

So far, she hasn't mentioned the email she sent asking how well I know my husband. How does Ethan fit into all of this? I thought I was coming here to find out, and now she's telling me she saw Isla die. She seems to know a lot about me. Who my husband is, my friends.

She has to be the woman Ethan's seeing. Who else would take such an interest in our lives?

"I'm going to ask you again. If you want me to believe anything you say, you'll tell me the truth," I say, adopting the tone I use at work when I'm coaxing a patient into a procedure they're not comfortable with. "How do you know my husband? And how did you know Isla was my friend? She was on the dance floor for most of the night. She wasn't sitting with us. So you knew who she was before you saw her in the bathroom."

I can see I've rattled her. She fidgets with her hair, tucking it behind her ear. She eyes the door, making me nervous she might up and leave without answering.

"I've been watching you," she says, lifting her shoulders in an apologetic shrug before correcting herself. "Actually, I've been watching your husband. He's gone to a lot of trouble for you, and I wanted to see why." There's a bitterness in her expression. As if she doesn't think I deserve the "trouble" Ethan has gone to for me.

She pauses, building the anticipation, making me suffer before she crashes into my world. The ascent is like a giant wave looming over my head, ready to trap me beneath the surface.

I've never been a strong swimmer.

My breath stays locked inside my chest. I'm so nervous I forget to exhale.

And then she says it, the hushed tone too small for the implications. "I think your husband killed your friend."

I feel like I might be sick.

"Why would my husband kill Isla?" I ask. Accusing someone of murder isn't something you do unless you're pretty sure.

She leans back, her smile gone as she again pushes her hair behind her ear in a practiced gesture, working her way up to something even more uncomfortable. "Your friend lived in my building. I've seen your husband there a few times. I've watched things get more heated each time he visits."

So that's how she knows Ethan. She saw him talking to Isla. Maybe they're not having an affair. Maybe she got involved in this against her will.

She must notice my surprise because she leans back, tucking her legs in, and says, "She discovered a secret. He was trying to convince her not to tell you, but it sounded like she refused. I saw him at her door. I couldn't hear what they were saying, but it looked as if he was about to hit her. He changed his mind at the last second."

I look at the woman sitting in front of me and wonder how much time she spends spying on her neighbors and meddling in their business. If she were a guy, she would be coming off as a creep right now. But I can't help it—I want to know what else she saw. I want to know badly enough to ignore my instincts.

Maryann Webb

Is she a fantasist who believes that everyone around her has secrets only she can uncover? Does she create scenarios and attempt to solve them for entertainment?

Except not everything she's saying is false. Isla is dead. She didn't imagine that. Who else did she tell? I think of the article I read about Isla, the information about a man being seen arguing with her, and now Monique is saying the same thing.

Maybe she has some sick vendetta against Ethan, and she's setting him up to look responsible for Isla's murder. Is it about revenge for choosing to end their fling?

My hackles shoot up, my limbic system on high alert. I can't reconcile how she ended up with Ethan's wedding ring if she's just Isla's neighbor. So much of what she's saying almost makes sense, but not quite.

I ask her outright, as if I can surprise her into answering, but she doesn't bat an eye. "How did you get Ethan's wedding ring?"

I fidget with my wedding band, the tip of my thumb twisting it around my finger. She watches, a stale smile spreading across her face, never reaching her eyes.

"I found it outside Isla's apartment. I tried to return it, but he was already inside. They were arguing, and I didn't want to get in the middle of it, so I didn't knock."

Her nonchalance rattles me. How can she go from being worried about disturbing an argument to being fine with breaking and entering?

Two of the college students leave the sofa, calling back to their friends as they leave. I wait until they're gone before resuming our conversation. "What were they arguing about?"

Her smile disappears, as if my question is unexpected. I need to convince her to tell me what she heard, even if it rips my world out from under me.

She's enjoying my ignorance, leaving me in the dark while she dangles the truth in front of me. Maybe other people's lives are a game to her. If she hid Ethan's wedding ring in the nightstand drawer, what's stopping her from slipping Isla's necklace among Ethan's luggage?

Who is Monique, and what does she want from me?

"They were arguing about you. He didn't hit her or anything. He's not the type to get his hands dirty."

Her words irritate me. What would she know about the type of person Ethan is? Is she trying to tell me they're involved? Or was it nothing more than a poor choice of words?

She's talking again, her tone authoritative. "You think you know your husband? You think he loves you, but how do you ever know? Does he want the same things you want? I had a husband once, and I believed the same things about our marriage as you do about yours. I thought he loved me, that he'd never hurt me." A hitching laugh spills, as if she regrets her naivety. "I was wrong." There's a sudden edge to her voice, a hardness, as though she's steeling herself against what she believes she lost.

Is that what this meeting is about? Is Monique upset because Ethan and I seemed happy? Did she want the happiness we shared? Was she testing what it would take to come between us, reminding herself it could happen to anyone?

She looks directly at me, emotion seeping into her tone, cracking her voice. Whatever happened had hurt her deeply enough that she'd involved herself in a stranger's life, convinced Ethan murdered Isla simply because they'd argued.

"I'm sorry you went through that," I say, meaning it. It was obviously hard on her, and I suspect she's not over it.

"You don't understand," she says. "I'm trying to save you from the same mistakes I made."

Listening to the way she said it, I could almost believe she cares what happens to me.

"What do you mean?" I pretend not to notice her loud repositioning as she sits up and flops back down, the chair moving beneath her. She looks around the room to make sure her discomfort hasn't drawn too much attention, but the din of twenty different conversations drowns out the scratching of the chair legs against the floor.

I can sense her hesitation, as if it's tough to talk about it. Maybe too tough to tell a stranger. I can't imagine anyone disappointing her. She is the kind of woman people want to be seen with—who men want to wear on their arm as proof they are desirable.

At least one man didn't see it that way from what she says next. "The worst thing. I thought I had one kind of life. I gave up a lot. I did things you only do for people you love before I realized he didn't love me, that he was using me."

The way she says it makes me wonder what she's done and whether she's justifying it.

Like killing Isla?

"He fell in love with someone else. I didn't realize what was happening," she says weakly.

Her words hit, each one landing an invisible blow, speaking my deepest fears out loud. I've been obsessing about whether Ethan is having an affair, trying to prove myself wrong instead of facing that I could be right. I'd prefer to follow him to Los Angeles than ask him outright what's going on, unsure what comes next. I'm scared he loves her, that he'll choose her, just like Monique's husband did.

Most of all, I'm ashamed of my inability to act badass about this. I'm supposed to be mad, unflinching in my resolve to find out as quickly as possible and move on, but as confronting as it is to admit to myself, I'm not sure I'm ready to lose him just yet.

I wonder if Monique would understand. She's looking down at her hands. Is she feeling the same shame I feel? It's clear she isn't talking about the little things you don't mind overlooking when you love someone, like compromising where you live, or ignoring their annoying habits, but things that make you question who you are. That turn you into someone you would never want to be.

"You're doing the same thing," she continues. "The person you think you're married to isn't who he says he is. Your life is one big lie. And it got your friend killed."

Is she blaming me for Isla's murder? Anger ripples through me like a current. "Listen, I don't know what you think you're playing at, but stay away from me and my husband. If this is some revenge rant because your husband left you, don't take it out on my family. If you come near us—or our home—again, I'll get a restraining order, I swear."

I stand to leave, unconsciously placing a hand across my abdomen as I do. It's too late to take back my words. My hand drops from my stomach.

Monique looks at me with renewed interest. "You're having a baby? Is that why you don't want to let Ethan go?"

"No," I say, but it's too fast. All I have is a test with two lines. It's not concrete.

Without speaking, I gather my things and leave before Monique can drop any more bombshells. I've heard enough. Although I'm angry with Ethan, going home is better than sitting here listening to a stranger tell me my husband could be a killer.

I take a rideshare home, replaying my conversation with Monique. By the time I arrive home, I'm convinced she knows Ethan. The way she said his name suggests she's said it a hundred times before.

When I reach our front door, I hesitate, imagining his response, picturing all the lies he could tell when I ask about her.

I've avoided Ethan long enough. I need to face this. If he tries to kill me, at least I'll know the truth.

Chapter 28

Ethan is pacing when I get home. His hair has dried into an uncombed wave, his feet are still bare. He looks like an alternate version of himself, disheveled and anxious, as if he's been waiting for me to return. Was he figuring out how to continue our talk? Or was he thinking about *her*, planning the next time they would see each other, carefully making sure I wouldn't find out about it?

He takes my purse and hangs it before leading me to the sofa, but I shrug his hand away.

"I was worried. I tried messaging you," he says.

I look at my phone. There are seven messages. Usually I would have responded, but not today. Not after waiting days for a response from him.

He hesitates, unsure where this conversation might go. Maybe he's deciding whether he should walk away before things head in a direction he can't change. I steer the conversation before he can hijack it.

"Who is Monique?" I ask, hoping she didn't give me a fake name. "And why haven't you mentioned her?"

Had he met her during one of his visits to Isla?

Maybe he doesn't know her, and she's just some woman who's obsessed with him. A past employee, perhaps, or a competitor from a rival company.

As much as I want to believe that, I'm not fooling myself. The way she said his name was too familiar, but I guess it's a common name. Maybe she knows another Ethan.

His jaw tenses at her name. Recognition flashes across his face. It's so quick I almost miss it.

"What are you talking about?" He studies my face before breaking into a grin. "Is this why you've been acting so strange? Because you've convinced yourself that I've been hiding some woman from you?" He snorts, as if it sounds even sillier out loud.

Usually, I would question myself about now, but his arrogance and disdain so soon after I lost one of my best friends makes him seem like an asshole.

"I found the receipt in your pocket, Ethan." I pause, hoping he'll explain without me needing to dredge the truth out of him. "From Matrix."

He opens his mouth and closes it like a fish. I watch him squirm, feeling petty satisfaction. He's not speechless often. There's no way he can talk his way out of this, but it doesn't stop him from trying.

"Why were you going through my things?" he asks, insinuating I'm the one with something to answer for. He's trying to turn the conversation, but I'm mad enough not to let him.

If he didn't give me a reason to, I would never have gone through his things.

I cringe, my logic that of someone using control tactics, before realizing I'm too fed up to care. This is about trying to discern the truth when I have a liar for a husband. It has nothing to do with control.

I expected him to deflect my words and have an answer prepared. "You never leave suits in the closet without plastic wrap. I figured you'd want it dry cleaned, so I was emptying the pockets before I dropped it off."

He sits on the sofa, his body perched tensely on the edge of the cushion. I can see how badly he wants to ask if I read it, but he can't ask without admitting there's something there worth reading. Ethan will play a long game. Does he know about the blood on the inner seam? Is he waiting for me to mention it? He can't fault me for helping out, but he finds a way.

"You shouldn't worry yourself about the laundry. I pay Willow to take care of it so you don't have to." He somehow makes me seem ungrateful and meddling. "You especially shouldn't worry about it in your condition." His eyes move to my belly and I realize he's talking about the baby.

I had forgotten about it for a moment, and his mentioning it throws me. I know he's concerned, but it bothers me. Is he going to oversee everything I do for the next eight months, deciding what is acceptable and what isn't?

Considering the things he's done, the lies he's still keeping from me, I wonder if he's the real threat. To me. To our child. Am I safe here with my husband? A few weeks ago, I would have been blissfully unaware of what he was capable of. I would've felt safe sleeping beside him, my head resting in the crook of his shoulder. I picture lying against him now, his arm snaking around me until it's choking the air from my lungs like a boa constrictor. When I'm limp and lifeless, I imagine him finally letting go, having tied up his biggest loose end to be with *her*, without an ex-wife complicating things.

"Are you sleeping with her?" I ask, a bitter taste in the back of my throat, warning me I might need to empty my stomach soon.

"Who?"

"I don't know. Monique? Isla? Is there someone else I should know about?" I let their names settle between us before I go on. "People saw you arguing with Isla. What were you arguing about?"

His jaw squares up, ready to take me on. "First," he says, annoyed at needing to explain himself, "I'm not sleeping with anyone, including Isla."

I take a throw pillow, tucking it against me, shielding myself from his words. He pauses, and I know he's figuring out what he should tell me.

I keep my eyes locked on his, letting him know he's not off the hook. Not even close.

"But Isla and I *were* arguing. I shouldn't have gone there, but I had to."

I can't think why he would even visit Isla, let alone why he would *have* to.

"We were arguing about you," says Ethan.

It's not the revelation I was expecting, but it's consistent with Monique's account. I expected him to deny visiting Isla, like he denied an affair. A heavy guilt grips me. They were arguing about *me*, and it could land Ethan in trouble when the police realize he fought with Isla days before she died.

A shudder runs through me. A few days isn't long before being murdered. Who else was mad at her in that time? If my husband was a killer, wouldn't the police have figured it out by now?

Chapter 29

I want to pretend it doesn't matter and continue on with an uncomplicated life. But I know I won't be able to. I need to know the truth.

Were Ethan and Isla really arguing about me? Why?

"Isla wanted to throw a surprise party for your thirtieth. She had already started organizing it, and I asked her not to. She wasn't the most thoughtful person, and you were stressed out about wanting a baby. I didn't want to remind you that you were turning thirty on top of everything else," says Ethan, resting an elbow against his knee.

I can see why Ethan would think a party might be too much, but I smile because Isla had wanted to celebrate my birthday. Why would Ethan think I wouldn't want to share my birthday with my friends?

Okay, I was dreading my thirtieth. I had joked about it since my twenty-eighth, and I guess Ethan took it literally. Something about entering a new decade made me feel like I'd aged ten whole years at once, and Isla likely knew turning it into a celebration would stop me fixating on it. It might've made me forget about my failed baby plans, at least for a while, but now that Isla's gone and I have a potential life growing inside of me, thirty feels more confusing than ever.

"She wanted to have a cougar-training party and get everyone to dress up in their best cougar clothes," says Ethan, scrunching his nose in distaste.

A smile tugs harder at my mouth. That sounds like Isla. Taking a stressful milestone and turning into something better, something we could laugh at. Remembering what I loved about her makes her absence real, and it grips me like a hand around my throat.

Ethan's voice cuts through my memory. "It would've been a glorified sex party with Isla organizing it. It was just an excuse to line up the next round of throwaways." Ethan has never liked Isla much, but I won't tolerate his rudeness, especially when she was trying to do something nice.

I shoot him a warning look. The way Isla lived her life is none of his business. She was single and having fun. At least she had the decency not to string her "throwaways" along like he was doing to his fling. At least Isla was honest, not hiding away like some dirty little secret.

"So who was the lingerie for?" I ask, so angry at what he said about Isla that the words shoot right out of my mouth.

He pretends he doesn't know what I'm talking about. His dumb expression makes me even madder. Is he really going to play it like this?

"Monique seemed to know you pretty well. She had your wedding ring," I say. "How do you think she got that if you don't know her?"

"What do you mean she had my ring?"

"She came into our home and left it here, in the drawer beside our bed. She was in our apartment while we weren't home, but there was no sign of a break-in, so I guess she got in another way."

I let the implication hang in the air. Someone either let her in or she already knew how to get inside. I know I closed the outside windows and pulled in the furniture from our balcony before locking up to go to LA. I double checked, thinking I could be gone for a couple of days. I would usually ask the neighbors to monitor things, but I didn't want to answer their questions about where I was going and why Ethan wasn't with me. Questions like that could lead to awkward conversations.

When Ethan doesn't explain how Monique not only got hold of his wedding ring but knew where to return it, I press harder. "You never take your ring off," I remind him. "Did she take it from you?"

He winces, placing a hand across his eyes as if trying to manage a headache. When he opens them, something has changed. He looks caught out.

Chapter 30

I can't look at him as he confirms I've been right all along.

"I'm sorry," he says. "I had an affair, but it's over. I swear." He sits back against the sofa. I mustn't look convinced, and he apologizes again.

I think back, trying to remember the last time I noticed a ring on his finger, but I'm not sure. When we snuggled together at night, I hadn't noticed it was missing. I had felt safe lying together, not realizing it was a trap, a lure. A pretty illusion designed to keep me from the truth.

If his ring had been missing for more than a few weeks, I'm pretty sure I would've noticed.

Why would he insinuate I was jealous and paranoid when he knew I was right? He could've confessed, tried to fix things. If I hadn't caught him out, if Monique hadn't made me question how well I knew my husband, I might never have found out. How long would he have kept it to himself?

It's true what they say. The truth hurts. He reaches out and I recoil, keeping the distance he has created between us.

"Aria, I'm so sorry. I was stupid," he says.

"Why?" I ask.

He shakes his head, still deciding what to say. Eventually he talks. "We were having problems."

He should have thought harder, and it comes across as a lame justification, but he's not finished.

"Everything we did revolved around becoming parents. You forgot about us. What we ate. Which exercise we did. How many hours we slept." He scuffs a toe on the rug, straightening the corner he's folded over in his agitation. "When we had sex. I missed those times when you'd fall into my arms because you wanted to be close to me."

I want to tell him it's not fair to blame me for his feelings, that he chose someone else instead of coming to me, but then I think maybe he was trying to slow things down before he finally said it.

Would he resent our baby for coming into the world when he had finally admitted he might not want to be a father?

"You should've told me you changed your mind, that you weren't sure you wanted to be a dad. I deserved to know," I say with a fierceness I don't expect.

He looks wounded, but it's not enough to make me apologize. If he felt there was a problem between us, he should've come to me and sorted it out instead of having an affair.

"Aria, I wanted kids. I just wanted an 'us' too."

He asks if I can forgive him. I think about it, but I'm not sure I can, so I don't answer. Instead, I ask him to give me time to think it through. I'm not sure there will be an "us" left to fix.

He finally agrees. "You shouldn't be alone. You're upset and you're dealing with pregnancy hormones."

I shoot him a look of pure loathing. "It's nothing compared to what you did. I think I can handle it," I say.

He takes the sting of my words, biting his lip. "Call Cassandra," he says. "You shouldn't be alone right now."

He clearly wants to say more. I wait as he agonizes over it.

"If Monique calls or tries to contact you, promise me you won't answer. She's unstable and angry. I don't trust what she'll do."

That's rich, given that he introduced her into our lives. I would've happily ignored her if she hadn't barged in on my life, but there's no point mentioning that now.

"Please, Aria. I'm not playing around. If Monique tries talking, I want you to ignore her. Don't tell her about the baby," he adds, and I'm glad the baby can't hear us.

Is he trying to protect me and our baby, or is his agenda more self-serving? Maybe he's worried Monique will be mad enough to tell me more of his secrets when she finds out.

It makes me wonder if their fling has ended, like he says. Maybe he intended to end it and couldn't. Maybe she convinced him they didn't need to.

The questions are circling like vultures, swooping in to feast on my corpse. Why else would Ethan hide this from her, especially when it gives him the perfect reason to stop seeing her?

Even backed into a corner, he's still trying to call the shots. "Are you worried she'll tell me what else you've been doing behind my back?" I know it's childish, but the words are cathartic, and I feel a little better.

His posture hardens, as if he's protecting himself against my comments, but he isn't swayed. "Swear it. You won't tell her," he says.

I nod, humbled by the urgency in his tone.

Ethan disappears and I hear his footsteps inside our ensuite as he rustles inside the bathroom cabinet. Bottles clink together as he gathers his toothbrush and toothpaste, throwing them into a bag.

Next he moves to the closet, moving aside hangers to get to the items he wants. Of course he would pack his suits. I laugh at how ridiculous it seems, given our marriage is crumbling.

He returns to say goodbye once he's done, but I'm too upset to respond. His eyes are sad as he says, "Listen, you have every reason to be mad, but I meant what I said about Monique. If she contacts you, let me know right away, but don't respond."

I toss the throw pillow aside and stand. "If she's such a threat, why did you let her into our lives?" I ask, reminding myself that none of this is my fault. I deserve answers. He brought her into our lives, and now he's asking me to pretend she's not there?

"I didn't know . . . I wouldn't have—" His explanation splutters to an end like a stalled engine. He starts up again, one hand swooping to gather his bag, two plastic-wrapped suits draped over his arm. "I love you." His voice breaks a little. I believe he means it as much as he's capable of meaning anything, but I can't let him get to me.

We've never fought without talking it through afterward, but words won't fix this. For the first time since I can remember, I don't say it back.

I watch him leave, his feet dragging. I pretend to myself that I don't care—a clear sign I care a lot.

"Call me when you're ready to talk," he says, closing the door behind him.

I'm not sure I'll ever be ready, but I keep it to myself as I listen to him walk away before finally falling into a restless sleep.

Chapter 31

I wake up the next morning with a stiff back feeling unrested as the night before comes creeping back. I take a seat in the kitchen, my body numb with shock. Ethan is really gone and I slept all night with the door unlocked. I struggle to find the motivation to lock it, but the fact that the door was open all night is like an alarm bell going off. Anyone could walk in.

What if he's right about Monique? If she comes back, I don't want her to let herself inside. I go to the door and test the lock. The handle is rigid beneath my fingers.

Ethan was serious.

Even if he's trying to stop me from talking to Monique to protect himself, she has been inside my home before. It doesn't matter whether he invited her to our home; she knows where I live and there's nothing stopping her from coming back.

A sickening thought strikes like a punch to the stomach. What if I've pushed him right into her arms by telling him to leave?

He's probably feeling vulnerable. Rejected. I imagine her laughing at me for being so stupid, offering the comfort I refused to provide.

I blink back tears—how quickly our perfect life has disintegrated, becoming something I don't recognize. I stay lost in my own head for hours moping around the house feeling sorry for myself until an email pings in my inbox. The sound breaks my reverie and I reach for my phone. I don't get a lot of mail sent to my personal email besides the occasional bill, and the spam that used to arrive semi-regularly is now (mostly) filtered and trashed.

There is a new message from Monique with an image attached. It can't be a coincidence that she's emailing now, right after Ethan left.

I should delete it. Whatever's inside can't be good, but I can't bring myself to trash it. Instead, I hit open and find a shot of Monique and Ethan with their faces so close together they're almost kissing. The intimacy of the photo leaves no room for questions. I look for a date to see when it was taken, but the metadata is blank.

Maybe I can figure it out by what I can see. I study the picture, taking in the freshly painted white walls behind them. They are unremarkable and don't tell me anything. To the right is a sofa and what looks like an ottoman. Both items of furniture are crisp and new, with nothing to suggest anything about the owners. No books. No throw pillows.

Did Monique just snap this picture? Could Ethan be okay enough just hours after our argument to smile and act this happy? I don't see how he could pull it off so convincingly. Did he want us to make up and get over our argument, or had I given him an easy out so he could be with her?

Why had he told me it was over between them when this photograph suggests it's very much still a thing? If he was acting, I had fallen for it. He played his part well. But I'm jittery and heartbroken, and it's only now I consider she may have taken the photo *before*, perhaps during one of the visits he had hidden from me.

I force myself to look at Ethan's tousled hair, his clothes. The image doesn't clearly show what he's wearing, but it doesn't matter. I'm too upset to remember what he was wearing when he left. I look at Monique instead, her body language suggesting she's at ease with Ethan, an arm draped around his neck as if he belongs to her.

I angle the photo, wondering if I'm imagining her self-satisfied smirk.

Chapter 32

In the photograph, Ethan doesn't seem aware of the camera like Monique is. Did she take the photo before he realized what she was doing? Did she hide it from him so she could torture me with it without him knowing?

I zero in on his face. He's half-smiling, but it looks strained, the muscles gathered tight around the edges of his mouth. There's a good chance this picture was just taken. His hair gives it away, the waves unruly like when he finished showering.

There's a message in the body of the email this time.

What's yours is mine.

I don't have time to process the message before my phone vibrates with an incoming call.

It's Cassandra. I answer without hesitation.

"Hey, Aria. Are you okay?"

Her timing is impeccable. "Uh, yeah. Sure," I lie. "Why do you ask?"

"I was expecting to see you tonight. You have a shift."

Shit. I had got the day wrong. I thought my next shift was in a couple of days. My argument with Ethan has thrown me, and I've neglected everything else, trying to figure out what happens now.

"Oh, my God! Cassandra, I'm so sorry. I thought . . . never mind."

"If you need more time, I can ask one of the casual staff to fill in. Don't worry about it."

It could be good to get my mind off Ethan and Monique. If Ethan and I are over, I'm going to need as many shifts as I can manage to pay the bills. "No. It's fine. I can be there in forty-five minutes." I start racing around the house, grabbing my work clothes as I go. "I'm on my way."

"Only if you're sure?"

I feel awful for leaving her short-staffed. "Absolutely," I say, holding my phone under my chin as I pull on my uniform.

"Okay, well, I can cover until you get here."

"You're the best," I say, ending the call. The picture of Ethan and Monique glares at me from my phone. It's painful to look at. The way she's staring at him stays with me, even after I close the image. They look great together.

For a moment, I wish Monique didn't exist.

If I never saw her again, it would be too soon.

Chapter 33

By the time I arrive, the hospital is buzzing. I check in at the nurse's station and do handover with Cassandra, who has already taken over from the nurse working the shift before me.

I apologize again, but a look of frustration washes over Cassandra's face before disappearing. How patient can she be with me before she snaps? I won't push my luck to find out.

She runs me through tonight's list so far. I have four patients to attend to. There's a man who had a car accident. Luckily, he was thrown in the right direction as his car hit a tree, and wound up with a minor wound from a tree branch instead of more serious injuries.

Next is a girl with a suspected broken foot. I visit her first. She hunches over in pain, cradling her foot. She is in her early twenties, but her mother is there to support her, demanding someone take her in right now, flashing me an impatient look when I apologize and say the doctors on tonight are currently attending to other patients and someone will review her daughter's x-ray as soon as possible. It's a familiar exchange that doesn't always end pleasantly, but there's nothing more I can do. The nurse on before me administered pain medication and gathered the required medical information, ready for when the doctor arrives.

Next up is an elderly man who was experiencing chest pain. He has already undergone a bunch of tests, which showed he wasn't having a heart attack, but he's awaiting further results to see why he is in pain.

Cassandra mentioned the last patient came in with injuries to her face. The patient claims she fell down some stairs, but it's a known—if not obvious—code for domestic violence, and her injuries don't look consistent with a fall. A fall down a set of stairs is usually accompanied by other injuries, usually on the hands and forearms, but Cassandra said only her face was affected.

When I enter the patient's room, she is lying in bed with her back propped against some pillows and an ice pack pressed to her face to keep the swelling down. "Hello," I say, and she lowers the ice pack, carefully sizing me up.

I've seen domestic violence before. I know the telltale purple bruises and the raised, broken cuts peeking through skin. It's my job to remain impartial, not to make judgments, so I smile and move closer, hoping my horror doesn't show. Her cheekbone is so swollen it distorts her features. It looks like she was hit hard, right in the middle of her face. Whoever did this was angry enough to want to hurt her.

Her nose looks unaffected—if that's where they were aiming, it looks like they missed, landing a fist against her cheekbone instead. I can almost hear the sickening crack it must've made as it shattered. It gives her face an eerie look, with some parts swollen and others deflated. It's lucky she didn't get knocked unconscious. A hit to her head as she fell could have caused irreversible damage. She's lucky to be alive.

Despite her contorted features, something about her is familiar. She watches me, her right eye partially closed from the swelling. It's as if she's waiting for me to realize where I know her from. I look at her chart to see who I'm talking to, almost dropping it when I read her name.

How could I not recognize her?

Chapter 34

"How are you feeling, Monique?" I ask, the words like sticking glue in my throat.

"It hurts worse than you'd think." She speaks through her teeth, her voice gritty with pain. She's avoiding movement in her jaw.

I want to ask how it happened, but I can't bring myself to do it. Instead, I look through her notes to see what I can find. The nurse on the shift before mine made observations and administered pain relief. Monique's notes mention a fall inside her apartment. Whoever wrote them placed a large question mark after "fall." There is no mention of anyone else at home when it happened. Apparently, she called a rideshare and got herself to the hospital. I can't help but respect her tenacity. It would require extremely high pain tolerance to organize transport with a broken bone, waiting for the ride to arrive and making the trip alone.

"I'm sure it does," I say.

"I'm sure it's nothing compared to what Isla went through," she says, placing the ice pack against her face, the effort of speaking clearly painful despite her attempt to hide it.

Why would she bring up Isla? Do Monique's injuries have something to do with what happened to my friend? "Who did this to you?" I ask.

Did Ethan visit Monique after our fight? Did he do this to her? They might have argued, just like he did with Isla before her murder. Had Ethan hurt Monique? I still can't see him doing something so violent. It takes a lot of pressure to break bone, but I've seen Ethan exert that kind of force to open a jammed jar lid.

"I fell down some stairs," she says defiantly.

"Who pushed you?" I shoot back.

"I think you already know. He was at my house. Said you were fighting."

In all my time with Ethan, he has never once hit me. I remember the times it seemed like he might. The times when his temper flared, and he grabbed hold of my wrist. He usually realized what he was doing and dropped it, horrified by what he had almost done. His most out-of-control moments occurred when he felt scared. Like the time he thought I had stepped on the watch his mother gave him before she died, and he had squeezed my arm so hard, as if he wanted to crush it. I don't think he was trying to hurt me, he just forgot, in his frustration, that he was holding on to it.

What would trigger him to attack Monique? I feel bad think-ing it, like I'm victim blaming, but I doubt Ethan's temper would get out of control enough to break a bone. Was he angry at her for telling me about their relationship?

I think of his warning to stay away from her, how he said she was dangerous. Could he have visited her to warn her to stay away?

It feels like a weak excuse. What did he think he was protecting me from?

"He got mad when I told him I didn't want to see him anymore, that it was over between us. He said it's over when he says it is." She stops to rest her face. When she speaks again, the sound is more compressed. Her mouth barely opens for the words to escape. "He forced his way into my apartment. I didn't know what he planned on doing, but I knew he was angry and that I needed to keep him out in the hall." She sniffs. "He had other ideas."

I think of the photo she sent. He didn't look mad then, but perhaps she took it before she told him it was over. Or maybe she's playing me.

"That's assault. Why didn't you report it?" I ask, testing her story. If she wanted to punish Ethan, that would be the perfect way to do it.

"He warned me that if I said anything, no one would believe me over him, and he's right." Her shoulders shrink with defeat. "No one saw what happened. What if he got away with it? If I made it difficult, he said he'd come back and finish what he started."

I offer her some ibuprofen, which she accepts.

She swallows the pills with a gulp and says, "The nurse who came in before is your friend, right?"

"Cassandra? Yeah. But you can talk to her about what happened."

I look at her bruises and feel my stomach hitch. I still can't believe Ethan would do this.

Monique scoffs at my comment. The suggestion is clear. She thinks we would believe Ethan's version of what happened.

"Your friend mightn't care about Ethan, but she would probably throw me under a bus to protect you. I wouldn't want to take my chances."

By the way she says Cassandra *might not* care about Ethan, I wonder if she knows Cassandra isn't Ethan's biggest fan. Would Cassandra believe that Ethan hurt Monique?

My phone lights up. It's Ethan. I hit the button on the side and the screen immediately dims. I can't answer the call now, not during my shift. Especially not while I'm treating the exact person he warned me to stay away from.

When I leave the treatment room a few minutes later, I feel my phone vibrate in my pocket again. I check who's calling without taking it from my pocket, edging the screen up just enough to see. Ethan again.

I set my phone to "do not disturb" mode and continue on with my shift, dreading the moment I'll have to return. Either Monique's lying, or Ethan is.

While I should easily trust my husband over a stranger, I don't. Not after realizing he's a cheater who has been lying to me for weeks.

I spend a good part of my shift traveling from one patient to the next. Because I was late, I skip my break, stuffing crackers in my mouth between patients, promising my baby I'll find something more nutritious when the nausea eases up a little. My mind wanders, trying to decide how to tell if Ethan injured Monique.

It comes to me while attending to a man in his mid-twenties. I wash blood from his arm to see how many stitches a drunk walk home is going to cost him, silently thanking him for not getting behind the wheel as I pull tiny shards of glass from his skin with a pair of tweezers dipped in antiseptic. The cuts form a pattern so that I can tell how he fell, and how he landed. The glass cut deeper across his right palm, and this section requires more attention.

I fall into a rhythm—pick, remove, antiseptic—and my thoughts return to Ethan and Monique. Similar to the shape of the wound, patterns will emerge. Things Ethan said. Actions he took.

I just need to look for them.

Chapter 35

I can't believe I didn't question the changes in Ethan's behavior earlier.

It's only now that Monique is forcing me to look closer that I realize I should've seen it long before I did.

Maybe she has done me a favor by ruining my marriage before my baby is born. I would bet this wasn't the first time he cheated. All the business trips and late nights.

I had trusted him. Now I know I should've asked more questions. I hadn't been suspicious enough, which makes me feel like it's my fault for not noticing. I didn't ask, so there was nothing to tell.

But there was always a hidden side to him. I had mistaken it as a way to protect himself after losing his parents. I hadn't pressed him, thinking it would bring up painful memories, but I should have. I might have saved myself a lot of grief.

Ethan was protecting himself, but not from being hurt. He was making sure his deceitfulness wasn't exposed.

Ethan misdirected me with affection, lavishing me with gifts and sweet words so that I wouldn't think anything was going on. He is an unflinching liar, and I believed his act because it was nice to feel loved, to feel I was enough. Ethan made me feel special. Even now, I'm finding it hard to believe this is real.

I finish removing the glass and cover the wound to let the antiseptic work its magic. The man thanks me.

"Anytime." I smile and go to visit my next patient before heading back to check on Monique.

Outside of her room, I prepare myself, hoping I'll wake up from a bad dream before I have to go inside. I try to convince myself that none of this is real. Monique isn't really at the hospital with an injury she claims was caused by my husband after a lover's quarrel.

Before entering, I brush invisible cracker crumbs from my uniform and self-consciously sift my fingers through my hair. Why does this woman make me feel so insecure?

I take a deep breath and enter the room before I change my mind, afraid of what else she knows about my husband.

The room is quiet when I enter. The bed is empty, sheets thrown back. Someone must've moved her to another room. Or perhaps she was taken in for surgery.

My relief is short-lived as I notice something left behind on the bed.

It looks like another photograph. Flipping it over, I find an image of Monique and Ethan. The white walls of the hospital feel like they're closing in around me. I blink hard, making sure my eyes aren't playing tricks on me.

Their fingers are laced together like lovers. I absorb the details, trying to learn what I can about their relationship from the picture. The idea of Ethan and Monique as an entity stings, their entwined hands tying them together, making it impossible to think of them as anything else.

Ethan's tailored black suit is formal and stylish. He looks years younger, the lines on his face less pronounced, his skin smoother. He is smiling at Monique, who is dressed in white beside him.

Did Monique edit the image? It wouldn't take much to photoshop a few things, change up their clothes in two separate shots and throw them together. I search for evidence—a missing elbow or a cropped ear, but I find nothing. Monique's dress makes my stomach turn. There's no veil, but she is wearing a wedding dress.

Despite the blurred background, I can still make out two faces just behind Ethan. I don't know them, but they're familiar. I've seen them in other photos Ethan has shown me. One of them he keeps on a wall in our apartment. His mom and dad—except that makes no sense, because Ethan said they died when he was a teenager.

If Monique used old photographs, how did she identify Ethan's parents? How did she access their old pictures?

I look closer. If it is fake, she did an amazing job. The lighting falls across each person in the same way, a golden glow illuminating the shadows, making the white of Monique's wedding gown light up like there are fairy lights strung across it. Ethan's skin glows too with a healthy bronzed tan, suggesting he had spent hours outdoors enjoying the sun instead of working overtime at the office, developing the sallow hue he has now.

"Aria?" I hear Cassandra behind me before I see her and slide the photograph inside my pocket, hoping she doesn't notice. "Found you," she says, as though she's been searching.

"Has someone moved the woman who was in this room?" I ask.

Cassandra looks confused.

"The one with the broken cheekbone," I elaborate.

Cassandra shakes her head. "Not that I know of. She's been waiting for the maxillofacial surgeon. They're stuck in surgery. There was an accident, so it could be a while."

I duck my head into the bathroom. There's no one in there. "She's gone."

"Well, she has to be somewhere," says Cassandra, hands on her hips while she thinks.

I wait while Cassandra calls to check if they have moved Monique.

I thumb the edge of the photograph in my pocket, the corner layered and thick with wear. First Monique left Ethan's wedding ring, and now this photo of the two of them together on what looks like their wedding day. It feels as if she's showing me a story, waiting until I figure it out myself so that she doesn't have to spell it out.

Now would be the perfect time to tell Cassandra who Monique is and what I've found, but I stay quiet, needing more time to think about what this all means—the ring, the photos, Monique's hospital visit.

Ethan has never brought up a divorce, even when we discussed past relationships. I told him about old boyfriends of mine, none of them very meaningful, and he told me about the girl he used to love, but he was light on the details, saying it didn't work out because they wanted different things.

He didn't elaborate beyond that, and I assumed they were high school sweethearts. When I asked about her, his reaction had stopped me from ever asking again. That one question had shifted our light, flirty conversation into a dark, moody fog that wouldn't lift. He'd spent the rest of the night brooding, until I gave up on lightening the mood, suggesting we watch one of his favorite movies instead so we could pretend the silence was a choice. When I'd tried to snuggle against him, he'd pulled away, and I had pretended it didn't hurt, trying to read his expression in the TV light as he watched a guy on the screen hiding in the shadows with a gun.

Was Monique that girl he didn't want to talk about? Nobody wanted their new girlfriend to find out they had a stalker ex who wasn't beyond breaking into their apartment. He said Monique was unstable, but why has she shown up now?

I search the nightstand, dreading that I'll find something similar to the ring she left at my apartment.

I breathe a sigh of relief when I see the drawer is empty.

"How did this get here?" asks Cassandra. Her phone call has finished, and she stands at the end of the hospital bed, retrieving something wedged between the sheet and the mattress.

My skin prickles at what she may have found. There's something small and delicate in her hands.

I swallow hard when I realize what it is, moving close to inspect it, making sure it is what I think it is: a tiny sock, small enough to fit a newborn baby.

Did Monique leave it? I cover my belly with a hand. Maybe Monique knew I was lying when I said I wasn't pregnant. What seemed like strange behavior before seems less crazy now I know they might've been married.

204

I probably seem just as crazy in my attempt to find out who my husband is under the shiny veneer he has created.

Ethan must have ended their marriage. Is she trying to win him back? Maybe she's struggling to let it go. Is that why she let herself into our home?

I force myself to consider the most dreaded question of all. Does Ethan still have feelings for her?

Maybe he wasn't ready to let her go either, even after we were married. So why did he ask me to marry him?

Would they have gotten back together if I hadn't come along? The thought that I might be a rebound that stuck makes me feel sick. No wonder Monique hates me.

I could torture myself with the possibilities, but there's no point. It's not like I knew.

I reach out a tentative hand and take the pale pink sock, smoothing the cotton between my finger and thumb, thinking how pink has become symbolic for girls, though it used to be worn by boys. It's too early to know if I'm having a boy or a girl. It seems like such a silly distinction, but I somehow know that if the sock was meant for me, Monique would've picked a gender-neutral color like yellow or green.

A code green is called over the hospital speakers, alerting staff to an elopement. I hope it's for Monique's disappearance, or it means we have another missing person on our hands. Cassandra swears under her breath and excuses herself.

Announcing an elopement triggers images of weddings instead of missing patients. Monique and Ethan all dressed up, celebrating their love. Me and Ethan years later, content to say our vows to no one but the open ocean and a sunset on the yacht we hired. I feel a tiny tug in my stomach. I had thought getting married in front of friends and family wasn't that important to Ethan, but seeing the people blurred in the background of his wedding with Monique, I'm questioning everything he ever said.

Was it less meaningful the second time around? Maybe he was over the big hurrah of doing it all again. His first marriage hadn't worked out, so maybe he didn't want to announce he was trying again, only to fail a second time.

Perhaps his parents' absence made celebrating too painful. Each holiday made him sad, almost as if he felt guilty for having a good time without them there. He spent a lot of time jogging during the holidays, channeling his sadness.

When he proposed, he had said, "We only need the two of us to make a promise." It had felt like the rest of the world didn't matter, and I agreed to marry him. It feels like a lifetime ago now, buying our apartment together, planning a family. Now, I'm standing alone at a precipice that no one would cross unless they had a death wish.

I clasp the tiny piece of fabric still in my hands, wondering where its pair is. Does Monique still have it? Perhaps it's special to her, and she kept it as a memento. Does she have a baby of her own? It might explain why she kept one, thinking giving me the other would scare me off.

Is Ethan already a father?

Chapter 36

Cassandra finds me when my shift is over late Tuesday night, startling me when she lays a hand on my shoulder. She finished her shift an hour ago, but she has been catching up on work. It's only now that I realize she was waiting for me to finish so we can talk. "It's not your fault," she says in a soft tone. "You couldn't have known that patient would take off like she did."

She's mistaking my lack of chatter for guilt about Monique leaving the hospital, but I can't tell her she's wrong, that I'm completely selfish, worrying about my own problems.

I don't meet her eyes, afraid she'll see the stress that is eating at me and start asking questions I'm not sure how to answer without telling her everything.

After Cassandra slipped out of Monique's hospital room earlier, I emailed Monique to ask where she had disappeared to. I hadn't received a response, but I spent most of my shift trying not to check my phone too often to see if she had replied.

My phone beeps. I slip it from my pocket and find a new message from Monique's fake email address.

"I've never seen someone leave the hospital with a broken face before. She must've had a good reason," says Cassandra, elbowing me gently, trying to make me see the lighter side of the situation.

It has the opposite effect, darkening my mood. I know I shouldn't be hiding the truth from her. Cassandra is my boss now, but I have to believe she's my friend first, that I can still trust her with my secrets. I don't want to involve her in something that compromises her professional boundaries, but perhaps it's time to share what I know. "Cassandra, the woman who disappeared— I know her."

"You what?"

"I mean, I don't *know* her, but she's the woman Ethan's been seeing."

The shocked look on Cassandra's face hurts. "Why didn't you say something?" she asks. What she's really asking is why didn't I trust her, especially after she had tried to help me figure out what was going on.

"It's complicated." There's no point in telling her I needed to process it, that I was afraid of the repercussions if I acknowledged Monique's existence in my life.

I want to find out why Monique left the hospital despite needing help. She was obviously in a hurry to get somewhere, but I can't imagine anywhere so important that she would endure the pain she must be in to be there.

"What the hell, Aria?" Cassandra looks at me for an explanation.

"She left this," I say, handing her the photo before I can change my mind. I had looked at it plenty more times over the course of the night, trying to figure out if it was fake. I photographed it in case Monique returned for the original, to remind myself this was real and not my imagination.

Cassandra studies the photograph, flipping it over to search the back for information.

"I kicked Ethan out of the apartment. Before he left, he told me to stay away from her. He said she's unstable, that she might try to contact me, but I didn't expect her to show up with a broken face," I say, suddenly feeling vulnerable.

Cassandra grabs my arm and starts leading me out of there. Eventually she lets go and we walk outside where she looks at the photo again. "What the hell? Ethan was *married* to her? Is this real?"

I wish I could answer her question, but right now, her guess is as good as mine. I shrug. "Let's find out," I say, taking out my phone.

Ethan has been trying to call all night, but I've ignored him, needing time to think. I'm sure he will pick up, but the longer it rings, the less certain I become. I try again, but his phone goes to voicemail.

"Maybe he left you a message," says Cassandra, but I'm already checking, listening as his recorded voice tells me he needs my help. I turn the phone to speaker and hold it between me and Cassandra so we can both hear.

"I'm at the police station. They're questioning me about Isla. They seem to think I killed her. Tell them I would never do that, Aria."

"Oh, my God. You're not going to help him, are you?"

"No," I say firmly. It's not like I can help anyway. I don't know what really happened. I need to find Monique if I want the truth.

Ethan's words stay with me. *I'm at the police station. They think I killed her.*

If he's looking for an ally, that's not me. I don't know whether I believe he's innocent. If the police find out he killed Isla—which they will if it's true—it won't matter what I say.

I make a snap decision, hoping it's the right one. "I need to find Monique," I say. "Ethan can wait."

"Do you know where she is?" asks Cassandra.

"She lives in Isla and Zoe's building," I say, remembering what she said about hearing Isla and Ethan arguing. Was any of it true, or was it to cover up how she knew Ethan? "She might've gone back there."

"You think she went home?" asks Cassandra, and I can tell she's skeptical.

"Where else could she go with a broken face?"

"That's where I've seen her before." Cassandra's eyes light up, like everything is finally coming together for her. "In the hall, when I was visiting Zoe. What if she knows what happened to Isla?"

What if Monique hurt her? I don't say it out loud, but Cassandra must've thought it, too. It seems strange that Monique turned up after Isla was murdered.

"Let's find out," I say, curling my hands into fists, preparing for battle. What would it take to get inside Monique's home, to see what else she's hiding? I'm tired of playing the game her way, waiting for the strike. It's time to confront her, and where better than her home, where she can't run?

"I'll come with you," says Cassandra, but this is something I need to do alone. Somehow, having Cassandra there would feel like coercion. I don't think Monique will speak freely if she's there.

I thank her and walk into the night, leaving Cassandra in the darkness. I promise to call when I know more, encouraging her to go home and rest. She looks like she hasn't slept since Isla died, her sleep haunted like mine. I'm scared that the killer is someone I know, someone who will kill again if I don't figure out what they want.

It's only as I'm walking away that I realize Cassandra didn't even try to change my mind. Perhaps she knows I would go anyway, but I'm surprised she agreed so easily. Does she want answers as badly as I do? Does she think Monique knows how Isla died?

There's a saying about shooting the messenger. Maybe Cassandra knows more than she's willing to admit, but she'd prefer me to be mad at someone else.

Chapter 37

When I arrive at Monique's building, I realize I don't know which apartment is hers. Sliding into the shadows, I hope no one notices me. It feels voyeuristic, trying to figure out where she lives.

When I reach the stairwell, I step out of the darkness, keeping close to the wall. The smell of paint lingers, the walls glistening with a fresh coat since Isla's death. The change makes me sad. The world has already moved on.

I picture my visit with Zoe, the way she kept glancing toward the entrance. She had seemed jumpy, nervous. She was afraid to even open the door, and I thought she must've been anxious, trying to adjust to living alone in the apartment she used to share, haunted by her memories. What if her fear was justified, and the killer lives in one of the apartments?

Perhaps knowing Isla's secret has put Zoe in danger.

I trace the trajectory of her gaze, remembering with my finger pointed in the air. Her eyes wandered across the wall as we talked, as if someone might break in if we didn't maintain vigilance. I picture where she was looking beyond the walls. What was on the other side?

I open the front door and follow Zoe's invisible gaze across the stairs.

It tells me exactly where Monique's apartment is and that Zoe might know about Monique after all.

I move up the stairs. To my left is a white door, where Zoe's gaze would have landed. Outside, I stop and listen, hoping to find something to suggest Monique came home.

I hear someone shuffling around inside, leaning in closer to listen to make sure my ears aren't playing tricks on me. The sound of a cabinet door swinging shut makes me jump. These apartments are cookie cutter. I would bet the layout is the same as Isla's, which would mean the sound is coming from the bathroom.

I press my ear against the door. I can hear a tap running inside the apartment. Someone is home. I make a snap decision and try the door handle. It's unlocked, and I quietly push it open, stepping inside as it closes gently behind me.

The tap has stopped, replaced by approaching footsteps. Did she hear me come inside?

It's too late to leave. I search for something to hide behind, but the sofa's four legs leave me nowhere to go. I freeze, exposed.

A woman appears from the bathroom, her eyes framed by dark bangs, but it's not Monique. She looks vaguely familiar, but I can't remember where I've seen her before. She finishes drying her hands on her shirt and eyes me warily.

She must be Monique's roommate. I expect her to scream, demanding to know why I'm in her home, but she stops still, a slow smile spreading across her face like a stain. "Hello," she says, as if my presence is expected.

It's the pretty woman who was at the bar the night Isla died. I remember wondering if she was the woman Ethan was seeing. It was the way her eyes had watched me. Until she had disappeared.

"I'm sorry. I knocked, and no one answered, but I think I have the wrong apartment. I'm looking for my friend," I say, my voice harried.

She takes a step closer, and I realize the smoky lights of the bar didn't do her beauty justice. Her features pop, as if each one was meticulously created with the rest of her face in mind. The only thing missing is the warmth I thought I noticed at the bar.

"I should go," I say, my instincts screaming for me to flee.

Her eyes flick back and forth, eyeing me. "Probably," she agrees, watching as I fumble for the door handle, trying not to expose my back to her. "You wouldn't want to be late to visit your friend."

She folds her arms, waiting to see what I'll do now that she has caught me trying to break into her apartment. She seems to know I'm lying about ending up here by accident.

My eyes move past her, searching for clues that something is as off as it feels. The tension thickens, neither one of us trusting the other. A picture frame hangs on the wall behind her, a photograph blown up and trapped inside the glass prison. The woman in the picture is beautiful, but it's not the woman I'm talking to. This picture is different from the one that was left behind on the hospital bed, but it captures the same scene. Again, it's Monique and Ethan. I'm beginning to think they really were married, that Monique is right and I don't know my husband at all.

The woman notices my horror before I can mask it and turns to look at the picture.

I move toward the door and fumble for the handle, desperate to leave. Whoever the woman is in Monique's apartment, I don't think she's supposed to be here either.

She wore the same curious look at the bar that night, just like now. She remembers me too. I'm suddenly afraid of this woman.

It's as if, now that I've started looking, there's a hidden underbelly with people who have been hiding just outside of my peripheral vision suddenly coming into focus.

It could be a coincidence, but I don't believe in coincidences, especially when I've seen her in two unfortunate places.

Without another word, I turn, ready to slink back out and pretend I was never here.

"Wait," she says as my hand catches the handle.

I move faster, eager to escape.

"Aria," she says firmly.

The handle falls from my grip. I mightn't know her, but she knows me.

Chapter 38

The woman holds her hands out in front of her, surrendering.

"Where's Monique?" I ask, nodding toward the photograph so that she knows there's no point in lying—I know this is Monique's place, just as she does.

"I don't know," she says, unbothered.

"What are you doing here?" I fire questions at her, hoping to leave her with no time to concoct untruthful answers.

"Probably the same reason you're here," she says, perhaps hoping I'll provide a good enough reason for the both of us. She cocks an eyebrow.

"Tell me where Monique is," I press.

Satisfied that I'm not about to turn and rush out the door, the woman relaxes, her arms dropping to her sides. "I don't know where she is," she says.

"Then what the hell are you doing inside her apartment?"

She looks amused. "I could ask you the same thing."

"Monique needs medical treatment. I'm trying to find her," I say, waiting for a reaction. Does she already know Monique has a broken cheekbone? Is that why she's here? Maybe she was the one who gave her the broken bone.

If that were true, why would Monique blame Ethan?

"Your turn," I say, trying not to stare at the photograph of Monique and Ethan behind her. I've been staring at it long enough to decide it definitely doesn't look like a fake, but it would be easy enough to create a happy imaginary life for her and Ethan using AI.

Is Monique so fixated on Ethan that she had fake wedding photos printed? If that's true, who knows what else she's convinced herself is real?

I look at the photo again, at the way their hands are clasped together, Monique squeezing Ethan's gently as if she doesn't want to let go, the pressure lifting her wedding band slightly.

It's the detail that tells me it might be time to accept it could be real. Ethan and Monique may have been married.

Are there more pictures throughout the apartment? I want to check, but the woman's presence stops me.

If Monique and Ethan's marriage was real, something had disrupted it, and I'm wondering if that disruption was me.

"I was looking for Monique too," says the woman, borrowing my excuse as I suspected she would.

"Why were you at the bar the night my friend was murdered? Who are you?" I don't trust her and I want answers.

I check her clothes, her hands, her face, looking for blood or bruises. Anything to suggest that she attacked Monique, but her delicate hands are unblemished, without even a chip in her polished nails.

She sighs. Resigned. "I was hoping you wouldn't remember that."

We're still standing in the space leading to the living room, a tiny square patch a realtor might try to pass off as an entrance in order to make the apartment sound bigger.

"Have you been following me?" I wait for her to deny it, but she doesn't.

"My name is Shannon. I'm a private investigator."

I let out a breath I didn't know I was holding. A private investigator. That would explain the way her eyes followed me in the bar. The way she didn't seem worried when I walked in here. I realize with embarrassment that she must've known I was there before I went inside.

What would she have done if it had been Monique coming home instead? I doubt she would've told Monique she was a private investigator.

I feel my cheeks flush at my hubris, thinking I could sneak in here unnoticed, when even someone trained to do so hadn't managed it.

"Who told you to follow me? Was it my husband?" I think of Ethan right away. He's the only person I can think of with a reason to spy on me. I have no idea how he even knew I was out that night, but he hadn't seemed too pleased at me drinking with the girls. What else did he think I shouldn't be doing?

Shannon's presence here, despite Monique's absence, raises a few questions.

A horrible thought occurs to me. What if Monique had already returned home, and Shannon was waiting for her? Perhaps she lied about being a PI to hide a more sinister vocation. I listen for Monique, in case she's locked inside a room somewhere, unable to call for help.

Shannon rests her hands on the back of her hips, her face expressionless while she considers whether to tell me who hired her.

She probably signed a non-disclosure agreement to protect whoever hired her, but it was worth a try.

"It's not my job to ask questions. I take the information I'm given, and that's it. It's better that way. It stops any bias. I'm given a job and I report back on the information I collect."

"What was the job?" I ask, doubting she will tell me.

Shannon flicks her fringe with a hand, revealing the startling blue of her eyes. Up close, they are glittering with different shades. How does Shannon succeed as an investigator when she stands out enough to attract attention?

"I'd rather not say." She shifts her weight from one foot to the other, waiting to get back to whatever she was doing before I interrupted.

"Did my husband hire you to follow me?"

"I don't know," she says, her tone even.

"Was it a man? A woman?" I ask, determined to break her silence. With the right leverage, I'm confident I can get some answers. "Listen, if you tell me what I want to know, I promise I'll turn around and won't look back. It'll be like I never saw you."

Except I would've already left if she hadn't stopped me. Maybe she was trying to distract me while her accomplice carried out what they came for. I probably don't have long to figure out what they're up to.

"You know what? It's fine. I shouldn't have asked," I apologize. "I'll let you get back to it."

I turn and open the door in one swift motion. She has to believe that I've given up on questioning her for this to work, that if I leave now, I might discover what they're up to.

She speaks just before I leave.

"I don't think it was your husband. I've only ever spoken with a woman. She wanted me to find out whether you were alone throughout the day."

Maybe Ethan got his secretary to call the job in for him. I wouldn't put it past him. At work, he avoided unpleasant tasks— why should home be any different? It would explain Stella's discomfort when I asked about the "business meeting" she didn't remember booking. She probably thought I was on to her, that I was making something up to find out what I wanted to know— whether my husband had her hire a stalker to follow me. Or was it simply that she knew about Ethan's infidelity?

I think before saying any more. She answered too easily but hasn't given away any useful details, just vague bits that I could have figured out myself. I already knew she was following me. I had asked as much. It wasn't a stretch that I might've noticed she followed me at specific times.

"Did the person who hired you have a name?"

"I don't ask for real names. It protects both me and my employer if a job goes wrong," she says.

It seems risky to me. If the wrong person caught her and tried to torture information out of her, she'd have nothing to bargain with.

"There are plenty of reasons to follow someone," she says, her voice mellow, "but I got the feeling they weren't trying to catch you out doing something awful. It was more like they were trying to protect you. The instructions they gave me were to report anything threatening, to never approach you, and above all else, to keep you safe."

When she finishes, I'm more confused than ever. Why did Ethan hire a private investigator if he was the one having an affair? Did his infidelity make him paranoid I was doing the same to him, or was he looking for something else, something that would be obvious to a hired spy without telling them what to look for?

The thought sends a shiver through me. All the moments I had thought I was alone, Shannon could have been watching. She would have seen Cassandra and me rifling through Ethan's things. Had she followed me while I was in LA, watching while I went through Ethan's trash? Had she watched as Monique and I met up, listening like a fly on the wall?

And how much had she told Ethan?

"If you're following me, you know my husband is having an affair."

She looks away. "I—"

"No, I know. You can't tell me," I say, repeating her own line back to her. "But you're in her apartment, so I'd say there's a good chance you already know."

The front door is open. I could leave now, take away her bargaining power. She knows that once I leave, I will confront Ethan. Her cover is blown, her employment is all but ended, which gives me something to work with.

"What else can you tell me about the person who hired you?"

She doesn't answer.

"If you tell me what I want to know, I'll reward you for it. It might even pay better than what you're currently getting."

She doesn't seem interested in the money, but she hasn't stopped me either.

"You were there the night my friend was killed. You were sitting at a table with a group of women."

I remember how she had disappeared, replaced by another woman from their group. It's only now that I realize that despite sitting there with the group, Shannon had not talked to any of the women there. She had laughed at their jokes, but she hadn't actually joined in the conversation.

She wasn't part of the group at all. She must have been resting at the table when a seat opened up. She was watching me, just like I had thought.

"You disappeared around the time she died," I press. It feels like I'm getting close to figuring out how it all fits together.

She bites her lip, revealing straight white teeth.

"Tell me what you saw."

Chapter 39

Her eyes widen, as though she's surprised that I noticed her disappear. If she's hiding something, it won't be so easy to hide now that I have a name to give to the police.

She knows it too, and it's enough to get her talking.

She pulls in a long breath before she begins.

"I saw her in the bathroom, fixing her face in the mirror. A few girls came and went. Her hands were shaking. She applied pink gloss but had to start over, they were shaking so bad. Usually I would've asked if she was okay, but I couldn't . . ."

"Without someone realizing you were following me," I finish when she hesitates.

She looks ashamed. "I got an alert. I was going to leave through the window. The person who ordered the job wanted me to . . ." She stumbles to find the right words, clearing her throat. "They wanted me to go inside your apartment to see if there were bugs planted."

Did Ethan think I'd bugged our house, trying to catch him out? Did he want to make sure it was safe to take her there without me knowing?

"Did you find any?" I ask sarcastically, expecting her to say no. Until recently, there had been no reason to think I needed to install cameras. I had trusted Ethan, which feels naive now that I know better. It must've seemed so easy. Me, the gullible fool. He mustn't have thought twice about getting caught, assuming I wouldn't realize his "business" trip was actually a romantic getaway.

Shannon looks guilty for snooping around my home. I wonder for a second if she might've left the bloodstained suit jacket or placed Isla's necklace in Ethan's bag while she was there. "I found two. One in the kitchen and one in the living area."

The blood drains from my face. This whole time, someone has been watching me. I think of Monique's story about wanting to protect me from the same thing that happened to her, the husband she had trusted who turned out to be an asshole.

What if she was trying to save me from the *exact* same thing? What if Ethan was the husband?

"Why should I believe you?" I ask. "Anyone can call themselves a private investigator. It's not like you need a badge like a real detective."

"Actually, you do. Well, not a badge, but you do need a license," she interrupts. I wait for her to stop talking and continue.

"I'm pretty sure private investigators don't break into apartments to check if someone has bugged them."

"Okay," she says. "You're right. They don't."

"So, you're not a private investigator then? You're just some thug my husband hired to follow me?"

"Did you think maybe I didn't break in—that someone gave me a key to get inside?"

The thought had crossed my mind, but something tells me that's not what happened. "How could he give you a key? He was in LA when your call came in, so I doubt it."

By her account, she would've been gone before someone slipped inside the bathroom, locking the door behind them. She would've been spared the sound of Isla's last moments.

"You didn't see who killed my friend, did you?" I ask, disappointed by the dead end.

"No. But I've been watching for a while now, and I think I know who did."

Chapter 40

"Is that why you're in Monique's apartment? You're looking for evidence that Monique killed Isla?" I can't think of another reason she'd be here, but from the look on her face, I've missed the mark. "Or were you hired to bug her home, too?"

It's too early in the morning for this. Tuesday has ticked over to Wednesday and sleep is calling, but I feel like I'm close enough to some real answers that I push through.

"I didn't bug anyone's home. I came here to figure out what she's planning."

That didn't sound right. If Ethan and Monique were married, why would Ethan need someone to figure out what she was planning? Wouldn't he have a pretty good idea based on what she'd done so far? He already knew she went into our apartment to return his wedding ring.

Couldn't he just ask her? Or were they no longer on speaking terms? The photo she sent of the two of them would suggest otherwise.

Maybe he hadn't asked what her plans were because they didn't share their secrets with each other anymore.

I relax a little, my hands dropping to my sides as I search the room, no longer afraid Shannon is going to attack me. "Did you find anything?" I ask. "The apartment is filled with pictures of Monique and my husband."

Shannon averts her blue eyes. She definitely found something, something she's not sure I should know about.

"Were they married?" I ask. There's no point stuffing around. If Shannon was here, snooping around, I'm guessing she already found out everything she could about Monique online, including who she was close to and whether she was married.

"Yeah," she confirms.

I laugh, realizing there's not a lot I trust about this woman. If she's a private investigator—which I doubt—she's not the legal kind. Ethan may have the authority to grant permission to enter our apartment, but he can't give her permission to break into Monique's home.

"Here," says Shannon, moving toward the bedroom. "See for yourself." She gestures for me to follow, but I wait while she disappears from the room. The way she moves around the house is too comfortable. She must've been here for a while before I got here.

I could run now. Open the door and disappear before she returns. But then I might never know if she's telling the truth. I might never know who Monique really is, or how she got a broken cheekbone. Is Monique Ethan's ex-wife? Is she a killer? Or is she just some woman who's obsessed with Ethan?

A drawer opens, closing a few moments later. Shannon returns with an official-looking certificate in her right hand. She holds it out for me to see. It's a marriage certificate. I move closer to read the small print, noticing my husband's name immediately. Ethan

Dolan, scrawled next to Monique Suarez. It's dated almost ten years ago, before I even knew Ethan.

Ten years. That would have given him plenty of time to get married, start a life with Monique, get divorced, and meet me.

"Is this real?" I ask Shannon, noticing she's still holding something in her other hand.

"Yeah," she says, opening up a little blue passport. Inside is a picture of Monique that looks like it was taken recently.

Why would she want me to see Monique's passport? I humor her and look, searching for details she might want to highlight.

I don't have to search long, as Shannon points out the date. The passport was issued just two years ago. After Ethan and I were married.

The name on the passport rips away the fog of denial.

Monique Dolan.

Why would she keep using Ethan's last name after they were divorced? Didn't people go back to their previous name?

Is that why my husband didn't want me to take his surname? Had Monique kept it for herself, tainting the meaning? I can't imagine why she would want to do that. It was strange, but Monique didn't seem like the most conventional person.

"I would know if my husband had been married before we met. He would've said something." *We don't keep secrets from each other*, I almost add, but the thought dies on my lips because I know it's a lie.

I'm still wondering whether this is all just some cruel joke where Ethan's about to appear from behind the sofa, laughing, telling me he pranked me good, that I can watch the replay on one of those "pranking my wife" reels for the amusement of complete strangers.

When that doesn't happen, I wait for Shannon to give up the ruse, but my personal hell stretches on without relief.

I look at the certificate again, their names together on the page. United. The paper drops to the floor as if the words have burned through my fingers.

Shannon looks at me with pity, coaxing me to the punchline. "I'm sorry, but it's real."

"She's obsessed with Ethan," I say, shaking my head in disbelief. "She's been sending me emails. She left a photograph she created of the two of them with his family in the background. She's deranged." Ethan was right. Monique is unstable. Dangerous. She refuses to let Ethan go. She's trying to get me to leave so she can have him back.

"You didn't know they were married?"

"No. I didn't even know she existed until she sent a weird email asking how well I know Ethan."

Humiliation stains my cheeks. She had been right. I didn't know him as well as I thought I did.

"She said he hurt her." I feel the conviction of my words slip away as the memory replays, Monique saying she was trying to warn me so that the same thing didn't happen to me.

I dismissed her warning, assuming she was angry because I had something she didn't. What if I was wrong, and she was trying to help me? She's known Ethan for more than a decade—longer than I have. She knows him better than I thought she did.

Whatever terrible things he could do to me he had most likely already done to her.

I move past Shannon and toward Monique's bedroom. I can see more photos encapsulated in frames on the nightstand. Sightseeing on their honeymoon in a lush rainforest. A snap taken a few years later, her hair grown out at a costume party. They're dressed as Scarlett and Rhett from *Gone with the Wind*. The perfect life Monique planned with Ethan looks very real.

Shannon's expression softens, some of the warmth I saw at the bar returning.

What was Shannon looking for when she broke into Monique's apartment? What else did she find before I arrived? She had obviously got a fair way through her search, given how fast she found the documents.

"The police are questioning my husband right now. What are the chances that the next time he calls, it'll be from a jail cell?"

Chapter 41

Shannon doesn't seem surprised the police are questioning Ethan. I ask what he's told her about me, Isla, and Monique.

Her face masks her thoughts, but I notice her shift with a kind of recognition when I mention Isla.

She could be lying. Maybe I'm feeding her information, but I want to test her reaction.

"You should talk to your husband. Find out what his end game is," she says.

Her brow twitches, but it could be involuntary.

"And if it turns out he's your mystery employer?" I say, wondering what kind of person accepts criminal work from a stranger with the risk of being caught. I couldn't imagine doing what she does without losing sleep.

"Listen, even if he was, I wouldn't want his money if he killed someone. I won't help a murderer get away with it." Her eyes harden like cold blue ice, as if I've accused her of something.

"This job is about finding out what you know, not just protecting you," she says, as if she can read my thoughts.

"About Isla?"

"Maybe, but mostly about Monique. Someone knew you would find out about her. Maybe they knew she was going to confront you." She waits, as if I might tell her what Monique and I spoke about.

Is that why someone hired Shannon, to find out what Monique told me? Or did someone else think Monique was as dangerous as Ethan did?

If that's why Shannon's here, my secret is safe. She's not about to go digging into my past and find things I've fought to keep hidden.

I need to stop her from thinking there's a reason to dig, so I play along, telling her just enough to seem cooperative. Maybe I can convince her to share what she knows.

"I thought she followed me home a few weeks ago," I say. It's easy to sound believable when you're relaying something that scared the shit out of you. "I thought she was going to attack me, but she didn't."

I never got a clear picture of the person following me. What if it wasn't Monique at all, but Shannon? There's no way to ask without creating a rift, so instead I watch for her reaction and continue.

"She said she was trying to warn me, but I guess I'll never know. I thought she might've killed Isla, thinking it was me in the dark bar. We were about the same height, the same build."

I might've said too much, but Shannon has said enough to incriminate herself too—including admitting to breaking into my house as well as Monique's apartment.

She still hasn't said what she thought happened to Isla, and I hate myself for wanting to know. "Do you think Monique killed Isla?" I ask uncertainly, desperate for answers.

Shannon shifts her weight. "I don't know, but I agree with you. Whoever killed your friend didn't mean to kill her. I think they slipped something in a drink that was meant for you."

"They poisoned her," I say under my breath, still reeling from how fast the night turned from a celebration to a tragedy. The police hadn't called with the tox results yet, and even if the results were in, the report could only show the toxins they tested for.

"Yeah. I saw your friend come back from the dance floor and grab your drink from the table. It seemed like a harmless mistake, but she drank from it, and not long after, she stumbled into the restroom."

I swallow hard. How close had I come to being poisoned? I only took a few sips of champagne, and none were from Isla's glass. I feel sick as I remember handing my glass to Isla to drink. After months of not drinking, despite my bravado, I couldn't bring myself to do it, scared that it might tip the scales.

"We didn't leave the table all night. How could someone spike my drink?" I think back. Cassandra and I had table-sat, happy to sit and chat while Zoe and Isla twirled on the dance floor. "It could only have been someone at our table," I say. Unless someone spiked the champagne before they gave us the bottle? But how could they isolate my drink without affecting the others?

Cassandra had poured the fizzing liquid into sparkling clean glasses, but I don't for a second think she would do that.

I move on to a more plausible explanation, my memory tinted with champagne toasts and plenty of refills. I didn't drink as much as Zoe and Isla, but after months of abstaining, even a few sips were enough to make me feel light-headed.

Could it have been something else in my drink that made me feel woozy?

Zoe had handed glasses to each of us, but there wasn't enough time to slip something in my glass. I remember her insistence that I have a drink. I had taken it as good-natured ribbing, but what if it was something more sinister? What if she needed me to drink it for whatever she slipped into my glass to take effect?

I excuse myself hastily, telling Shannon there's somewhere I need to be.

Zoe is just a few doors down. Of course, I can't ask her if she tried to drug me, but I can ask if she saw anyone tampering with our drinks.

Shannon watches me leave. She doesn't stop me like before.

Soon, I'm knocking on Zoe's door, hoping she forgives me for interrupting her sleep so early on a Wednesday morning. I'm vaguely aware of Shannon standing outside of Monique's apartment as if she's curious to see how this will unfold.

I wait for Zoe to answer, ready to disappear inside when she opens the door—a mouse escaping an apex predator for a lesser one.

I press my ear closer to the door and listen, expecting movement inside. There's silence. I try the handle—something I've done a hundred times before, but this time it feels intrusive.

The handle gives and I slip inside, away from Shannon's prying eyes.

Inside the apartment, something feels off. The silence is stifling, as if no one's home, but Zoe always locks the door when she goes out.

Someone got here before me. I find her sprawled on the living-room floor. It looks as if she's sleeping, and I think for maybe a second that she's taken a sleeping pill and rolled off the sofa, too deep asleep to wake up. That idea is forgotten when I notice her waxen skin.

"Zoe? Honey, wake up!" I say, shaking her gently at first. "Zoe!" My voice becomes panicked, but still Zoe doesn't move.

I bring a hand to the side of her face and feel her cold skin under the warmth of my fingers. Her eyes stay slightly open, unblinking under dark lashes, telling me what I already know. I check for a pulse just in case there's a faint flutter whispering under her skin. I wait for the tickle of movement far longer than we're taught to at work, but there's nothing.

The hue of her skin tells me it's already been hours, and an attempt to revive her won't do much except make it harder for the police to figure out what happened.

Reluctantly, I remove my hand.

Zoe is dead.

Chapter 42

What are the chances this was just an accident?

Deep down, I know it wasn't. That's two friends dead. What's stopping them from coming after Cassandra or me next?

Shannon's voice startles me, her hushed tone making her seem far away. She must have followed me into the apartment. I vaguely register her calling 911.

I find my phone and call Cassandra. She answers, making a sound like pressure escaping a soda can when the tab is pulled. "Aria! I was worried. You didn't message."

There's silence as she realizes she's right. "Oh, my God, what happened?"

"It's Zoe. She . . ." I look at Zoe's body curled up on the floor. Where do I start? Do I tell her about Shannon and Monique's apartment?

I turn. Shannon is gone, leaving me to wait for the EMTs. Is she avoiding needing to explain why she broke into Monique's home?

My nerves prickle when I hear her voice deep within the apartment. She didn't disappear after all.

She emerges and looks at Zoe still lying there. For a minute it looks like she's figuring out what to say, maybe something comforting. She gives up. "There's no one else here. Whoever did this is long gone."

"Who's that?" says Cassandra from the other end of the phone. I'm not sure how to explain who Shannon is, so I don't.

"It's a long story," I say. It's not much, but it'll have to suffice. "She was looking for Monique when I got here."

"Where's Zoe?"

"She's . . ." I stop. This is the part I've always hated about my job, having to explain to a family that we couldn't do anything to save a loved one. It's ten times harder when telling Cassandra. "It was too late by the time I got here. She's dead," I say, the harshness of my words making me stop.

"When did you find her?" Cassandra's voice is pitchy.

"Just now. I'm worried that whoever did this might come after you next. Where are you?" My voice is frantic, scared that my warning has come too late, that the killer is looking for Cassandra.

"I'm at home," she says.

I hear sirens in the distance, closing in until the sound is almost on top of me.

"Lock your doors. Stay away from the windows. Don't answer if anyone knocks."

I end the call once she agrees, turning to Shannon. "Go," I say, hoping I won't regret letting her leave.

"What?" She's looking over Zoe's body, trying to figure out what happened, circling without getting too close, touching nothing, as if trying not to contaminate the crime scene. She doesn't look as horrified as I would expect. It's as if she's been around dead people before.

Was Shannon used to seeing people die in her line of work? Would she kill for the right price?

"It looks like someone shot her." She points out something, but I can't see a gunshot wound.

"How can you tell?" I ask skeptically, not wanting to think about what happens to your body when it's shutting down.

"There's a small hole in the side of her T-shirt," says Shannon matter-of-factly. I look for myself and sure enough, a tiny hole that could be a small tear mars the fabric.

I expected more blood, like in the movies, but there's no sign she was shot. She looks peaceful.

Shannon must notice how skeptical I am.

"There could be blood pooling underneath her," says Shannon quietly. "Her shirt will soak some of it up, and some of it's likely pooled under the sofa. I'm guessing the shooter is really skilled and shot her straight through the heart, or got lucky with a clean shot."

I nod, too numb to make sense of what she's saying. I can't peel my gaze from Zoe, her lifeless eyes giving her the appearance of the sleeping doll I had as a kid, whose eyes would close as I lay her down to sleep and open when I picked her up. Zoe looks stuck somewhere in the middle.

"I'm sorry for your loss," says Shannon. "Do you know why someone is killing off your friends?" Her tone dips gently, like she's easing me into something I mightn't have thought about yet.

I don't tell Shannon about Zoe and Isla's secret. It doesn't matter now that there's no way to figure out if it's related. Perhaps she already knows about it if she's been following me, and she's trying to figure out their secret, too.

"Wish I knew," I say. "But then we might have stopped this from happening, and we wouldn't be having this conversation."

She flicks her head, hands on the back of her hips while she sizes me up. "If we can figure it out, maybe we can stop you from being next. Think hard. Why would someone want them dead?"

I remember Zoe saying Isla knew something but was afraid to say it. How Zoe seemed to know what it was but didn't tell me. There's no way of knowing now. Their secrets will die with them.

Help is almost here. I hear the sirens, even closer than before. It feels redundant, with Zoe unsavable and the killer already gone.

Deflated, I decide Shannon is more useful away from the prying eyes of the police. "Unless you want to spend the night in a jail cell for breaking and entering, and maybe murder, go now. I'll wait for them."

She looks at me with uncertainty. "But I didn't—"

I stop her, the glow of red lights hitting the window. "Go," I say firmly. I don't think she murdered Zoe. She sure as hell wouldn't call emergency services if she had.

"Thanks," she says, considering my offer. "But what about you?"

The small part of me still wondering if I'm helping a criminal vanishes. I can't imagine a criminal waiting to make sure I'm okay when they have a free pass to leave.

The sirens change timbre like the low call of a whale. Zoe's legs are curled to the side, her back flat against the rug, just like I found her.

The killer could have rolled Zoe up in the rug, taking a good chunk of evidence with them. They could have attempted to clean up and hide what they'd done. But it's as if they don't care who knows, like they're not afraid of being found out.

Or perhaps someone scared them off before they could do any of that.

The EMTs will arrive any minute now. If Shannon wants to take up my offer, she needs to go now or figure out how to explain why she was here in the middle of the night, rifling through Monique's apartment.

If she left, she'd be doing me a favor. I wouldn't need to mention finding her here when I arrived, or tell the police about the stop I made at Monique's apartment.

"They're almost here," I say, but Shannon is already gone.

Chapter 43

The EMTs storm in to assess the situation.

It doesn't take long for them to figure out Zoe is dead, and the mood changes from urgent care to gentle preparation. An EMT in green-framed glasses guides me away from where Zoe lies. The glasses amplify the intensity of her gaze, and I see the hesitation in her expression, how she's unsure whether to treat me like a patient in shock or a suspect.

I'm too numb to protest as she leads me to another room, away from the sofa and Zoe's lifeless frame. She checks me over for injuries I already know I don't have.

Not long after, a police car arrives, red and blue lights dancing across the shadows, coming to a stop somewhere below. I hear the clang of a police belt at the door; the attachments jingling like a horse's bridle, reminding me of the weapon tucked in their holsters.

Detective Kinsley Scott walks through looking about as pleased to see me as I am to see him. An EMT tells the detective Zoe is dead. His face falls as he thanks them and looks at me. I know that look. He's wondering why I'm here, and how another of my friends is dead. It doesn't look good, and I'd probably be doing the same thing if I were in his shoes.

"What are you doing here?" he asks, as if never seeing me again would have been soon enough.

"Visiting my friend," I say. "I found her like this when I arrived."

"At one o'clock in the morning?" Large circles rim his eyes, the puffiness made worse for each hour of sleep he's lost. I would bet money someone got him out of bed to attend this callout, his foul mood inevitable.

"I fought with my husband and needed to talk to a friend. Zoe was the kind of friend whose doorstep you could show up on at any time and she'd invite you in."

That part at least is true, but the detective is looking as if he mightn't believe me, lip curled to the side, biting the inside of his cheek.

I watch people in uniforms move around the body, securing the scene before a twenty-something woman in a stylish trench coat strides in, heels pounding against the floor, and takes a bunch of photographs from different angles, as if she's the lead creative on a fashion shoot. Zoe would hate this. Strangers seeing her at her most vulnerable, capturing it so they can scrutinize every detail.

I know it has to be done so that the detectives can try to make sense of what happened to her, but I wish there was a way to shield her from all of this, to make sure her last moments before they transport her to the morgue are dignified.

When they finish, Detective Scott offers to drive me to the station. I know it's not a real offer but a way for him to ask more questions. I'm not sure my mind is clear enough to make it to the station, so I accept.

I am an actual suspect now, but he won't arrest me before he has enough to hold me for a long time. Scott acts nicer than usual, asking if I'm okay, insisting that the EMT finish checking me over before we leave. Which means one thing. He thinks I might have killed Zoe. Isla too. He's making sure he does everything by the book so that poor process handling claims don't ruin a conviction later on.

He doesn't give a shit about my welfare, despite the convincing act. Scott's hoping the EMT finds something incriminating that will tie me to the murders so he can slap a closed label on the case. I comply with their requests until they ask what happened. Despite me telling them I didn't hurt Zoe, they don't seem to believe it, and I'm worried I'll say the wrong thing and incriminate myself.

I sit through the rest of the medical check, anticipating each of their requests from my medical training.

I don't trust myself to speak, thinking about how Zoe must have spent her last moments. Without meaning to, I keep glancing at the rug where detectives and crime scene staff swarm around her like flies, wondering about the last thing she saw.

The detective pulls me from my thoughts. He's been observing me since he got here, scrutinizing me with every response I've given. Finally, I find out what has him so suspicious. "Your husband was called to the station earlier today to answer some questions. That wouldn't be why you're so reluctant to talk to us now, would it?" He watches for a reaction, anything to give away what happened here, but being a nurse means I've had loads of practice at remaining impartial, and I maintain a neutral expression.

There don't have to be any secrets. I could tell them about Shannon, but if they get to her, I don't know what the implications will be. I don't know what she knows about Ethan or how deep she's dug into my past. If she *knows*, and I rat her out for breaking into Monique's apartment, I might end up in jail with her.

I want to ask if Ethan's still at the station. I'm curious how he's holding up, and whether the police believe him when he says he doesn't know who killed Isla. There's no way they'll disclose what they discussed, so I don't ask.

"Can I talk to a lawyer?" I ask, the words dry on my lips. I never thought I would request legal help to defend something I didn't do, but life is surprising like that.

Detective Scott's expression hardens, his eyes narrowing because of how difficult I'm making things. I expect him to tell me I don't need a lawyer, that they were just asking a few simple questions to help with their investigation, but he doesn't. He gives me my options, agreeing to organize a phone call so I can find a lawyer. "Aria, I'm not charging you. I want you to know I'm just looking for information to do my job," he says.

I thank him but stick to my request, saying I'd still prefer a lawyer if it's all the same to him. He leads me to his car and we ride to the station in silence, Detective Scott glancing at the rearview mirror, me pretending to watch the scenery passing by the window so I don't catch his eye.

Being a cop must be a lonely job. You question innocent people as if they're guilty, and you can't assume the guilty ones are guilty, ostracizing everyone. When you're not doing that, you're looking for answers to questions you wish didn't exist. *Was the girl murdered? Was the driver drunk? How well do you know your husband . . .*

Everything you do has the potential to piss people off, and yet you would still put your body on the line to save them because that's what you agreed to when you accepted your badge.

What made Kinsley Scott want to become a cop?

Chapter 44

The station is darker at night, as if it's operating on low power to save the precinct a couple of dollars.

I'm led through the foyer and to the back where the real business happens. My eyes dart like a nervous fish trapped in a small pond, searching anxiously for Ethan, who probably left hours ago.

I walk through to a small interview room, passing a desk cop who looks like he's lived out most of his life here on the night shift, away from sunlight. He stretches his back, his belt sitting tight as his belly presses out over the band, glad for the distraction from shuffling paperwork around his desk. He invites me to sit in a plastic chair at the bare white table, offering a cup of coffee despite the late hour. I guess time's not so important when you're a cop who needs to stay awake in case a call comes in.

He fixes me a mug before I can answer, and I accept it with a nod and a tight smile—I might need it if I'm going to be interrogated tonight. Is this how it feels to be a criminal? I take a small sip of the tar-like liquid, wondering if I'm even allowed to drink caffeine while pregnant. I've read so much about fertility and almost nothing about pregnancy, but I think I recall a colleague talking about it when she was pregnant.

I take another small sip, deciding I'll be no use to my baby if I'm too tired to stop myself from being thrown in prison—maternity care isn't exactly a five-star service behind bars. I hope it does the trick, that I'm ready to explain everything to a lawyer before Detective Scott comes back to grill me about Zoe.

Time passes slowly while I wait with little to distract me but my own thoughts. Despite Detective Scott's excuse about leaving to organize my phone call—something I easily could have done on my phone—I know he's discussing Zoe's death with his colleagues, theorizing how I ended up at another murder scene where I knew the victim.

"Is there something else I can get you?" asks the officer, whose name he didn't bother mentioning.

I shake my head no.

He pours himself a mug of black sludge. I wonder how many people have answered questions and taken coffee from that pot tonight. How many noticed the black ring that suggested it was in desperate need of a refresh?

I clear my throat. My voice needs to be clear and confident to ask what I'm about to ask. "My husband was in here earlier," I say, trying to sound conversational.

He sips his coffee, liquid moving down his throat with a gulp. He grimaces. Whether at the coffee or my question, I can't tell. They can't have so many murder suspects coming through that he doesn't remember Ethan.

"Ethan Dolan," I say pointedly. "Do you know what time he left?"

I look at the door, which is open just a crack, expecting Detective Scott to appear and begin asking more questions about Zoe, testing whether I've changed my mind about having a lawyer present.

"Dolan," he says, his tone suggesting he's accessing an invisible index system in his mind. He holds his coffee mug loosely by the handle, making me nervous it might slip and crash to the floor. "Oh yeah," he says eventually.

I feel my heart quicken. Ethan was here. If this cop's willing to admit that, he might tell me more.

"Ethan Dolan was here to discuss the girl who got killed at the bar. His wife picked him up earlier." He stops talking, as if he's just realized what I said. "Wait . . . you said you're his—"

"Sister," I state emphatically. "I missed his call earlier. I'm glad he found someone to collect him."

It takes effort to hide my emotions this time. I clasp my hands to stop them from shaking. Did Monique come to collect Ethan at the station? She was Mrs Dolan once. She might've let the cop think they were still married to avoid any awkwardness. If she came straight from the hospital, that would explain why she wasn't home, and why she didn't tell anyone she was leaving.

I can't imagine anyone forgetting her, given the condition of her face when she left the hospital. She clearly needed medical attention. Her broken cheekbone couldn't look good for Ethan if she picked him up, claiming to be his wife.

The officer rises from his chair. "Give me a sec. I'll go see where Detective Scott is."

He leaves the room, closing the door gently behind him, leaving me locked inside.

With nowhere to go while I'm waiting, I sift through phone messages, grateful it wasn't confiscated. There are multiple messages from Ethan and one from Cassandra. I check Cassandra's message first. If she mentioned my plan to pay Monique a visit, it could look incriminating.

I'm relieved to find no names mentioned in her message. She's only asking where I am and if I'm okay.

I check Ethan's message next. He says something about being at the police station and asks me to pick him up. Shortly after, there's another message saying not to bother. He found a ride home. Although it's typed, I can feel his annoyance in the wording. The accusing tone. The overuse of punctuation to emphasize his frustration.

I had been so preoccupied with Monique showing up at work that I hadn't even bothered checking if Ethan had messaged.

Where are you???!!!

I dial his number, wondering if he's annoyed enough to screen my call. I can see him now, fishing in his pocket, checking who's calling. Taking a moment to decide whether he's cooled off enough to talk. But he answers partway through the second ring.

"Where were you?" he says, an edge to his tone. "I tried calling like a hundred times."

His lack of concern about why I didn't call sooner irritates me. He assumes his situation is worse, that I should've answered right away.

"I was stuck at the police station. I asked to call you a bunch of times until I gave up. It was humiliating, and it made me look guilty as hell, Aria. Not even my wife wanted to come and get me."

He lets the words hang, as if the memory of it is too embarrassing. "I came back to the apartment later to see if you were ready to talk, but before I got there, a cop stopped me and asked if I would answer a few questions about Isla. They took me in the cop car. Jesus, Aria. They think I had something to do with her death." The way he says it makes it clear he thinks he doesn't deserve the treatment he's getting, but he's forgetting the reason he was outside our apartment in the first place. I'm tempted to remind him, but I have bigger issues than a cheating husband to deal with.

"*Did* you have something to do with her death?" The question is flat, like an opened soda can left sitting for too long. Maybe he didn't kill her, but perhaps he knows who did, and why they did it. Maybe the argument he had with Isla led to her murder.

"*What?*" He does a good job of sounding indignant. "You know I didn't," he says, but I know Ethan. Something in his voice isn't quite angry enough. It takes a moment, but once I place what's off about his tone, I can't shake the feeling that he should be more upset. I'm questioning whether he murdered my friend.

There's nothing in his voice to suggest that questioning whether he's a criminal is hurtful. He used the same tone when I asked him about Monique back at our apartment, when he was lying about their relationship. Now I know that it's the tone he uses when he's lying.

"Well, what did they ask?" I try to sound as if I'm on his side, like I think the police questioning him in the first place was unreasonable.

"They wanted to know why we were arguing outside her apartment."

"And what did you tell them?" I ask, feeling as if I'm prompting a child to do the right thing before I decide on what punishment they'll receive, depending on how truthful their answer is.

"I told them exactly what I told you when you asked about it. I said that Isla and I disagreed on what was best for your mental health, and that our disagreement blew out into an argument. She said I was being controlling, and I said she was looking for a reason to go ahead with the party anyway because that's what *she* wanted to do."

There is probably some truth to both sides. While Ethan probably didn't realize he was trying to control the situation, he can be forceful when he has a firm opinion on something. He's right though. Isla loved an excuse to party.

"Where are you now?" I ask, wondering if he would have the nerve to head back to our apartment as if nothing had happened after I asked him to leave.

He hesitates just long enough for me to notice, recovering quickly. "I'm at Jason's," he says. I listen for his old college friend in the background, the boom of his laughter, or the sound of the TV set, but all I can hear is Ethan breathing into the phone.

I almost ask him about the woman who went to the station claiming to be his wife—I doubt Jason would pass for anyone's wife with his stubbly face—but I hesitate, knowing Ethan will probably lie if he has something to hide. I have no way of knowing if he's telling the truth without seeing his face. In person, I at least have a chance.

I decide to wait, finding a more subtle way. "It's quiet," I say innocently. When Jason's around, he interrupts our conversations with a steady stream of things he wants to talk about, as if his thoughts are connected to his mouth.

Maybe Ethan had mentioned our argument so Jason had respectfully given us space ... but I doubt it. I would expect Jason chattering in the background, encouraging us to kiss and make up, saying nothing is unforgivable if you mean it when you say you're sorry.

"Yeah. Jason's not in right now," says Ethan, thwarting any attempt to confirm his whereabouts.

"Interesting that you went to Jason's. I thought you would've had other places to try first," I say, baiting out the lie.

He picks up on the innuendo and sighs, his patience wearing thin. "Aria, I know you're mad, but I won't do this with you right now. It's been a long day and I'm tired." His tone is pointed. He blames me for making it even longer, contributing to his tiredness.

"Did you know that Zoe's dead? I found her. Tonight. At her apartment."

A sound outside the interview room grabs my attention. I stop talking, expecting Detective Scott to walk through the door at any moment, but whoever it was passes by without stopping.

"Sweetheart, that must've been awful." He sounds distracted. Nervous even. "Why were you at Zoe's so late?" he asks, and I imagine him pacing, looking down at his feet like he does when he has a stressful client to deal with at work.

"I stopped by after work. To talk," I say.

The conversation has shifted. Somehow, Ethan has escaped my questions, moving the focus back to me.

"I don't mean to sound insensitive, but doesn't the timing tell you I didn't kill Isla? That whoever killed her probably killed Zoe too, while the police wasted their time questioning me?"

He's right. The timing suggests he didn't kill Zoe, but I remember something Monique said about Ethan not being the kind of person to get his hands dirty and letting someone else take care of his problems. Being at the police station answering questions would give him the perfect alibi while he had somebody else kill Zoe.

"This is silly, Aria. Why don't we talk? I can be there in a few minutes," he says, proving he's not at Jason's or exaggerating how soon he can be here. It's at least forty minutes from Jason's apartment to ours. I tell him not to bother, that I'm not home.

"Where are you?"

I expect more of a reaction when I tell him I'm at the police station answering questions, but if he's worried I might say something incriminating about his involvement in Isla's or Zoe's death, he doesn't show it.

"I told them what you did to Monique's face," I blurt. It's a test. He has no way to know I'm bluffing, no way to stop me from saying more, but his reaction tells me a lot.

"I didn't do that to her," he says. "I swear."

Then how do you know what I'm talking about?

I end the call without saying goodbye just as Detective Scott opens the door and lets himself in with a somber expression.

Chapter 45

I've always been skeptical about the loyalties of state-appointed lawyers, so I choose one of my own that isn't too pricey. Paying the bill on a nurse's salary, I can't be too picky.

I try to get some sleep in the interview room with my arms resting on the table as a pillow. By the next morning, I have a lawyer who's willing to drop their plans to speak with me.

She looks no-nonsense in a tidy, minimalist way that suggests she doesn't spend money on frivolous things—maybe she uses her designer clothes fund to help people like me instead. She shakes my hand, holding it for a moment, pairing it with a reassuring smile. The gesture is surprisingly warm as she introduces herself as Milly, not Milicent like it says on her LinkedIn profile.

I've never needed a lawyer before, and I wasn't about to pick a self-proclaimed expert by trawling through websites, so I compared lawyer profiles on LinkedIn. I selected Milly for the reviews referring to her as a "formidable and intelligent lawyer with a fantastic win rate." She has a ton of endorsements for criminal defense, where most of the others were divorce lawyers.

She looks capable enough that I almost ask why she's working so cheap, but decide that would be rude.

When the introductions are complete, I ask anyway, my curiosity winning out.

She smiles as if she's glad I asked. "My mom, basically."

I wait, hoping there's more to that story, and there is.

"She was an accountant, but she gave up her job to have kids. When a client passed away, she became the key suspect and my dad left her. She didn't have the money to pay for a defense lawyer, and her shitty court-appointed lawyer was bought off early, so she went to jail for something she didn't do. I was angry for a long time, so I channeled it, and here I am."

"Wow. That's impressive. I bet your mom's proud," I say.

Her smile drops. "Yeah, well. She died in prison. Cancer. But I hope so."

"I'm so sorry." I could kick myself for putting my foot in my mouth, but Milly's smile is back.

"Every win is for her," she says. "Now, let's see what we can do here."

Milly preps me to answer Detective Scott's questions—at least the ones she deems suitable for a response. "Scott pretends to have a hard shell, but it's all gooey under there. The guy's interested in the truth, not just a conviction, so he's going to ask you a lot of questions. Answer only the relevant questions about what you saw. Stick to the facts."

I nod along as she talks, feeling hopeful.

"First," says Milly, "tell me what happened. Leave nothing out. If there's anything I should know, anything that might come up later, tell me now."

I relay my visit to Zoe's apartment, how she was already dead when I arrived. I mention Isla and how the detective probably doesn't believe I had nothing to do with their deaths, because both times I was there. I leave out details from my distant past, deciding it won't come up if it hasn't already. It's a gamble I'll take if it means not reliving it.

When we're done, I answer the detective's questions. He maintains a practiced look of concern, making it impossible to tell if he believes me.

He doesn't ask about Monique's apartment, and I don't bring it up. If they don't already know, I'm not about to incriminate myself further. Perhaps Monique won't report it. Maybe she won't notice whether Shannon moved a few things around with a murder investigation happening a few doors down.

I'm exhausted by the time we're done. Milly slips me a business card, just in case.

I arrive home just before midday, the sun shining like a bad joke on my dark mood. I open the door to my apartment, keys jingling, and make it as far as the sofa before I crash, pulling a throw over my legs.

I sleep for a couple of hours and wake up to a knock at the door. Afternoon light spills through the window, duller and less energetic than the midday sun.

It rushes back. Leaving work the night before. Me and Cassandra trying to find Monique. I assume it's Cassandra at the door now, eager for details since I haven't updated her for a while.

"Coming," I say, rubbing at my eyes to remove the sleepiness that clouds my vision. I throw the door open, suddenly awake when I see who's there.

"Monique." My tone shifts.

Her face has the raw look of someone who has just been treated with antiseptic. Gauze and tape cover her face like strips of papier-mâché. I can tell immediately that her cheek has been reset by someone who knows how to mend a broken bone. If I looked under the gauze, I'd find a rainbow of bruising, but the bone is back in place, her symmetry restored, though warped by swelling.

"What are you doing here?" I blurt.

"Listen, I came to talk. I didn't tell you everything before, but I think I'm ready."

I hesitate. Ethan warned me about talking to her, almost preempting her visit. I consider closing the door, locking her out forever, but she might be my only way to figure this out. Screw Ethan—it's not like he's been truthful.

She lets herself in while I'm still considering my options, brushing past me with a familiarity that makes it seem like she's been here before, which she has.

"I know you were married to Ethan," I say. "That story about making the same mistakes you made—you were talking about Ethan?"

Now that she's inside, it would feel awkward asking her to leave. I don't offer her something to drink, hoping she doesn't stay too long, but I decide to find out why she's here. She sits on the sofa, and I join her, taking the spot closest to the door in case I need to get out quick.

"I thought he would grow tired of you," she says, her eyes welling up. "I told myself you deserved to be used and thrown away." The loathing in her voice is clear. She hates me. For taking Ethan's attention when she no longer held it. For spending hours that should've been hers, curled up with him watching Netflix, or sleeping against his shoulder while she waited to see him again.

I feel stupid, like I should have realized he had been married before. Divorced. That he was still seeing her. I feel even worse that the clues still don't seem obvious. He hid it too well, like he never wanted me to find out.

She touches her fingertips lightly to her face, trying to hide her pain. "When I found out about you, he lied. He claimed you were some girl from his office who was infatuated with him. He swore it was one-sided, but then I saw the two of you drinking coffee. You were sitting too close. Then you leaned against his shoulder." She gestures with her hand. "He kissed the top of your head and you snuggled into him. That's when I realized it was mutual."

She looks at the top of my head, as if the kiss still stains the happy image she's built of her and Ethan.

"You were in scrubs, so I knew you worked at a hospital. There was no way you met Ethan at work like he said. I figured that wasn't all he was lying about."

A few months ago, Ethan and I had gone out for hot chocolate at a dessert bar after I finished my shift. I was still wearing work pants. I usually changed into regular clothes at work, but after losing a patient that shift, I just wanted to leave. I had messaged

Ethan on my break, and he had insisted on taking me out afterward to cheer me up.

"You followed me into the alleyway," I say to Monique, feeling certain.

She frowns like she can't remember specifics. Like she had followed me enough that each time was less memorable. It was no longer the one time she did something devious, but a wrong she indulged.

She looks away, sheepish. "It was only for short periods. Until I followed you home. Ethan was away on a business trip—a real one this time." She laughs, the sound dry and scratchy, suggesting there's nothing funny about what she's saying.

I think about Shannon's claim that she had followed me, too. She would've known Monique was as well, but she never mentioned it.

"I couldn't understand why he needed both of us. I was trying to figure it out," she says.

I look around the room, avoiding her sad eyes, but she isn't finished.

"I wanted to know what kind of person would be selfish enough to ruin a marriage. You didn't even seem to care whether you got caught, because after a while, I figured you must've known about me." She leans back on the sofa, waiting for me to respond.

"I thought you were a fling. I didn't realize you used to be married," I say. It's a weak apology, because maybe she's right. Maybe they would've lasted if I hadn't come along.

I want to tell her she might've done the same, but then I think of Shannon finding their marriage certificate. What if Ethan manipulated me into believing she was crazy? What if he had made her crazy?

I had seen the pictures of their wedding, Ethan's parents smiling in the background. It must've been taken shortly before their death. But that couldn't be right. Ethan said his parents died when he was a teenager.

"When were you married?"

"Ten years ago. In April."

"I noticed Ethan's parents in your wedding picture, but they died when Ethan was a teenager."

She looks at me as if I've suggested the most ludicrous thing she can imagine. "Pearl and Doug?"

Maybe Ethan had miscalculated, or perhaps I misunderstood.

"Ethan's parents aren't dead," she says. "They live in Newark. His mom sent a card last week. It's been eight years since—" She waves a hand, abandoning her sentence.

Each time we speak, there is a new revelation unraveling Ethan's lies. I put them together, creating a Frankenstein's monster of a life cut up and restitched. Ethan left out the parts he didn't want me to see, cutting away until what we had together almost moved and breathed but never really lived.

"When did you and Ethan get divorced?" I ask, lacing my fingers together, unsure where to put them. My hands feel empty, and I wonder if the real reason guests are offered drinks is to stop the host from fidgeting.

"Divorced?" She seems confused by my question. "We aren't divorced. Let me guess." She pretends to think, and I feel like a child being reprimanded for my lack of judgment. I wish I could go back to just before she let herself inside and ask her to leave. "He told you he would leave me? You seem like a smart girl. Did you really fall for that bullshit?"

"You can't still be married," I say. "Ethan and I are married . . ." I trail off, wondering how that's possible if he's not divorced. Weren't there laws against marrying more than one person? Wouldn't I have received a notification to say our marriage license was revoked?

I remember getting a marriage certificate in the mail, and I hadn't thought much of it, slipping it away in a drawer. It looked legitimate, but what if it wasn't?

"Are you sure?" she asks knowingly.

I feel my cheeks flush and open a browser tab on my phone. Thumbing the screen, I search for our marriage certificate online, but the search returns nothing. She waits patiently, seeming to know what I'm doing as I try a few different combinations of our names, the place we were married, and our initials to find the correct certificate.

"We had a wedding and a honeymoon all in one," I say, still searching.

There doesn't seem to be a marriage registered under our names. Is that why Ethan wanted to elope? Had he already set up everything to make it seem spontaneous so I wouldn't question the smaller details or suspect that the celebrant was some hired guy with a fake certificate for us to sign?

I stop searching, knowing I won't find anything because there's nothing to find. Our marriage is a lie.

It explains why only Jason could make it to the wedding. Ethan had suggested we elope, saying it would be romantic. He made it sound like an adventure. We didn't have to organize caterers or go through endless options for flower arrangements and menu items. I had laughed and agreed that it sounded perfect. Days later, I was surprised to discover he had the whole thing organized. It was all so sudden.

I barely had time to arrange time off work, and I realize now that was exactly how Ethan had planned it. He had love bombed me. That way I had no time to question my friends being unable to take time away from work. With fewer people to witness our wedding, the chances of someone figuring out it was fake were much lower.

My parents would've found a way to be there had I invited them, but I didn't, worried their presence would remind Ethan that his own parents couldn't be there. Instead, I'd agreed to a couple of close friends and the two of us.

I place a hand across my stomach, as if the life growing there might be another lie I've believed.

Chapter 46

I look away.

I'm the other woman.

While I've been angry, confused, and hurting, she must have been feeling the same.

"Did you ever suspect?" I ask. "When he wasn't home for days on end? Or when he made excuses about why he couldn't be there for plans you had already made?"

Really, I'm asking myself, testing Ethan's excuses on Monique. When it felt like he was disappearing into work, expecting me to understand, I knew there was more to it. I want to know whether it was the same for her.

"I trusted him," she says. "Just like you did."

I look at her cheek, bruises peeking from under the dressing. "Did he hit you?"

She doesn't meet my gaze. "I didn't think you'd believe me. I know how charming Ethan can be." She sighs. "If I knew you were on duty, I would have gone somewhere else. I blamed you for Ethan's infidelity. I didn't want your help."

"Are you okay?" I ask, trying not to stare at her wound.

"They set the bone, but it's too awkward to operate on, so I have to wait for it to heal."

She's right. Depending on the type of break, sometimes the only option is to realign the bone and leave it.

I feel sick at the thought of Ethan hurting her badly enough to break her bone. What else is he capable of?

The room rushes in on me and I excuse myself, walking through to the ensuite bathroom, trying not to throw up until I reach the basin.

Once I've emptied my stomach, I rinse my mouth with mouthwash. I can hear Monique's feet on the rug as she shifts in her seat. Somehow, she seemed less scary than a stranger following me. Now that I know the impact she has on my life, I'm truly afraid of what else she could take from me.

I splash my face, placing a hand against the sink. The cool water clears my vision and I notice the pregnancy test Ethan found in the trash can. It's cracked into two pieces. One is in the garbage, the other on the floor.

Maybe Ethan accidentally stepped on it—or perhaps he wasn't as happy as it seemed about becoming a dad, and this was how he expressed it.

I take the two halves and try to fit them together, but there are missing fragments so it doesn't work. If Ethan had stepped on the test accidentally, it might have cracked, but it wasn't likely to snap in two without significant force. Whoever did this wanted to destroy it.

Outside, the living room has grown quiet. "Monique?" I call tentatively, but I can't hear her.

I hadn't heard her arrive downstairs either. I didn't buzz her in, so I assumed it was Cassandra at the door.

Security must've let her in.

Was she hiding in the building, waiting to confront me when I got home?

Or maybe Ethan was right and she really is unstable beneath that calm, collected persona she's trying to project.

Her voice is suddenly close, making me jump. "That doesn't sound good. Do you want something? A glass of water?" she calls. "Don't worry. It's normal to throw up when you're pregnant. Especially at the start. I know I did."

She knows about the baby. How? I only told Ethan, and I can't imagine him being in a hurry to tell his wife he's having a baby with someone else—especially when he warned me not to tell her.

I discard the pregnancy test, one pink line into the trash, and then the other. Did Monique break it?

A sudden fear seeps in. Monique is clearly upset about Ethan and me—so how does she feel about our baby?

Was Ethan's warning for more than self-preservation? Maybe he thought it would push her to her breaking point.

I find my phone, fingers flying over the screen.

Monique is here. Inside the apartment.

I leave the bathroom, lead her back to the sofa, and force myself to speak, sounding like a reluctant kid giving a class presentation. If I can keep her talking, it might buy me time. "You've had morning sickness? You have a child?"

"I would have," says Monique, her voice hitching. "She was born sleeping."

A pang of empathy hits me. It is my worst fear. I can't imagine the pain it must've caused her, losing her child.

"Ethan and I called her Lola," adds Monique, as if she needs me to know exactly what she's lost.

"That's pretty," I say softly, wishing there was more to say. I can't believe I'm just learning this about my husband now. He was a father.

Why didn't they have more kids? Was their marriage already over by the time they lost her? I think of my own brush with death, and the impact it still has on me. How sometimes I still snap awake in the night, thinking I'm in a car rolling down an embankment as the metal contracts and crunches around me.

I still dream about it, the car reaching the bottom, trapping me in the passenger seat alone. When I try to find Matt, I realize the doors are locked.

That's not how it really happened.

The familiar wave of guilt hits me. I remember trying to unclip him, giving up quickly when I realized he was already dead. The relief I felt at being finally rid of him. No more screaming or bloody noses when I disagreed. No more punishments when something made him unexpectedly angry.

The guilt that followed for surviving, for getting on with my life. I wonder if it's been the same for Ethan after his loss.

I can't believe my husband has kept such a life-changing secret from me, but I am a hypocrite with secrets of my own.

I wanted to tell him, but how could I after what I'd done?

No one knew I was out that night. I snuck out to meet Matt while my parents were sleeping.

Once the car stopped rolling, I left Matt inside and didn't look back. I told myself someone would find him and assume he had lost control of the car. I walked home on a sprained ankle to clean up the gash across my midriff and down my arm.

I finally convinced myself I did the right thing because Matt hadn't really lost control of the car. He had been drinking as usual, and we were arguing because I had broken up with him.

He was furious and sped up, trying to scare me. He told me to say it again, and stupidly, I hadn't recognized it as an invitation to change my mind. I told him once more. "I never want to see you again," I said, sealing my fate.

And I hadn't.

I'd seen it repeatedly since working as a nurse, but back then I thought domestic violence was something that happened to married people. I hadn't recognized my own relationship for what it was until much later. By that point, Matt was dead, and I carried what had happened in silence.

I never spoke about it to anyone. It was as if I had never been a part of his life. No one knew that we had secretly been dating for months.

After that night, keeping secrets was easier, and I became less shocked by the things others hid.

Until it became obvious I had only scraped the surface of what Ethan has been hiding.

Chapter 47

My phone vibrates softly, the volume down so it doesn't draw attention. I tap the screen and read Ethan's reply.

What?? I'll be there soon. Try to get her out of there . . . she might try to hurt you.

I pocket my phone and sit on the ottoman, distancing myself.

"How many weeks are you?" she asks. Under different circumstances, it might feel like an innocent attempt at small talk, but her question feels ominous, and I don't want to discuss my baby with her.

"I'm not sure," I say. "I haven't even confirmed the pregnancy with my doctor yet."

"Not far then," she says knowingly. Something in her tone unsettles me, as if the shared experience of pregnancy means we're in it together.

I'm about to stand and thank her for her visit, tell her there's somewhere I need to be, but she beats me to it. "Does Ethan know yet?"

I wipe my palms against my sides, trying to rid myself of the way she makes me feel. Like being trapped inside layers of sticky cobwebs, pushing their way down my throat and inside my ears.

"So, he does know," she says when I don't respond.

I jump from my seat too enthusiastically. "I have an appointment soon, but thanks for stopping by."

She raises her perfectly shaped eyebrows, blue eyes drinking me in. "Really? That's all you have to say? Thanks for stopping by?"

"I'm sorry," I say. "I'm just a little rattled by what you just told me. I honestly didn't know."

"Except you did," she says.

"Excuse me?"

"You may have buried it down, pretended you didn't know. But you *knew*. It's not even the first time you've done this, is it?"

How could she know about that? No one knows.

When I met Matt in college, he was married. I was only in his class for one semester, but afterward, we kept in touch and eventually started dating. We'd drive down the coast to a spot outside the city we liked to go to. Somewhere no one knew us, where no one could judge us.

It all sounds familiar now. He told me he was miserable in stolen phone calls. He'd call while his wife was out. He said he would leave her—the exact things Monique asked if Ethan had said. Maybe she wasn't just asking about Ethan.

You're a smart girl . . .

Except, this time, I'd fallen for worse. I accepted a lie, justifying it to avoid reality.

I hadn't even told Cassandra about Matt. And yet Monique was quoting words only Matt and I knew about.

Matt had a whole life that stretched well beyond my eighteen years. I dreaded his wife finding out and confronting me. I told myself that if they were happy, he wouldn't need me. I felt *sorry* for him, for how unhappy I thought he must have been.

I hadn't realized he was grooming me since the day I arrived at college.

Had I fallen for the same shit again?

Matt ran right into me, a lost new student. He had caught my arm, steadying me with a strong hand. I might've fallen and twisted my ankle if he hadn't, but when I looked into his face, I noticed how the line of his jaw cut sharply, the hint of stubble dulling the edges. He stared at me with concern and interest, wondering who this girl was in such a hurry.

After making sure I wasn't hurt, that I didn't need help, he gave what felt like a reluctant goodbye. I hadn't been ready for him to go, and I had turned to watch him walk away with his smooth, athletic gait. My stomach fluttered as I thought about the sensation of his hands catching me, moving up my arms to steady me.

It flutters even now with the memory of the effect he had on me, before I even knew him.

Later that day, the butterflies returned when I walked into one of his lectures. He made a bad joke about running into me again. Each week I listened to his smooth tones as he discussed anatomy and physiology, thinking about his fingertips against my bare arms.

One day he asked to speak with me after class, so I stayed behind. He wanted to know if I was enjoying his lectures, and for a moment I was terrified he would suggest I pursue another career.

He had surprised me by asking what I was majoring in, guessing that I was on the path to become a surgeon. When I told him I was studying to be a nurse, he seemed pleasantly surprised.

After months of sneaking around, he finally acknowledged what we had was more than just physical. It was real. He loved me, but things changed quickly, and the bruises he gave me were also real.

The first time he hit me, he apologized, saying he cared so much that he got upset when he thought I didn't feel the same. All I had done wrong was choose a study partner Matt didn't approve of.

He demanded to know why I chose the only guy in the class, forgetting that Cassandra was usually there too, or that I was capable of having friends that stayed friends. He accused me of being a slut, saying I would sleep with anyone, that Bailey wasn't even attractive, and that I didn't take my study seriously.

I feel an ache in my ankle. A reminder of the night the car crashed. It still flares occasionally, especially when it's about to rain. Matt's words whisper in my ear again, like a ghost returned. *"You're a smart girl . . . did you really believe him when he said he just wanted to study?"*

I had decided to break up with Matt after that fight. I couldn't take the controlling behavior anymore. The constant phone calls, worrying he could snap and hurt me even worse than the last time. I kept everything about us to myself, including the anger I felt when I figured out he was a creep. Who would believe me over a well-respected, intelligent professor?

Looking at Monique's broken cheek makes me think of the time Matt might have broken my rib. I never had it checked, scared someone would find out how it had happened.

Perhaps Monique is bluffing, and she doesn't really know about Matt. Maybe she just assumes I must have cheated before if I'm doing it now. She needs to justify what she has planned for me next.

"What are you talking about?" I say, daring her to say it.

"You seem to be around death a lot, but I don't think it follows you. I think you invite it. Two friends dying so close together can't be a coincidence. You pretend you're the nice girl, nursing people back to health, when really you like their misery. They're so grateful when you rid them of their pain. It makes you feel alive."

My hands grip the side of the ottoman. Is that what drew me to nursing? Am I drawn to suffering? To death? I think of how Matt died—another person I knew who died too early.

Monique continues. "And somehow nature decided you should be a mother, when all you care about is yourself. How can you care for a baby?" Her words sting and I notice her body is rigid. Her chest rises and falls in shallow breaths. I see it now— the rage no longer hidden. She resents me for having what she lost. Is it any coincidence that she chose now to confront me about Ethan when she must have known about us for weeks?

My pregnancy is the one thing that has changed within that time.

I slide my phone from my pocket and message Ethan. Finally, I know what she wants. This isn't about me. This is about her, about Ethan. And mostly it's about the child they never got to see grow up. Monique watches me tap the screen. I send the message before she can stop me, because as angry as I am at Ethan, there's no one else that will understand the danger I'm in.

She knows about the baby.

Chapter 48

I have to try harder to make Monique leave.

"I really have to go," I say. I stand, but she mirrors me, challenging me to walk out of there.

She moves so we're standing inches apart, so close I can smell the salty scent of sweat on her skin. She is nervous about being here, about confronting me. From the outside, we could be close friends sharing a secret, but my body is alert, telling me I need to be ready for anything.

"Are you going to keep it?" Her words are like needles, closing the distance between us with barbed thread.

Her eyes drop to my middle, looking for something she can't see.

"I—" My voice stalls.

I'm not the threat she wants to eliminate. I'm not even close. She waited until now, until she was certain. It's written on her face. She had been waiting for this moment since she found out about me and Ethan. Maybe she wanted to be sure. About what? Ethan and me? Or about the baby?

I think about the pregnancy tests in the trash each month, reminding me I was another month away from having a baby. Until that one test that changed everything.

The one Ethan placed in his pocket, which ended up in pieces in the bathroom trash. Had Monique sifted through and found it? How else would she have found out? Did Ethan tell her about the baby?

Somehow, that feels like a worse violation than if Monique broke in and went through the garbage.

"Do you even want to be a mother?"

"Of course. We've been trying . . ." I stop myself from saying more, hoping my words don't aggravate her further. Is a baby even what I want anymore, with Ethan as their dad?

I had wanted nothing more when I thought I was bringing a child into a loving family with a warm, safe space to grow up in. Now I know I had been wrong, did I still want to be a mother?

It's as if Monique can sense my hesitation. "There's no shame in giving up your baby now that you know Ethan isn't really yours. I would love him as if he were my own."

She's looking at me with new hope, her tone sickly sweet. I have something she wants, and she will do whatever it takes to get it. A knot forms in my stomach. What happens if I say no?

My phone beeps. A message from Ethan flashes across the screen.

Monique is right. You should give her your baby. You would be a terrible mother.

What the fuck? Why would Ethan say something so cruel? Why would he tell me to give her our child when he said she's unstable?

How did he know what Monique said? I check my phone to confirm I haven't accidentally called.

I struggle for another explanation, my pulse thumping in my throat. What if he's in the apartment? He could have easily slipped in while I was sleeping, hoping we could talk. Maybe he's part of this charade, mocking me, waiting to see how far I can be pushed before I break.

"Ethan?" I call, my voice shaky. I know it's risky, but so is being here alone with Monique. "Ethan! Are you there?"

He doesn't respond, and disappointment fills me as I remember Shannon saying that she found bugs inside the house. Was he listening remotely to our conversation?

"Oh, honey. Ethan isn't coming to save you. He has about as much love for you as I do. He just wants a baby so badly that he's willing to do whatever it takes." She clears her throat loudly. "Even if it's with you."

"Ethan wouldn't do that," I say. Hurting me is one thing, but involving a child is another.

"Wouldn't he?" She raises an eyebrow.

I take a step back, watching the door get farther away as I retreat.

I hold my phone, typing in three numbers. I almost hit dial, but she snatches it from my hand. "I don't think we need to call the police about this. We're just talking. If you hear me out, you'll realize it's for the best."

Her voice is eerily calm, as if she's soothing an unreasonable child.

"Please, I just want to leave," I say, holding out my hand for her to return my phone. "Ethan and I aren't even together anymore. He left. He isn't coming back here. You could go back to the way things were . . . and try again." I hope I'm still as good a liar as I was when Matt died.

My life depends on it.

I keep my hand out, waiting for her to give up the phone until she eventually relinquishes it. I wrap my hand around it and unlock the screen with my thumb. "I'm going to call Ethan and ask him to stop by," I say, looking for the security cameras that he may have had installed, hoping he can hear me.

She doesn't look convinced, so I keep talking. "Don't you think he should be part of this conversation? If he says he wants to raise a baby with you, I promise to consider it."

I put everything I have into sounding believable.

Monique doesn't disagree, so I hit dial.

"Put it on speakerphone," says Monique. I hit speaker and wait as the phone rings.

My ears must be playing tricks on me, because after the first ring, I hear an echo. Ethan has his ringtone set to mimic an old-school phone because he claims no one does that much anymore and this way he always knows when he has a call. By the third echo, I'm sure I can hear Ethan's phone inside the apartment. "Ethan?" I call again.

"I guess he left his phone when you kicked him out," says Monique sarcastically. "He must've been in a hurry."

"He's gone, I swear," I say, trying not to seem as shaken as I am. I watched him leave. If he came by while I was sleeping, surely he would have made himself known when he heard Monique.

His message suggested he was on his way here. He didn't say he had already arrived.

A second, more sinister possibility crosses my mind. Is this a setup? Are Ethan and Monique having some fun before they kill me? Is that what they did with Isla and Zoe?

"What did you do to my friends?" I ask. "They didn't deserve to die."

I back up toward the sound of the ringing. It's coming from the guest room, which Ethan uses as an office when he's working from home. Monique watches me trap myself deep in the apartment like a spider leading its prey into a sticky web.

"Ethan lied to both of us," I say quietly, paranoid Ethan is listening from somewhere inside the apartment. "I didn't know about you. I swear," I say, hoping she will see me as a person, that it'll stop her from whatever she has planned.

The phone stops ringing. "Ethan," I say, relieved.

"Who is this?" A woman's voice crackles, annoyed at the interruption.

"This is Ethan's—" I stop myself before I can say wife. "This is Aria. Who is *this*?" I ask, catching sight of Monique, who looks just as shocked as I am. "Can I speak with Ethan, please? It's urgent." The only person I've heard answer Ethan's phone besides him is his secretary, Stella, but she always answers in a professional tone and says Ethan can't get to the phone before offering to take a message.

This woman isn't Stella, but her voice feels familiar. I try to remember where I've heard it before, but I can't place it without hearing her speak again.

"I'm sorry, Ethan can't come to the phone right now," says the woman, the rounded end of her sentence suggesting she's about to hang up on me.

"No, wait!" I say. "Please. Can you tell me where I can find him?"

I'm almost level with the hall now. Just a few more steps and I'll be outside the guest room. If Ethan's in there, ready to convince me to give up my baby—our baby—there's nothing I can do about it, but I have to believe he wouldn't set me up, that there's another explanation for Monique's visit.

I walk as quickly as I dare, throwing the door open to the guest bedroom, expecting to find Ethan.

What I find instead shocks me.

Chapter 49

"Mrs Dolan. Can I help you with something? I'm almost finished up here." Willow is tidying the desk in the guest room. The sheets look immaculate, and the wardrobe is closed. I don't recall her ever calling me Mrs Dolan before. I'm *not* Mrs Dolan. I have never been Mrs Dolan. I have always been Aria Miller.

Had she heard my discussion with Monique?

The *real* Mrs Dolan, I remind myself, although I still can't understand why Ethan would create such an elaborate lie.

I must have been in a deep sleep when she let herself in. I hadn't even heard the door open.

"I didn't realize you were working today," I say, relieved to have someone else here. Surely Monique wouldn't hurt me while Willow's here, would she?

I'm sure Willow wasn't scheduled to work today, but she might have switched days, and Ethan just forgot to tell me. I force a smile—a hard task under the circumstances. My senses are on hyper-alert as I look around the room for Ethan's phone. I can't see it on the desk or on the floor.

Could Willow be the woman who answered Ethan's phone?

I look at her thin hands, her nails chewed down. If she answered, she has since put the phone away.

"Did you hear Ethan's phone? He must've left it in here," I say, giving the performance of my life, still listening out for Monique's footsteps in the hallway.

"What?" she asks, pulling an earbud from her ear. "I heard nothing."

I know she's lying. Even with earbuds, if she could hear my question, she could hear the phone. At the very least, Willow would've heard Monique and I arguing for the last thirty minutes, and yet she hasn't said a word. She couldn't have missed the heat in our voices or the friction in the air.

I doubt she was in here cleaning. Though the room looks immaculate, every crease kneaded out of the fat duvet so that it rests smoothly against the mattress, plump pillows at the head of the bed. The desk is tidy, with a filing tray neatly lined up on the side. Maybe she didn't want to get involved with my personal business.

"Willow, have you seen Ethan?" I ask, still searching the room in case his phone is hidden.

She levels her eyes with mine. "Not since I collected him from the police station."

Chapter 50

So it was Willow who went to the station. I suppose I can see the officer assuming she was Ethan's wife. But where had she taken him once they left?

"Please, Willow. I just want to talk with him." I lower my voice, hoping Monique won't hear me if I'm quiet enough. "His, uh . . ." I try, but I still can't bring myself to call her his wife, the words too real outside of my head. "There's a woman here. I think she's angry at something he did. She might want to hurt him."

Then I remember how far back Willow and Ethan go. She has cleaned for him since he was old enough to leave home, long enough to know about him and Monique. She was probably at their wedding. If anyone can shed some light on what's going on, it's Willow.

"You must mean Monique," she says knowingly.

"Yes! Monique," I say, suddenly hopeful she can explain everything, but we've never exactly talked much before. I've never felt comfortable starting a conversation with her. When I first met her, I got the distinct feeling she wasn't interested in small talk, giving one-word answers to my questions without offering to elaborate.

"I know they were married," I say carefully. "Do you know when they got divorced?" I ask, hoping it sounds like an innocent question.

Willow stops tidying the desk, having nothing left to do to avoid talking to me. "They're still married."

Shame floods me like a burst dam, catching me off balance. So it's true.

Willow sidesteps the desk, folding her arms, waiting to be dismissed.

Out of the corner of my eye, I notice a glimmer of amusement playing on her lips, tugging at the corners so that she's almost smiling.

I've never looked at her up close before. In fact, I've avoided making eye contact altogether, assuming my attention makes her uncomfortable. I never questioned why. Did she know things about Ethan that I didn't? I had assumed she was a little awkward, the kind of person who liked to keep to herself, and I had respected her right to get her job done and go home.

"What do you mean they're still married?" I say.

Now I have her full attention. Her eyes are alert and interested. She seems entertained by my misery.

"What?" she says. "You seem surprised. Did you think you were special to Ethan?" She gives an ironic chuckle deep in her throat. "You aren't the first. And you probably won't be the last."

My face contorts. She knew what was happening all this time, and she never thought to mention it? All the times she came in and loaded our dishes, changed our sheets. She probably laughed about it, wondering when I'd catch on. "Why didn't you say something?"

"Would you have believed me?" she asks pointedly. The smell of lavender-scented cleaner is in the air, cloying in the small space.

I mightn't have believed my husband had some secret wife I didn't know about, but something tells me that isn't the real reason she didn't tell me Ethan was married. "You could've warned me when we were first dating," I say. "I would've left."

She raises an eyebrow. She doesn't believe I would have left without making a scene. "Ethan is my friend. He pays my wage. Why would I help you?"

She is finally free to say what she really thinks, but her words still sting. I was right—she doesn't like me, but there's more to her words. She's angry.

"Help me get Monique out of here," I whisper. "She needs to go home before she does something she'll regret."

"I think it's way too late for that." I turn, noticing that Monique has crept up behind me. How much of our conversation did she hear?

A look passes between them. Familiarity. Willow more than knew about Monique. They seem like they could be friends. But it's her lack of surprise that Ethan's wife is inside my apartment that concerns me. It's as if she expected her to be here.

Chapter 51

I slip a hand in my pocket for my phone. I subtly angle the screen so I can see it and dial Ethan again, waiting for the ringtone.

I was sure the ringing was coming from inside this room. He's not in there. Does Willow have his phone?

Now that I've woken up properly, it doesn't seem so strange to hear his phone ringing. It seems feasible that he would come home hoping to talk and find me asleep. He might have napped, hoping to talk later. When I slept through longer than he expected, he probably left me to sleep undisturbed.

Why didn't I hear him come in or leave? I must've been out cold if I'd missed the telltale bang of the door that always announced his departure.

The tinny sound of a ringtone comes through my speaker. I wait for the echo. When it comes, I look at Willow, watching as she takes the phone from her pocket, holding it up to show my name flashing on the screen. My instincts tell me something is wrong. I can't think of a reason Willow would have Ethan's phone.

I remember what Willow said when I asked whether she had seen him. *Not since I collected him from the police station.*

"Why do you have Ethan's phone?" I ask unsteadily. "You responded to my texts, pretending to be Ethan."

That means Ethan doesn't know Monique is here. He isn't on his way now to talk some sense into her.

"Where is he?" I demand.

"When you didn't pick up, he asked me to get him. The police refused to release him unless someone accompanied him home. He was pretty drunk. He's lucky they didn't keep him in to sleep it off."

"Aria," says Monique, and I immediately pick up on the warning. "Come back to the living room." She's trying to lure me away from Willow, away from anyone who can help. "Now," she adds, leading the way.

I'm sandwiched between them, a rabbit between two hungry foxes, unsure of who I should be more wary of. Monique hates me because I ruined her perfect fairytale with Ethan. It couldn't have been easy for her. I never intended to hurt her, but I can't take away her pain.

Monique's anger makes sense. But why does Willow hate me?

She looks at Monique's broken cheekbone and winces. "What happened to you?" she asks.

"Ethan got mad," Monique says brusquely. "He broke into my apartment after Aria kicked him out. I told him to leave, and he attacked me."

"Oh, please," says Willow, moving closer to inspect Monique's face. "Ethan hates blood. He couldn't stomach looking at you like that."

I jump as Monique grabs hold of my arm. "Go. Now," she says calmly, eyeing Willow. Her voice rings in my ears, and I shrug my arm free, cradling my stomach with my other hand. The fear in her voice makes me back away from Willow.

"You were right about Monique, Aria," says Willow, suddenly sounding concerned. "Monique made me tell her everything I found out about you. What you do for a living. Where you work. Your friends. I'm sorry."

She stops, as if daring Monique to deny it, but Monique is silent. Had Monique planted Willow as a spy this whole time?

The thought of being watched by Willow creeps me out, but the mention of my friends unnerves me. The insinuation Monique had an ulterior motive combined with Zoe's and Isla's murder makes it sound like Monique could have killed them.

"She was furious when she found out about you," says Willow, turning on her friend.

"Willow, please," says Monique, pleading with her to ... what? Back away? Stop before she reveals more?

I'm not sure how it happened, but the mood has shifted, the energy between them loaded and explosive.

"That's not true," says Monique, addressing me. "I was curious about you, because Ethan was, but Willow came to me." Monique runs her palms over her thighs. "She told me you were wearing a wedding ring. I thought it must be an engagement ring, and that Ethan was making false promises, but then I dug a little deeper. I was curious about how he made you believe you were married. I realized you didn't know about me, so I left his ring, hoping you'd figure it out. I figured he took you to some shady Vegas chapel. The son of a bitch didn't even use a different ring. He used the ring I gave him at our wedding, probably so he didn't have to keep track of who he was with and which ring he was wearing," she says.

Ethan told me that the ring had belonged to his father and that he hoped we would be as happy as his parents were.

Willow knew Ethan was married. She had spent three years working in my home and had never mentioned any of it to me. Had she avoided me to stop herself from revealing Ethan's awkward secret? If I knew a secret like that, I probably would've mentioned it.

Heat rises in my cheeks. Shame that I had hidden something much worse for much longer. But I can't think about Matt. Not now.

Willow laughs. "I thought you would kill each other when you found out Ethan had fooled you both," she says, and looks directly at me. "But then your friend Isla saw Monique leaving Ethan's car. She assumed Ethan was cheating on you, just like you thought. She made the mistake of confronting Ethan, saying she was going to tell you. He had to shut her up."

I try to suppress a rumble in my stomach. Now's not the time to lose my lunch.

"Don't listen to her. Ethan would never kill—" says Monique.

"Wouldn't he?" screams Willow, shocking Monique into silence. "You gave him no choice."

At first, I think she's talking to me, then I notice her approaching Monique. "You knew he was going to leave you. You wanted to make sure he had nowhere else to go, hoping he'd come crawling back. It didn't matter that he didn't love you anymore. You've been guilting him into staying for years."

I flinch at the harshness of her words. She has gone too far. Monique's face changes and she stops in front of Willow. "What did you think would happen?" she asks Willow. "That he'd get sick of us and finally notice you?"

Willow stops, her mouth gaping like a fish. Monique's words have struck a sore spot.

I can't believe I didn't notice before. The hostility she's had toward me from the first day we met. It was never aimed at me personally. She didn't like me because I was another obstacle standing between her and Ethan. Willow was probably already in love with him before he met Monique.

"He doesn't love either of you." She looks at me. "You're the latest toy. He'll get bored with you, like he did with her." She gestures to Monique with a nod.

Monique positions herself between me and Willow.

Willow's arm rises, swooping in an arc. By the time I notice, it's already too late. At first I think she's holding Ethan's phone, but as she raises her arm higher, I realize she has pulled out a gun. The barrel points somewhere between Monique and me. She hasn't decided who she will need to use it on yet. With a flick of her wrist, she could choose either of us.

"He'll notice now. Because I know his secrets. Things he wouldn't risk anyone finding out that he only trusted me with," says Willow, and I wonder if she's waiting for an excuse to shoot. I stay as still as possible. She has completely lost it, her hands twitching. It won't take much for her to pull the trigger.

I need to talk her down.

"Willow, someone will hear you shoot," I say. If working as a nurse has taught me anything, it's that people are likely to respond to self-preservation.

I keep talking, hoping she'll see there's only one option if she wants to survive this with her freedom intact. "You can walk away. Whatever Ethan has done, that's not your fault."

"He's all yours," says Monique. "I don't want him, and apparently neither does Aria."

Without hesitation, I agree. I promise Willow she doesn't have to see either of us after today. As I say the words, I realize I'm not just saying it to convince her to drop the gun. I really am done with Ethan. He's been lying to me since I've known him.

Meeting Ethan felt like a serendipitous moment. It was my very own love story. It's clear now that every moment was fabricated from the moment I stepped into Starbucks and saw him in line ahead of me. He whispered something to Megan, the barista that usually worked mornings. I went there so often that we'd become acquaintances, bonding over our shared love of sugar, especially cookies.

They say when you face a life-or-death situation, your life flashes through your mind. Maybe that's why I'm thinking about how Ethan and I met.

I had noticed Ethan there before, too. He was the cute guy in the business suit. I had imagined what he might do for a living—my favorite guess being that he was a living manne-quin for an upmarket department store.

He was ahead of me in line, so his drinks were ready before I ordered. He must have asked what I usually drink because the barista handed him two drinks and he immediately turned and offered me one. Chai. Exactly what I would've ordered.

I accepted the drink gratefully, in all my awkward glory, spilling a little on my hand but trying not to show my discomfort as it scalded my skin. He said he hoped we could drink them together because he really didn't like the anticipation of first dates—the asking, worrying whether it would go okay, and the nervous build-up that made you act unnatural and rehearsed no matter how much you tried to avoid it. This way, he didn't need to go through all that.

The joke instantly put me at ease. Now, I see how manufactured it was, putting me on the spot, making it uncomfortable to say no. Even if I hadn't wanted to go on a date, I would've found it hard to decline under those circumstances.

I snap out of it. I won't figure out Ethan's motivation now. There are more pressing things to deal with.

Willow contemplates what I've said, clearly considering whether she can ride off into the sunset with Ethan like I thought I had. It seems ironic that the three of us are here fighting about Ethan when he's gone. He has caused so much turmoil, and I'm not sure he even knows it. The barrel of the gun turns until it's pointing right at me.

"It's too late to walk away from this," says Willow, the barrel pointed at my midriff. She looks at my abdomen. "He can never be rid of you once the baby's born. You will always be in his life. You'll always be the mother of his child."

"Willow, no!" says Monique, trying to get Willow's attention now that she's threatening the one thing Monique might care about. "What do you think Ethan would do if you hurt his child?" She answers the question herself. "He would never forgive you."

Willow wavers, her attention taken by something behind me and Monique. She looks as if she's been caught doing something she shouldn't.

I turn instinctively, dreading seeing something even worse than the gun Willow has aimed at me.

And there he is.

Walking through the door, almost smiling, as if our marriage isn't in shambles. As if he hasn't turned my life into complete chaos.

Ethan.

Chapter 52

As angry as I am, I'm relieved to see that Willow didn't shoot Ethan before she came here.

He's already talking before he takes a moment to look up and see what's happening inside. "Listen, Aria. I don't want to fight. You deserve the truth. I'm going to tell you everything."

He stops when he sees we have company. As Ethan closes the door behind him, Willow raises the gun.

He doesn't run like I might've expected him to. "Willow? What's going on? What's with the gun?" I can tell he's trying to stay calm, asking the question as if it's unusual, but not completely unheard of, to point a gun at somebody.

She looks less sure now that Ethan's here. She finally has his undivided attention, like she's always wanted, but he's looking at her like a chore he needs to take care of instead of the woman she wants him to see her as.

"You said it was over. First Monique. And then it was Aria. It'll never be over, will it? After Aria, it would've just been someone else. It was never me, never us."

I want to ask what she means by "us." Was there ever an Ethan and Willow, or is it a fantasy she's entertaining?

"Willow. I *couldn't* leave Monique. Not after we lost our baby. It would have been cruel."

"You promised me you'd leave her. I thought you meant it, or I never would have . . ." Willow stops speaking, but the insinuation is clear, and Monique doesn't miss it either.

"Ethan—" she starts.

"We were going through a rough patch," he says, and I don't think I've ever felt as indifferent to him as I do now. "Willow was there when I needed her. I'm sorry."

There's a dismissiveness, as if Willow was a filler while he waited for his real life to pick up again.

Willow looks hurt. "What about *before* that?" She looks at Monique. "We were good together."

Ethan's tone is soothing. "I didn't mean it like that. Of course we were."

"And then it was Aria," Willow continues. "You wanted a baby, but not with me. I could've given you that."

I thought no one knew how much we wanted to become parents, but Willow had been in our home during some of our discussions about trying vitamins and tracking ovulation. She knew we were struggling to have a baby, and she probably knew the last pregnancy test I did promised that everything was about to change.

Except she's not looking at me when she says it. She's looking at Monique, talking about how badly Monique and Ethan wanted a baby. How Ethan would do anything to make up for the baby they had lost.

And finally I realize. I was the anything. The fake courtship. The romantic wedding that we ran away for, escaping into our own fairytale.

I never imagined it was because he was using me. What I thought was the happiest day of my life was like the worst April fool prank ever.

I look down at my belly. I think about Monique asking me to consider giving up my baby. It had seemed like such a strange request, but now it makes sense, because that was the plan all along.

She asked me to give up my baby because that is what Ethan promised her.

Willow's hand moves against the gun, and I know she's turned the safety off, preparing to shoot. She shifts her weight, ready for the kickback. I watch her fingers curl tighter around the handle, the tip of her index finger kissing the metal trigger.

The tension in the air is palpable. Ethan is almost level with Monique and me, creeping closer, and I hope he doesn't say something to make Willow angrier.

Maybe she needs a diversion to allow her to calm down and change her mind. No one has to die today. "Ethan's not worth going to prison over," I say, trying to shock her out of ruining her life and someone else's.

I catch Ethan's eye. My words have hurt him, but at this point I don't care. "Yeah," I say. "Look at what he did to Monique."

Willow laughs. The sound startles me. "If only you knew," she says, as if there are even worse things I don't yet know.

I see Monique out of the corner of my eye shaking her head, pleading with Willow not to say more.

Willow ignores her. "She set you up, Aria. She *chose* you. Not Ethan. You were never supposed to find out. She would've done anything to have the family she wanted . . . even if it meant sharing Ethan for a while."

I step away from Monique, her proximity making me uneasy. I don't know where this is going yet, but I get the feeling it's nowhere good.

"Why?" I ask. Losing a child is traumatic, but if she wanted children, why didn't they try again?

"Because you deserved it," says Monique. "You took my baby from me. I came to the hospital looking for help, and you let my baby die. By the time she was born, it was too late to save her. You should've done something, but you didn't. You let her die. My uterus ruptured, and I needed a hysterectomy, so I couldn't have any more children."

I chance a look at Willow, but she's still holding the gun. Not quite at me now, but between Monique and me, as if she's not sure whether she can trust either of us.

I watch the gun from the corner of my eye, worried about spooking Willow, who looks like a skittish dog.

Monique blames me for her baby dying, and I feel awful for not being able to save her. I can almost understand why she would think I owe her, but I can't give her my baby to make up for what she lost.

Monique cries as if the weight of everything has caught up to her. Ethan places a hand on her arm, trying to calm her, and as strange as it is seeing them together, I can't help but notice that his touch doesn't seem like someone trying to console their wife.

It's dutiful; the action is there, but his heart isn't in it. "Don't do this to yourself, Monique," he says, but she interrupts.

"He was supposed to *pretend*. Enough so you'd believe it, enough to want a baby that we would raise together. When you didn't get pregnant in the first year and a half, we agreed the plan hadn't worked out and Ethan was supposed to end the relationship."

I try not to look at the gun, afraid of angering Willow, who is nodding at Monique's words, encouraging her to tell me what happened. I keep the rest of my focus on Monique, who is sounding as unstable as Ethan said she is if she thinks that plan ever would have worked.

But I'm embarrassed it might have. That if it wasn't for that feeling in my gut telling me that something was wrong, so insistent that I had to pick at it, I might still be living a lie.

Although I know it was fake, parts of our marriage still feel real. Ethan saying he loved me as we lay curled up in each other's arms, both reluctant to leave in the morning. If you asked me now, I would swear he meant it as much as I did.

His eye catches mine. I have had years of practice reading his expression. I can see he feels bad for deceiving me, but there's something else there. Affection? Love?

I look away. There is no way the two of us are walking out of here together.

If their end goal was a baby, why had Ethan suggested we stop trying?

I think of the child I'm carrying. The child Monique believes I owe her, and I feel a sudden protectiveness. As sorry as I am about what happened to her, she will not take my baby.

"Why didn't you adopt?" I ask. It's the logical path if they wanted to be parents but couldn't have a baby of their own. Why go to all the trouble of setting me up? I never would have agreed to give my baby up, but perhaps the plan wasn't to ask. I think of what they would have needed to do to claim my baby. The only way they would have succeeded is if I were dead.

"Ethan has a criminal record. It was going to be difficult to convince an adoption agency that he should be a father. Especially because it was a violent crime."

I hadn't known this, and it shocks me to hear it. An image of Isla grips me, followed by one of Zoe curled next to her sofa. My mind still can't believe Ethan was involved in their deaths. "When?" I ask, wondering how I could miss the fact that I've been living with a violent offender.

"It was years ago," says Ethan. "I got into a bar fight with a guy who grabbed my friend's ass." He looks at Willow. "He threw the first punch, but mine landed better and broke his nose."

I look at Monique's face, the purpled skin like a stain. "I see," I say, but he corrects my insinuation.

"Aria, I didn't do it." He sounds confident. Believable.

"Your *wife* said you did," I say. He has lied about so many things. I have no reason to believe him now.

"Because he did," says Monique.

"I tried to stop her," he says. "She was going to hurt you, Aria. When she realized we were still together—that I was in love with you—she went crazy. She's been planning it for weeks. I tried talking to her. When she tried to leave, I wasn't sure what she was planning on doing, so I grabbed her arm to stop her, and that's it. I swear." He assesses the damage to Monique's face and shakes his head before continuing. "My hand caught her arm wrong, and she fell. She hit her face on the edge of the marble coffee table. That's how she broke her cheekbone."

Monique scoffs but doesn't disagree.

"I've tried talking her out of it. She's hurting. I even took her to California to try to sort things out. I would've gone to the police, but I couldn't." He looks at me, pleading for understanding, but I owe him nothing.

Because she would have told them what your part in this was, I think. If he believes his story is eliciting sympathy, he's wrong. I'm madder than ever.

"You told me you ended things with her!" screams Monique through her tears, frustration spilling over. "How could you love her after what she did to us . . . to Willow?"

Ethan is talking to Monique, but he looks at me, saying the things he can't say without upsetting Monique more than she already is. "I told you I stopped seeing Aria because you wouldn't let me leave." He stands close, our arms almost touching. I can feel the heat radiating from his body. He lowers his voice, keeping the conversation as intimate as possible with Willow and Monique in the room.

I look away, unable to separate myself from the person I thought I knew and the real him, the guy who has lied to me since we met. I want to skip the part where my emotions flip-flop back and forth and get to the part where I'm sure I'm better off without him.

"At first, I hated Aria too," Ethan admits. "I wondered if she could've saved Lola, but I never thought Monique would go through with her plan. I thought once she had time to grieve, she would see that what happened was a horrible tragedy."

"You weren't there, Ethan. While you were off on one of your business trips just weeks before the due date, I was in the hospital losing our daughter. Alone. You have no idea what that was like."

He apologizes again, but it can never be enough.

He takes my hand in his and I resist the urge to pull it away. "I fell in love with you. I knew we could never have the life you deserved if I left Monique. She wouldn't let us. So, I tried to let you go. Except, I couldn't eat. Couldn't sleep. I know it's selfish. I couldn't marry you like I wanted to, so I married you the best way I could. Even if it wasn't technically real, it was real to me."

"I'm sorry about what happened to your daughter," I say. I can't deal with Ethan and me right now, but it seems wrong to ignore his pain. "I can't even imagine."

He reaches for my other hand, which I slide from his reach. I feel bad for him, but it doesn't justify the lie he let me live. He looked me in the eye and said he loved me, that he was lucky I married him, knowing the whole time it wasn't real.

Willow moves the gun forward, stretching her arms out straight toward me. "He *thinks* he loves you because he doesn't know you. The real you. Tell him . . ." She gestures with the gun, encouraging me to do what she says. I stay quiet, trying to work out what she might be referring to.

"Tell him how you left a man to die alone in a ditch because you didn't want anyone to know you were there. You didn't want to get kicked out of college. Your future, your happiness, was more important to you than his life."

Her words catch my attention, my body tensing as she lines up to pull the trigger.

"You don't care who you hurt if it gets you what you want," she says, growing tenser by the second. I worry she will misfire, landing a bullet straight through my middle where my baby is growing. She's losing control of her emotions.

I need to take the gun without setting it off. I consider wresting it from her grip, but she would see me coming and have plenty of time to shoot before I even got close. If it were Monique holding the gun, I know she wouldn't risk hurting the baby, but Willow I'm not so sure.

"What are you talking about?" asks Ethan.

"Tell him," Willow says, thrusting the gun forward, the threat clear. If I don't talk, she will shoot.

Monique folds her arms, looking unfazed by Willow's performance. She doesn't seem surprised by Willow's revelation.

Monique knows too.

They think I deserve to be treated the way I treated Matt. This is about Monique's baby, but it's also about what I did all those years ago. That's why the two of them decided on me.

They had multiple reasons to think I was a shitty person, making it easier to justify hurting me and taking my baby.

Maybe they thought they were saving my child from having me for a mother.

If I don't get out of here now, they're going to kill me. Maybe not right now, but eventually, once they get what they want. The thought of them raising my baby, of what kind of life my child would have with them as role models, makes me feel ill.

Part of me feels like I deserve to die, that death would mean being free of the guilt, because while Matt veered off the road that night, planning to end his life and mine, his family never had a choice.

I had wondered how they were coping after his death, but I was too much of a coward to find out. I think I feared the truth, because it was still my fault. If I wasn't involved with Matt in the first place, we wouldn't have been in that car.

"Please, Willow. Put the gun down," I breathe, but her eyes are unforgiving as she points it in my direction.

I hear the pop of a bullet exiting the barrel, exploding with the clarity of an epiphany. Now that her rage is no longer disguised, I see it. Her anger is a living, breathing thing, warping her. I've seen anger like that before. Hot. Raw. Explosive.

Willow's face crumples as she realizes what she's done, but it's too late to take it back.

It's the same expression Matt used to get just after he hit me, before he started apologizing, saying he didn't know what got into him. Suddenly, the likeness is unmistakable.

I knew Matt had a daughter, but I didn't know her name was Willow. I had never asked. I knew nothing about his family. I didn't want to know.

It takes seconds to realize the bullet has gone past me, burrowing into the wall.

"I'm sorry. He drove off the road. He was angry and—"

I don't know what kind of father Matt was, whether Willow had been on the receiving end of one of his bad moods, but I can't bring myself to ruin any good memories she might have of him by telling her that her father veered off the road on purpose. "He was already dead when the car finished rolling," I say, as if that somehow makes what I did forgivable.

Some girls dream of their father walking them down the aisle on their wedding day, but I had taken that from Willow, along with a hundred other memories she would never experience.

Her response chills me. I could almost pretend to myself that I misheard, but I can't ignore the shock it sends through me.

"You're wrong. He was still alive when you left him there to die."

Chapter 53

Could I have been wrong? All this time I'd been telling myself that what I did wasn't good, but he was already dead. If I had stayed, if his family found out about me, it would have destroyed their memories of him, and I didn't want that.

Had I left a man to die alone in the dead of night? Would I have called for help if I knew he might live?

Once I thought I was free of him, I felt relieved. Finally, I could do as I pleased without worrying how he would react. Would I have walked away if I had noticed his heart beating faintly against his chest?

No. It's why I became a nurse, so that I could save people and avoid the overwhelming feeling of despair that haunted me days after the accident as I realized how final death was.

Was Matt suspended upside down inside the car, waiting for someone passing by to stop? Did he die knowing I had left him there?

"How long before someone found him?" I ask. I owe him enough to find out if he suffered, and for how long.

"Five hours. Someone driving home from their night shift found him. He was barely hanging on, but somehow he managed to. I immediately knew he was with you. I heard your phone call earlier that night. He didn't notice me listening. There was a lot he didn't think I heard."

The rest of what she says is hard to follow. I can only think that Matt didn't die that night on the road. He survived. At least for a little while. I remember the spot where the car hit the dirt, careening through the air. I remember seeing a sign promising scenic views of the valley and the ocean. It had felt surreal passing by the sign, tires skidding off the road, waiting for the impact.

I realize Willow is still talking.

"Dad wasn't the same after. He was constantly in pain and had to leave his job. He was more difficult to deal with than before. Angrier. He lost his temper faster. Mom bore the brunt of it. It seemed unfair that after what he did, she was the one to suffer. She had to get a job cleaning houses to support us."

She stops, and I try not to look at Ethan, giving away his position. I risk a glance anyway. He is almost beside Willow, who is looking down, hiding unshed tears. "After the accident, he told Mom about you," she says, the gun still pointing at me. "Never your name. Just vague details. You're the reason she finally left."

I remember Ethan saying Willow understood him because she knew what it was like to lose a parent too, and I dread what's coming.

"Mom started taking antidepressants, but they didn't help. She couldn't eat. She didn't sleep properly. Her work suffered. Then she started taking sleeping pills, because she couldn't function during the day. She overdosed one night and didn't wake up."

Willow grips the gun in both hands, steadying her arms to make sure she won't miss this time. Of course she blames me for what happened. How could she not? I barely checked Matt's pulse before leaving him to die.

The regret I couldn't muster back then in my desperation to be free of him finally hits. I hadn't for one second thought that he was alive. Now, Willow would make sure I suffered for what I had done.

"You killed her," she says, and I feel awful about what happened to her mother. Not just for the way her life ended, but for the way it must've been with two young children and Matt as a husband.

"A life for a life," says Willow. I can see this has always been her plan. "After everything we lost, it seemed like the obvious choice. Why should you get to live a happy life after what you had taken from us?"

"You were working the night Lola died," adds Monique, startling me. "That's two people you got away with killing."

She's moving toward me, the flash of something glinting in her hand.

"Why did you kill Isla and Zoe?" I ask, looking from Willow to Monique. I know it was one of them, but I don't know which.

"Your friend with the big mouth found out about Ethan and Monique," says Willow. "Just after I realized you were pregnant."

So, it had been Willow who killed Isla, not Monique. Monique approaches, the shiny object coming into focus. A knife. Did she bring it intending to stab me?

"I didn't know I was pregnant until a couple of days ago," I say. "How could you have known?"

Uneasiness settles over me. I let Willow into my home because Ethan trusted her. I didn't know who she was, or that she blamed me for what happened to her family.

"It was obvious. You were moody and felt sick a lot. You finally realized your 'husband' was cheating on you." She says the word husband like it's an inside joke, one that I might finally get after meeting Monique. "I clean your trash," she continues. "I know what you eat and what you throw out. The bathroom bin has been empty for over a month. No tampon wrappers. Then I heard you throwing up in the toilet I'd just cleaned. I waited to clean it once you were done, but you're so wrapped up in yourself that you didn't even notice I was there."

I had mistaken Willow's loathing for apathy, thinking she had no interest in being my friend because we didn't quite mesh, but she had been paying more attention to me than I realized. I hadn't thought about it before, but I suppose she would know exactly what happened in my home.

It must've been difficult knowing who I was and staying silent all this time. She was bound to snap, seeing me moving on with my life while her family had fallen apart.

I can see she wants to send another bullet flying straight for me, the muscles in her hand shifting. As she's about to fire, Ethan lunges, grabbing her wrist as I dive to the side.

"Go," he screams, and I realize he's talking to me. The gun is in his hand now and he's looking at me, his eyes filled with remorse.

"Did you know?" I ask. "About the car accident?"

"I knew about Willow's family, but I didn't know about you and Matt. It wouldn't have mattered. I would have fallen in love with you anyway." His voice trails off as Willow escapes his hold and scoots around him, heading straight for me.

I could leave like Ethan suggested, letting them battle it out, but I've been running from this for too long, waiting for that night to catch up with me. It's almost a relief to have it out in the open—proof that monsters can't stay hidden forever, even if the monster is me.

I face Willow head-on. "I'm sorry about your mom," I say. She crashes into me anyway, and I hope my baby is small enough to be protected from the impact as I fall.

"No!" shouts Monique. "The baby!"

Willow claws at me, trying to erase me and everything I've taken from her. Ethan and Monique are on her, trying to pull her back.

The reality of my escape is nothing like the streamlined action shot in a movie as I roll ungracefully. I hope someone called the police after the gunshots, but there are no sirens, so I'm not sure what to expect when the front door swings open.

Chapter 54

I expect to see an exasperated Cassandra, tired of calling, taking matters into her own hands like she usually does, but it's not her familiar face that appears around the door.

Ethan pulls Willow backward, holding her in place.

My attention shifts back to the door and the person standing there.

Shannon, the self-proclaimed private investigator, looks like she came here on a mission, her eyes passing over me without a second glance as she lets herself inside.

"Willow!" she screams.

She must have seen Willow arrive while scoping my apartment. But why is she calling out to Willow, and what makes her think she'll listen?

I edge to the corner of the rug, out of the confrontation, unsure how this will play out. Is Shannon on my side? Or is she part of their crazy plan? Maybe I wasn't her target after all, and my instinct that she lied about being an investigator was correct.

Willow looks at Shannon and stops struggling, as if Shannon's presence is enough to muzzle her rage.

Shannon moves deeper into the room and the mood changes. Ethan releases Willow, who stands defiantly, hands balled into fists, looking at Shannon.

Shannon is the first to speak. "What did you do?" she asks. She is angry, but there's something else. Concern?

"You didn't care before. Don't pretend to now," says Willow between gritted teeth.

Ethan seems to know Shannon too. "She was going to kill Aria," he says. "She had a gun . . ."

The gun is now tucked into his waistband. Did he turn the safety on?

Shannon spots me huddled against the sofa. She looks embarrassed—she clearly lied about who she is.

"She isn't responsible for what happened, Willow."

I notice a look pass between them, their expressions almost identical as they seem to communicate in that unspoken language siblings have. They both have the same wide-eyed expression, each in different shades. They don't look identical, but there's a definite resemblance. Sisters.

To confirm, I ask Ethan, "Did you hire an investigator to follow me?"

He looks confused, as if I've asked a nonsense question he's not sure how to answer. "No," he says.

"Mom wouldn't want this. If you're telling yourself you're doing it for her, don't."

Willow flexes her hands, rolling and unrolling her fists like a warmup exercise. She lunges for Ethan, pulling the gun from his waistband, and pivots so she can see everyone.

Ethan dives to stop her, but her finger is already on the trigger, gun pointed at me. This time she doesn't miss.

The bullet leaves the barrel, hurtling toward me. Pain explodes in my chest and I see Monique's face close to mine, her eyes wide with shock.

This is it, I think. *This is how I die. This is how my baby dies. This is what I've been running from.*

Chapter 55

I wake up to find a blanket draped across my legs up to my waist. There's a metallic burn in my mouth. My first thought is that I've awoken from a nightmare, but the relief is short-lived when I move my toes and notice the cart I take around to patients at work.

I'm on the wrong side of the rail, lying in bed as Cassandra shuffles over in her uniform, taking my hand in hers.

My voice is croaky as I ask what happened, but Cassandra shushes me. The crushing pain in my chest tells me the bullet wasn't a dream. I try looking around, as if Willow might still be here, gun in hand.

I mutter something about the gun, about Willow wanting to kill me, and how it's not her fault.

"It's all right," says Cassandra. "She's getting the help she needs."

My next thought is of my baby, and I move my hand over my belly, realizing that despite everything that's happened, I want this baby more than ever.

Cassandra knows me too well, and she rests a hand on my arm, soothing me. "You just had surgery, honey. The bullet entered your side and caught a couple of ribs. A small area of the lung needed to be repaired. It's too early to tell if the baby made it."

If the baby didn't make it, it mightn't be obvious. The hCG levels would slowly decline and it's still too early to reliably detect a heartbeat. I feel under the sheets, looking for blood. My rib catches, sending pain shooting down my side.

The fabric feels dry, but I know the chances of the baby surviving aren't good if my body reacts poorly to the trauma, so I force myself to take a deep breath and center myself.

"I took some blood anyway," says Cassandra, and if I could move, I would hug her. "The levels are normal for this gestation. I hope the little guy makes it." It's her way of telling me there's hope. "You had a laparoscopy, and you'll make a full recovery."

"She shot directly at me," I say, trying to put together a picture of what happened. "Only Superwoman could survive that."

Cassandra frowns at my joke. Not a good sign.

"What happened?" I ask.

"Monique saw Willow raise the gun and tried to shield you. She didn't get out of the way in time and got shot."

The explosion in my chest must have been her pushing me to the ground, making it feel impossible to breathe. "Did she—"

"She didn't make it," says Cassandra, and despite everything, despite what she put me through, I can't help feeling sad for her. She had taken a bullet to save me and it had cost her her life.

I don't trust myself to speak, but there are questions that need to be asked. "Where's Ethan?" It seems important to make sure he's all right. He was so close when Willow fired the gun.

"He's waiting outside. I told him to wait while you slept. I didn't know if you would want to see him."

"Send him in." I try to sound decisive, but I'm suddenly nervous about seeing him.

There are so many things I need to know before I can begin healing. After what I've learned, it may take longer than I thought.

What is he now, this man who was once my husband?

Chapter 56

Ten months later

I wrap my baby in a pink blanket that's so soft it feels as if it's made from a cloud, pressing her soft little cheek against mine, drinking in the love I feel when I'm holding her. I named her Ella, mixing Zoe and Isla's names as a way to remember them. Ethan said he loved it when I told him what I'd chosen.

He seemed just as horrified as I was that Willow had killed Isla. She had been planning it for a long time, apparently. Zoe was a message to scare me. She wanted to take everything that mattered from me, and if we hadn't stopped her, Cassandra almost certainly would have been next.

Ethan edges closer now, desperate to hold her, to breathe in her soft scent, but he doesn't want to take her from my arms. The visiting room is small, but not so small that it's suffocating. It's strange visiting Ethan in prison.

"It's Daddy's turn to spend some time with you," I coo, running a hand across her soft, plump cheek. "But I'll be back in a couple of hours."

"Aria, why don't you stay," he says as I place her carefully in his arms.

The prison clothes look ridiculous on him. They fit like a bad Halloween costume, the cuffs wide around the arm, the pants like a potato sack engulfing his waist. He has lost weight since being here, and his lean muscles have become ropy and tight. The green of the uniform makes him look like a nurse, the bags under his eyes suggesting too many night shifts. "Ella would like you to stay," he says, cradling our daughter in his arms, holding her up so I can see her face—a face he knows I find it hard to say no to.

Seeing the love in his eyes when he looks at her reminds me of why we visit. I never imagined I would bring my child to a prison, but I want her to know her dad, to decide for herself when she's old enough whether she wants him in her life.

If it were up to me, I wouldn't have pressed charges for what he did to me, but he was part of a conspiracy, and once the police learned what had happened, it was out of my hands.

"You know I would have left Monique if I could," he says as I turn to leave. "She meant it when she threatened to hurt you. She hurt me. It's lucky she didn't break my nose. I still have the blood on my jacket. It's why I needed to get her away from you."

I look away. This isn't the first time he's tried to explain what happened. Maybe if I hear him out, he will see that it's too late for any of it to matter.

"So," he continues, "I bought her a gift and said we were going to California on vacation. I wanted to keep her happy while I figured out what to do." He looks at me, pleading with eyes that used to make me melt with just a look, as if he needs me to believe him.

The problem is, I do. I remember the photo Monique sent me of the two of them just after I asked him to leave. I had looked at it many times, but it was only hindsight that showed the things I hadn't noticed. How he subconsciously pulled his body back as he leaned toward her, acting out a role she expected but not quite feeling it. Apparently she noticed, and they had fought afterward like Monique claimed.

I look at my baby girl and wonder if all this craziness between Ethan and me happened just so she could be here. If never meeting Ethan meant she wouldn't exist, then I don't regret it.

"The plan was to—" says Ethan.

"Stop," I say, my voice overriding his. Anyone could be listening to our conversation, and Ella will have already started school when he gets out—I don't want to give them a reason to keep him here until she has finished school. I've heard enough before, and I'm still convinced I'm better off without him.

My tone startles the baby and Ethan shifts her in his arms, resting her head in the crook of his elbow, rocking her gently until she stops wriggling.

"I went to see your mom," I say.

It had taken me a while to work up the courage to do it. I felt embarrassed about the situation and how I had accepted Ethan's story about his parents' death, but Ella deserves to know her grandparents, and they seemed happy to meet her.

Pearl Dolan is a kind woman with an easy smile, louder than her husband. It was easy to see where Ethan got his confidence. The warmth of their home enveloped me, with plush furniture and a gallery of photographs capturing Ethan's journey at every stage of life. There was a photo I sent of Ella inside a pretty frame in their living room.

Pearl said she always sensed there was something off about Willow, but she never thought Monique and Willow would conspire to do what they had done. She apologized on their behalf, explaining how Willow and Shannon struggled after their mother died, how they had a strained relationship with their father. I had blushed at the mention of his name, resisting the urge to ask what had become of him.

"Mom would've loved seeing Ella." Ethan beams, bringing me back to the present before I can worry over the past. It had been so long since I had seen Matt that I doubt he was a threat any longer.

"I have to go," I say, collecting my things and planting a kiss atop Ella's head.

I think of the message that pinged my inbox last night as I was settling down with a book and a cup of chamomile tea. It was probably sent by a random true crime fan who'd heard about the emails Monique had sent me, thinking it was funny to spook me. I wasn't exactly an innocent victim. I was just as guilty as Willow and Monique, leaving a man for dead in the middle of the night.

The clock is already ticking before I need to collect Ella, but I have an hour or two, just enough time to report the strange email to the police.

I take a deep breath and retrieve my phone, reading the email again. It looks the same as Monique's original message, but it's a common enough font that it could be a coincidence.

Are you happy now?

The words feel childish but seething. Something you'd say to a sibling who ratted you out.

It's most likely nothing, but Monique taught me a valuable lesson about how different things can be to how they seem.

I will need to report it.

Chapter 57

Someone is following me as I leave the prison and head back toward my car. I drove out here hoping to see the coast with Ella. I think about ignoring the stalker and disappearing inside of my car, but I've been avoiding this for too long.

"Aria?" He sounds older, but the voice is still distinctly *his*.

The lines that were beginning to creep across his face when we first met now form deep rivulets in his forehead. I'm glad Ella is inside the prison.

He looks me up and down with a smirk, as if he can still picture what's underneath my clothes.

"Matt," I say, making it clear I want to know what the hell he wants.

"Did you get my email?"

"Yeah," I say, unimpressed, pocketing my hands. Now that I'm all grown up, he doesn't seem as formidable. "I'm just about to report it to the police."

I try to sidestep him, but he keeps talking. "There's nothing to report. It was just a friendly question. I'm worried about you. This life, it isn't really you, is it? Don't you miss what we had?"

What used to seem like excitement now feels like an attempt to feel alive. I've found that in other ways now. Even if it's quieter, it's a lasting feeling that outlives the adrenaline-fueled risks I took before. Snuggling with Ella. Taking some time out to read a book and learn something new.

I meet his eyes, accepting his challenge in a way I never could before. "Not one bit," I say, hiding the old fear that threatens to return when he doesn't move out of my way. "Are you here to see your daughter?" I ask, knowing I'm dangerously close to making him angry. Surely he wouldn't be stupid enough to let his temper show his true self right outside of a prison?

He studies me, as if trying to determine whether the Aria he's speaking to now is the same girl who would crawl into his bed and let herself believe she didn't need to hear him say he loved her because she knew he did on some level, even when the angry black and blue marks of his fists stained her skin.

Or was she the girl who left him for dead, who could walk away hoping that if she pretended she wasn't there, it would be like she never was?

I'm not sure either of those girls still exist. They were both too scared to say no and too scared to ensure the job was done properly, completing what the wreckage couldn't.

"She's going to be in there for a long time," I say, feeling bad for using Willow to bait out his temper, but I know something now that I hadn't realized then. It wasn't just me whose skin he bruised. It was Willow and Shannon, too. It was his wife, and probably a myriad of girlfriends he'd had since. And I know from my relationship with Matt, right up to the point where he took us over the barrier and down the embankment where we were supposed to die, that it would only have gotten worse, the violence growing more creative as he figured out what I was truly afraid of.

He has the strangest look on his face, his voice low as he whispers words meant only for my ears. "You were supposed to die with me that night, in that car."

He can't really believe that it was supposed to end like that, that we were star-crossed lovers, when the truth was I knew I didn't want him in my life anymore. Maybe he realized I was serious that night when I told him no apology could fix what he had done. The crash was to stop me from leaving, because one thing Matt couldn't stand was other people deciding the trajectory of his life. He didn't care if I left, not really. It just needed to be at a time when he decided he was ready for it, and that time hadn't arrived. My escape wouldn't have gone unpunished, and yet he had waited until now to confront me. Why?

According to Willow, he had made them pay for it when he couldn't punish me any longer, but I know that wouldn't have been enough to placate him.

I move around him now and head straight to my car, hitting the fob to unlock the door. Matt calls out to me, but I ignore him. He hasn't been part of my life for a long time, and I want to keep it that way.

He grabs my arm from behind, squeezing hard enough to hurt. He taught me how to control my pain, and I retreat inside of myself, focusing on my breathing.

"There are cameras in the parking lot," I warn him, but he laughs it off.

"I don't care," he says.

I try to shake his hand off, expecting some resistance. To my surprise, he lets me go. I slide into my car before his mood changes, starting the engine. He jumps in the back seat behind me and curls an arm around the seat to reach me. I feel a knife press into my back. "Drive," he says, and I know from the rigid pressure of the blade that it's real. "Don't think I won't use it. I've done it before and they haven't found the bodies yet."

I allow myself a deep gulp of air and a moment to think. He would never have been allowed to visit Willow while he was carrying a knife, but he wasn't here to visit Willow. He must've followed me here, waiting outside until I came through the exit.

How long has he been waiting for this moment? Has he followed me out here before when I've brought Ella to visit Ethan?

I believe him when he says he's used a knife. That he's killed with it. I imagine him choosing them. Women whose families will never know what happened. I believe he will use the knife on me if I don't follow his instructions, but my hesitation is enough for him to inflict a warning bite with the tip, digging it underneath the fabric of my shirt. I feel the skin split and know he's drawn blood.

There is a sting and I wait for him to push the knife deeper. I can't wrest away without causing more damage, so I hope. I close my eyes and think of my daughter and the future she will have without me. I drive, my foot pressing the pedal, causing the car to jerk forward. The pressure releases as I get to speed, awaiting further instruction.

"Take the next left," he says, and I indicate. "It's lucky I survived," he says conversationally. "You were my introduction to what I could do, what I could achieve. I hadn't even known how far you could push the limits of survival until I made it through that night, but I was always coming back for you."

He leads us out toward the coast, away from the city. If anyone passing notices a man looming behind me in the back seat of my car, they don't seem to think anything of it and keep driving. No one can see the knife pressed low against my back, and I hope a cop pulls us over and finds it.

I don't give Matt the satisfaction of reacting to his words and instead focus on driving.

"I had to practice first. I needed to get it out of my system. I was saving you for last. It would've been much easier if Willow hadn't been so impatient and gone off script."

I think of all the times he gaslit me, making me think a fight was my fault, or that a hit he inflicted bruised up so good because he didn't really hit me that hard, I was just prone to bruising. How easy it would be to condition a child, to make them think that what they were doing was for the good of their family. How easy it was to hate someone outside of that, when the real monster was so much closer, pulling your strings.

"How did you convince Willow to kill Isla and Zoe?" I ask mildly, as if his actions are as predictable and boring as he is.

"She hated you for what you did to our family. Especially her mother. Your friends would have stopped her from getting the revenge she's been waiting for. I promised her I wouldn't let that happen," he says. "They were just another way to make you suffer."

As I drive, I know we're almost there as the road winds. I know exactly where he's taking me. The sign promising amazing views of the valley is just up ahead. We're nearing the point where the tires came off the road. He's bringing me back to where it was supposed to end.

"Someone would've seen you leave the prison. They'll know you climbed into my car," I say, gripping the steering wheel until my knuckles pale.

"You think I care if they catch me?" He leans forward, his breath hot against my ear. He can't be wearing a seatbelt if he's this close. "I want them to find you and know that you're finally dead."

I try not to grip the wheel tighter. He is going to kill me if I can't think of something. Although he thinks he will stop once he's achieved that, I know he won't. If he's been doing it all this time, if he trained his own daughter to do the same, he will only find new motivation to kill.

He instructs me to pull over as we navigate the bend.

I haven't been out here since the accident, but there's still a sign announcing the scenic routes.

I don't pull over as he asks. Instead, I calculate an angle, remembering the way the hill slopes downward, and just like Matt did years ago, instead of turning into the corner, I let the wheels veer off the road and into the valley, throwing Matt forward.

The car tumbles, the seatbelt hugging tighter against me as it locks to keep me in. At some point, the airbag releases with a whoosh and I hear Matt grunt as he's thrown around like clothing in a washing machine.

The car stops suddenly at the bottom of the embankment. It takes a while to reorient myself and realize that this time I'm not upside down, and Matt isn't suspended in the seat next to mine.

He is gone.

Chapter 58

I release the seatbelt and fumble for my phone, which I'm guessing went through the windscreen when the car crashed. The windscreen glass is shattered, gaping like an open mouth.

With a grunt, I try the door handle, expecting it to stick, the door warped into a new shape from the crash. The crumpled metal gives, allowing me to crawl from the vehicle. I try to stand, but my left ankle is heavy, and there's resistance in my knee. I don't have time to indulge the pain because this isn't over yet, not until I find Matt's body.

I look around. He can't have gone far, but I can't see him, which triggers a deep-seated fear that he's waiting somewhere, knife in hand. The sign above is too far away to read from down here, but the sight of it is enough to send a shiver through me. This is where it all began, and this is where he wants to end it. I turn and face the valley. The terrain weaves, and I pick through, combing for a glimpse of Matt's lifeless body.

I spot my phone first, a deep crack splitting the screen. As I scoop it up, my foot kicks something hard. It's the knife Matt was holding inside the car. I scoop it up, feeling slightly better knowing I have something to defend myself with. My side aches from the cut he made. I stop myself thinking how deep it might've gone, but I still feel the slick liquid like sweat against my back despite the tepid weather. If I were to look, I know my shirt would be stained red with blood.

I see a figure lying on the ground about twenty feet from the crumpled mess. It doesn't look as if it's moving, but what if it's an act to lure me closer?

If Matt's still breathing, am I willing to let him live this time?

I clench the knife. I would be doing the world a favor, stopping a monster from claiming more lives, but my grip loosens at the thought, and I don't know if I can do it.

I move closer to his body. I need to know if he's alive.

It doesn't look good. He hasn't moved. Hasn't attempted to call out for help.

I consider flagging down a passing car, but there aren't any on this stretch of road, and I could be waiting a while. Time is ticking on. I'm due to pick Ella up from her visit with Ethan, but my car is totaled and I'm not sure how I'm going to get back to the prison.

Thoughts of Ella give me the push I need to inspect Matt's crumpled body. Blood pools underneath him, but I can't see where it's coming from. He looks smaller, more fragile, with his arm twisted awkwardly at his side, his legs balled toward his chest, but that familiar fear still spikes at the sight of him. I almost expect him to strike, a punishment for not rushing to his side, for not loving him enough.

His chest is still and I force myself to close the distance between us to feel for a pulse. His hand unexpectedly reaches out toward me, two weak words on his lips. "Help me."

Instinctively, I jump back, fumbling with my phone to call emergency services. Once that's taken care of, I wait with Matt, doing my best to keep him warm. I can't move him. Whatever caused the blood loss, moving him could make it worse. Moving him could kill him.

"You were supposed to die with me," he says, an odd smile spreading across his face.

Looking at the pallor of his skin, the dull sheen in his eyes, it occurs to me that he already looks dead.

"We're already dead," I lie. It feels close enough to the truth, being out here with him, knowing what he has done. Knowing it was me he wanted to kill all along. "I was the last, like you wanted. Now you can tell me what you did to them, where you put them."

And to my horror, he begins talking. Telling me in detail the things that made each of them special and therefore a target. All seven of them.

He tells me how no one even noticed Willow at the bar the night Isla died. How she followed Isla to the bathroom to make sure the drugs in her drink had worked. It would have been me if Willow had done the job properly, but that near miss made Matt realize he would need to do it himself.

I force myself to listen as he tells me more, too scared to check if the record button on my phone has started in case he stops talking. His words drift further apart, and a couple of times I think he's passed out.

I think I remember hearing one of the names he lists in a news bulletin a few years ago, but there are still others whose names I haven't heard. How many would there have been if his plan had worked out and I had pulled over like he asked?

He is partway through telling me about the seventh, how her hair so closely resembled mine that he cut a chunk of her scalp to keep. I cradle my arms around myself to keep from falling apart.

Eventually, Matt grows quiet as light cuts through the darkening sky. I hear sirens growing louder. Soon I will be able to share what he told me.

I stop recording and flag down the emergency vehicles.

Detective Scott parks and steps out, slamming the door shut behind him. "Aria fucking Miller," he says, but there's a hint of respect in his voice now as he takes in the scene. I hand him my phone and point a couple of EMTs in Matt's direction, unsurprised when they report him dead on the scene.

I recognize one of them, Brady, from the ER.

"You okay?" he asks, concern in his blue-green eyes. "That was quite a crash."

"I need to get back to my little girl. She's with her dad."

"Okay. I'll see what I can arrange. Do you have an address?"

I tell him awkwardly that she's visiting him in prison, trying to explain that we're separated as he checks over my wounds. If I could stand up and leave, I would. It sounds like I'm hitting on him and doing a poor job of it.

We've recently started saying hello at work, though not much more, and even that has been enough to put me in a good mood and a bounce in my walk.

When I tried to come up with ways I could have more of a conversation with him, this isn't what I had in mind.

"Hey, no judgment here." He smiles, and I know it's his job to keep me calm, but it works. I'm immediately at ease as he checks me over for injuries, his hands soft and quick.

Chapter 59

Brady calmly tells me there's a gash on my back that may require stitches, spraying it with antiseptic while I put on a brave face and try to ignore the burn creeping up my spine.

"I'm divorced too," he says. "No kids."

Detective Scott lingers as Brady continues to work over the scrapes and bruises I gained from the crash, apologizing when he has to spray them.

Brady notices the detective too and leans in to say, "Listen, now's probably not the time to ask, but we always seem to be heading in opposite directions at work, so this might be the only opportunity I have. When you're feeling better, maybe you'd like to have dinner sometime?"

I smile, though it probably looks more like a grimace with the pain I'm in and agree. It'll be good to have something to look forward to once this is all over. It might be fun getting to know Brady. The thought triggers a memory. *How well do you know your husband?*

It's okay. This is different. Brady's different. It turns out, I didn't know my husband at all, but I've learned to be more discerning and I'm not afraid to walk away at the first sign that Brady's still married.

"I'll go call the prison, tell them you've been held up," he says, grinning. "Sorry," he says sheepishly. "It's just, I wasn't sure you'd say yes when I asked you out."

I grimace-smile even wider, as he leaves.

Detective Scott clears his throat, waiting patiently until Brady's gone. "You've got more lives than a damned cat," he says.

"Yeah, well, hopefully this is the last one I need to use for a while," I say.

Detective Scott sits with me and watches the video I took showing Matt relaying one by one each woman he murdered.

"What the fuck did I just listen to?" He scrapes at the ground with his shoe. "He sounds proud of what he did."

"When did you start cursing so much?"

"I've always cursed this much. You just haven't spent enough time with me to know that," he says. His tone turns somber. "I've been looking for a couple of these girls for a while now. Gut's telling me we'll find them exactly where he said he put them."

I nod. I have no doubt that's where they'll be.

"What's this shit about you being dead?" he asks, referencing where I started recording.

"The Aria he thought he was talking to died a long time ago. It wasn't a lie."

"You freaked him out pretty good." A smile plays at the edges of his mouth. "Probably because you look like a ghost. Sure got him talking though," he says, as if he can understand why I would mess with Matt the way he used to mess with me.

An EMT announces that everything looks fine, but just to be safe, they're transferring me to the hospital where they can run more tests and give me a few stitches for the knife wound on my back.

I decline, saying I really just want to get back to my baby girl.

"I'll take you," offers Detective Scott. I'm about to thank him when he places a condition on the favor. "But only if you agree to go to the hospital after."

"Deal," I say without hesitation.

Later, when I'm holding Ella in my arms at home, smiling as she coos, I realize that maybe I've finally figured it out.

This is how you learn to be happy.

One moment at a time.

Acknowledgements

Crafting a book is no solo endeavor, and I'm deeply grateful for every person who contributed to this journey. I want to extend my heartfelt thanks to everyone who read one of my books and shared the adventure with me. Hearing your thoughts and exchanging stories has been truly enriching.

I am especially thankful to those who lent their eyes and minds to early drafts—Donald, Angelle, Anna, Tam, and Julia—your insights were invaluable. My writing group and dedicated beta readers, your honest feedback helped shape this work into something I'm proud of. I also appreciate the patience and support from Oni, Zen, Quinn, Xari, and Nova; your encouragement and enthusiasm keep me going.

A special note of gratitude goes to Steph, Danielle, Emma, and the entire team at Embla. Your collaborative spirit and support has made this journey so enjoyable. Thank you all for being part of this story.

About the Author

Maryann Webb writes psychological thrillers and suspense novels, including the Oscar de la Nuit series. Her books have hit the Amazon best seller chart in the US. She studied psychology but prefers the fictional kind.

My Husband's Lies is a stand-alone psychological thriller, and her third release.

https://www.mqwebb.com
https://www.facebook.com/MQWebbAuthor
https://www.instagram.com/mqwebbauthor
https://mqwebb.com/media-and-reviewers

About Embla Books

Embla Books is a digital-first publisher of standout commercial adult fiction. Passionate about storytelling, the team at Embla believe our lives are built on stories – and publish books that will make you 'laugh, love, look over your shoulder and lose sleep'. Launched by Bonnier Books UK in 2021, the imprint is named after the first woman from the creation myth in Norse mythology. Embla was carved by the gods from a tree trunk found on the seashore; an image of the kind of creative work and crafting that writers do, and a symbol of how stories shape our lives.

Find out about some of our other books and stay in touch:

X, Facebook, Instagram: @emblabooks
Newsletter: https://bit.ly/emblanewsletter